Red

The Stolen

Publisher's Cataloging-in-Publication data

Witt, Amanda Beth.
        The Stolen / Amanda Witt.
        pages cm.
        Series : The Red Series.
        ISBN 978-0-9965761-1-6
        1. Totalitarianism--Fiction. 2. Dystopias. 3. Dystopian fiction.
4. Science fiction. I. Series. II. Title.

        PS3623.I8765 W38 2015
        813.4 --dc23   2015945736

River Jude Press
www.riverjudepress.com

Cover Image Pixabay, MysticsArtDesign

This is a work of fiction. Any resemblance to persons living or dead is purely coincidental.

For Sarah and Elizabeth

. . . for obvious reasons

The Stolen

Book Two in *The Red Series*

Amanda Witt

River Jude Press

~THE STOLEN CHILD~

WHERE dips the rocky highland
Of Sleuth Wood in the lake,
There lies a leafy island
Where flapping herons wake
The drowsy water-rats;
There we've hid our faery vats,
Full of berries
And of reddest stolen cherries.

Come away, O human child!
To the waters and the wild
With a faery, hand in hand,
For the world's more full of weeping than you
can understand.

Where the wave of moonlight glosses
The dim grey sands with light,
Far off by furthest Rosses
We foot it all the night,
Weaving olden dances,
Mingling hands and mingling glances
Till the moon has taken flight;
To and fro we leap
And chase the frothy bubbles,
While the world is full of troubles
And is anxious in its sleep.

Come away, O human child!
To the waters and the wild
With a faery, hand in hand,
For the world's more full of weeping than you
can understand.

Where the wandering water gushes
From the hills above Glen-Car,
In pools among the rushes
That scarce could bathe a star,
We seek for slumbering trout
And whispering in their ears
Give them unquiet dreams;
Leaning softly out
From ferns that drop their tears
Over the young streams.

Come away, O human child!
To the waters and the wild
With a faery, hand in hand,
For the world's more full of weeping than you
can understand.

Away with us he's going,
The solemn-eyed:
He'll hear no more the lowing
Of the calves on the warm hillside
Or the kettle on the hob
Sing peace into his breast,
Or see the brown mice bob
Round and round the oatmeal-chest.

For he comes, the human child,
To the waters and the wild
With a faery, hand in hand,
from a world more full of weeping than he
can understand.

--William Butler Yeats, 1886

Chapter 1

Surely I was dreaming—the bright sunlight, the sand, the girl standing beside the boat. Surely it was all a dream.

The girl came a step closer, her startled face reflecting mine exactly. It was like looking in a mirror.

Farrell Dean stood up. My feet were caught in the blankets, in the supplies at the bottom of the boat, but somehow I scrambled free and climbed out of the boat and stood facing the apparition on the sand. I stood toe to toe with her, not three feet away, and even that close I could see only myself in her.

Her hair, like mine, was long and flaming red, touched with gold sun streaks. Her eyes, like mine, were green. The shape of her face, the set of her shoulders, even the way she tilted her head—everything about her looked just like me.

She began circling around me on the sand, looking me over from every angle. I stood frozen in place, too stunned to move. So, apparently, was Farrell Dean. He was still standing in the grounded boat, staring at the two of us as if he doubted his own sanity.

"I'm a little bit taller," the girl said, coming back to stand in front of me again. "And a little heavier."

That was a tactful way of putting it. Beside her I felt half-starved, all elbows and angles. She was gently rounded, with curves I had just about given up on ever having. The other difference was that she was wearing a soft-looking dress in various shades of blue and green; a wide blue band kept her hair off her face; and a silver chain set with colored stones hung around her neck. She looked like a more elegant and civilized me. And definitely a cleaner one.

My face began to feel hot as I considered this unflattering contrast. I was wearing my usual rough gray uniform, in worse than usual condition. My pants and my shirt both were torn, streaked with bloodstains, and had been slept in for—I winced—four nights in a row. My hair was wind-tangled, my nose sunburned, my fingernails jagged, and my skin salt-caked; I'd been in the sea more than once over the past few days, not always intentionally.

Farrell Dean looked just as bad as I did, with stubble on his jaw, his golden-brown hair stiff with salt, and his clothes even more tattered and bloodstained than my own. But he wasn't standing beside a clean, elegant, well-rested, well-fed version of himself.

That I was even thinking such trivial thoughts at such a moment speaks to how out of my depth I was; the sight of this girl had all but short-circuited my brain.

"I hope you don't mind my staring at you like this," the girl said, a smile lighting up her face. "I've always known there were two of us, but Papa never said we looked alike. Maybe he couldn't tell—babies all look so alike anyway. And of course you died less than a day after we were born."

Farrell Dean made a choking sound and the girl turned around to face him.

"You're laughing at me," she said, smiling. "I don't care. All my life I thought my sister was dead, and she isn't."

Sister.

There was no question of me finding my voice at the moment, but Farrell Dean didn't speak either. Usually he was unflappable, but he'd been through a lot in the past few days, and now he was seeing double.

"He doesn't talk much, does he?" the girl said, spinning back around toward me, the skirt of her dress flaring out with the movement, her hair glinting in the morning sun.

"Shock," I managed to say.

She lowered her voice. "Who is he? Your husband?"

Husband? I didn't know what she meant; that wasn't a word we had, and somehow I didn't like to ask. I already felt awkward and barbaric enough.

"A friend," I said. "His name is Farrell Dean. He …"

How to put it? I decided to keep it simple. "He helped me escape from a man who was trying to kill me."

The girl nodded, unfazed by this explanation.

"How did you get taken away from us?" she asked. "Do you know?"

"I don't know anything," I said. "I didn't even know you existed. I thought I was born in Optica." Seeing her puzzled expression, I clarified. "That's the city on the other island." I pointed south. "It took us almost two days to get here. Did you call me *Valentina*?"

The girl nodded. "That's your name," she said, and her eyes went round. "You didn't know your own name. Then what do you go by?"

"Red," I said. It felt very short and plain.

The girl laughed. "It's fitting, I suppose," she said, reaching out to touch my hair, so very like her own. "I'm Fiona."

Then her expression shifted to one of concern, and before I knew what was happening she had her arms wrapped around me and started running on with so many new words, I began to feel dizzy.

"You must be very weary," she said. "And hungry too. We should get you to Papa. You were dead and now you're alive again. I'm putting it all wrong, I know, chattering on, but I didn't start screaming when you popped up from the boat. Be sure to tell Angus and Rory that, when you meet them. Be sure to tell them I was very calm and brave."

"Who is Papa?" I asked, pulling away from her. "A teacher? A cook?"

Fiona looked puzzled. "He is both of those, yes. Sometimes. Mostly he's a farmer. A dairy farmer."

I couldn't fathom why she thought she needed to get me to a dairy farmer.

Fiona met my baffled look with one of her own. "I must not be making good sense," she said. "I'm so sorry—I'm terribly flustered. Papa is just papa. Our father."

Our father.

The light reflecting off the water suddenly seemed strangely fragmented.

My father.

From the moment I'd seen this girl it had been obvious that we were sisters; but somehow the mention of a father made it real. All those years in Optica when I felt like a stranger, an outsider, a freak, I was. Here, on this foreign island that I'd never known existed, I had family.

And I'd never have found them, if Farrell Dean had listened to my pleas and curses and demands to take me home.

Blindly I turned toward him. "Did you know?" I asked. "Did you know about her?"

"No," Farrell Dean said, climbing out of the boat. "I had no idea. Maybe Sir Tom did."

We looked at each other. How much had that wily old Guardian kept from us? And yet he had helped us, and was still helping our friends in Optica.

We hoped.

I saw my thoughts reflected in Farrell Dean's eyes. We'd been gone almost two days. Was everyone back home all right? Were they even still alive?

Fiona was peering into our little boat. "Shall we carry your baggage with us?" she said, and then she answered herself. "I think we should. Gabriel Drewblood is around, so it might get taken if we leave it."

She reached into the boat and lifted out the near-empty food bag, the flattened water skin. We divided the rest among us—the blankets, the spade, the traps, various other items Sir Tom had stashed in the bottom of the boat.

If I'd seen all those supplies beforehand, I'd have known he intended to send me away, that the plan he presented to me was a trick. Then I would have refused to get in the boat, refused to come to this island, refused to be torn away from Meritt.

But I didn't see the supplies until too late. I had fallen straight into Sir Tom's trap, all the while thinking I was baiting a trap for someone else.

For two days I'd been furious with Farrell Dean for the part he had played in Sir Tom's ruse. Now I didn't know whether to be grateful or angry or both. I cast a sidelong glance his way, but he was gazing at Fiona. The sea was dancing behind her and the sunlight was catching in her hair, turning it into a fiery halo. Against its vibrancy her face looked very fair, her eyes very green.

"Oh!" she said suddenly, shifting her burdens to one hip. "It occurs to me—Valentina, please don't be offended, but I'm wondering whether I'm rushing you. Perhaps you would prefer to change clothes before meeting Papa?"

I felt my face flush. "I don't have any other clothes," I said. "We left in a hurry." Though even if I'd had time to pack, I'd still only have had gray uniforms. That was all I'd ever worn in my entire life.

Fiona nodded and for a moment stood there in thought, looking out across the sea. The sun was spangling the water with golden sparks, though the breeze was cool.

"Would you like me to fetch you something to wear?" she asked finally, then rushed on. "Though of course you're fine as you are, Papa will be so glad, it doesn't matter a bit how you're dressed, he won't even notice, no one will, they'll just be so happy to see you, but if you want clean clothes I can go get them—I'm a weaver and I have a pretty pink dress I haven't ever worn, I was saving it for my seventeenth birth-day—*our* seventeenth birthday—and I'd love to give it to you, if you'd like to have it, that is. As a welcome-home present."

A pink dress—something pretty to wear. The very idea silenced me.

Fiona, studying my face, misunderstood. "Of course most redheads can't wear pink," she said. "But it works for me—for us—haven't you found?"

Most redheads? All my life I'd been the only redhead anyone had ever seen.

Fiona was gazing at me anxiously, apparently still afraid she'd caused offense. I wasn't offended—I simply didn't know how to answer. No one had ever offered me a pretty pink dress before. No one had ever given me a gift of any sort, save for the odds and ends of food Farrell Dean stole to keep me from starving, or the little corncob dolls old Louie used to make for me when I was very small.

I glanced at Farrell Dean for advice, but he was still staring at Fiona, transfixed.

Somehow that made up my mind. She might look like me, but she was not me, and I didn't intend to try to be her.

"Thank you," I said, raising my chin. "But no. I'll wear my own clothes. Please—"

A lump rose in my throat and I could hardly say the words. "Please take me to our father."

We climbed the dunes to a golden leaf-strewn path that

wound back and forth up a steep hillside. Trees hung over us, their branches thin and bare; in the summer this would feel like a leafy tunnel.

Fiona hummed as we walked—she had decided to save her questions until Papa was present, she said, but really I thought she was giving me time to collect myself. She didn't look anywhere near as shocked as I felt. I supposed it was because although she'd thought I was dead, at least she'd known I existed.

Farrell Dean and I walked silently behind her. The leaves cushioned our steps, rustling gently as we walked over them. I couldn't help but glance over my shoulder now and then at the undergrowth beneath the trees. Farrell Dean, I noticed, did the same. Our woods back home were not a safe place for a stroll.

Once Fiona paused and turned her head as if listening; but she said nothing, and after a moment walked on, apparently unconcerned. Though I peered in the direction she'd turned, I could see nothing but trees and leafy ferns.

At the top of the hill I could see the path straightening out in front of us, stretching through a furrowed field of dark rich dirt, then passing a long pond, and finally weaving through a meadow dotted with black and white cows and edged by large, luxuriant willow trees. Another pasture, fenced off from the first, held a scattering of brown chickens bustling busily around.

Just beyond the meadow stood a collection of four buildings. They weren't the cinder block or corrugated steel buildings I was used to. They were made of stones, flat boards, or a mixture of the two.

A dog came tearing up the path from one of the larger buildings—a big dog, black but with tan thumbprints above his eyes. I hadn't had much experience with dogs, but I didn't think this one looked friendly.

"Here's Rex," Fiona said casually, just as the dog bounded past her and faced us, growling, the hair on the back of its neck standing up.

"Rex," Fiona said, spinning around. "What are you doing? Sit!"

He ignored her and began to inch toward us, crouching, baring his teeth.

Very slowly, Farrell Dean edged in front of me.

"Rex!" Fiona said, more loudly. "Bad dog! *Sit!*"

The dog lowered his rear end toward the ground, but didn't actually sit. He didn't take his eyes off us, either.

Fiona sighed and walked around him to us. "Angus can't seem to teach him manners," she said, then spoke to the dog. "Look, Rex, they're friends."

She patted my arm, and Farrell Dean's, then extended her hand to the dog, palm up. He leaned forward to sniff it curiously.

"Friends," she said firmly. "Be nice to the friends."

The dog seemed to relax a little. He straightened up, edged over to us, and gave us each a careful sniff before bouncing back. Now his tongue was hanging out and he looked like he was grinning.

"Come on, you idiot," Fiona said to him. "Let's go see Papa."

The dog gave us one last glance, then trotted at Fiona's side as we made our way down the path toward the group of buildings.

Fiona pointed to a stone building that had a wisp of smoke rising from its chimney. "That's our cottage," she said. "That's where you and I were born. For that one day there were nine of us, but only Papa and I live there now."

I silently tucked this information away, but Farrell Dean spoke. "You live with your father?" he asked. "Is that usual here?"

Fiona looked baffled. "Who else would I live with?" she said, and then her face fell. "Oh, you mean—Valentina, I'm so sorry. I should have told you right away. Our mother died when you did—I mean, when we thought you died. Right after we were born."

Mutely I nodded. I hadn't even thought about a mother—a father and a sister seemed such enormous riches.

Fiona's smile flashed at me. "I can't tell you how glad you will make Papa," she said. "All my life he's been eaten up by grief. People say he has never been himself, not since you and Mama died. And now—" she laughed. "Now I feel as if I'm bringing life itself to him." She tucked one arm through mine and led me along the path, Farrell Dean following behind us.

Clouds were coming in now, muffling the sun, but the stone house looked snug and warm. The door was wooden, painted a dark green that contrasted prettily with the gray and brown stones. The windowsills were painted green as well. Beneath one was a small kitchen garden; beneath another, clusters of white flowers—a little weary, this time of year, but well tended.

A short fence made of wooden slats surrounded the house; here and there vines twined over it, dry now with winter coming on. As we drew nearer I smelled wood smoke, mingled with a scent that made my mouth water and my stomach growl. Bacon and fresh bread, and something sweet. Cooked apples, perhaps.

At the gate to the little fence Fiona hesitated. "Would you mind waiting outside the cottage for a short moment?" she said. For the first time her expression was less than open, and I had the feeling she was choosing her words carefully. "It's going to be such a shock for Papa. He's been unhappy for so long—I think perhaps I should prepare him a little."

We nodded. She led us across the little grassy area, Farrell Dean carefully pulling the gate shut behind us. At the door to the cottage she set her burdens on the flat stone step and gestured to us to do the same with ours. Then she put a finger to her lips warningly and slipped inside. Though she shut the door behind her it swung back open a crack, and she didn't return to shut it more firmly.

Rex sat down between us and the door and fixed us with a firm stare. He was no longer grinning. Farrell Dean took my arm and pulled me back a step.

"Papa!" Fiona called. "I'm home!"

"So I see," a male voice replied. "You were slow this morning. Rory and Angus have already been and gone again."

"That's a shame," Fiona said. "Papa, I'm starving. Can we set out an extra loaf and some cheese for breakfast?"

"Of course."

"And we'd better set out extra plates."

There was a silence. Then, "Fiona, what do you have to tell me?"

Fiona didn't immediately reply; I could hear the clink of plates, of utensils. I looked at Farrell Dean, shifted a little closer to him. He smiled at me reassuringly, but his eyes were wary. We weren't exactly prepared for a meeting with a father.

Inside the cottage the silence stretched. Somewhere out of sight chickens clucked quietly. A light rain began to fall, misting my hair and face with cool droplets.

"Well, Papa," Fiona said finally. "It's just this. After all these years I finally see the point of going to the beach every morning."

There was a sound of sudden movement; something fell to the floor with a clang; then came footsteps, and the door flew open and a tall man dressed in a dark green shirt and brown pants came out. He looked strong and he wasn't old, perhaps in his mid forties, but he was leaning heavily on a walking stick. His eyes were brown, and his hair was a dark red streaked with silver. He saw Farrell Dean first, then me, and one hand came up as if warding off a blow.

For a long moment no one said anything. Rex circled around us. Expressions shifted on the man's face, amazement and relief, followed by—surely I misread it—something like dread or pain, before he seemed to gain control of his features and they became blankly courteous. I knew I was trembling but couldn't help it. I wanted to turn and run away, back to the beach, back to the little boat, back home to familiar Optica, however troubled it might be.

Out of the corner of my eye I saw Farrell Dean glance at me. Then, with a cautious look at Rex, he stepped forward and cleared his throat.

"This is Red," he said. "I think she's your daughter. My name is Farrell Dean. We came in the night from another island."

The man looked at him and nodded, then back at me. His jaw clenched; I thought he might be trying not to cry. Fiona appeared in the doorway behind him and smiled at us.

Finally the man cleared his throat. "My daughter," he said, holding out a hand to me. "My lost child."

Chapter 2

The fire was warm, its flickering light a pleasant contrast to the gray drizzle outside the windows. Little flames burned in sconces along the walls—gaslight, Fiona had explained. Its glow was warmer, softer, than that of the electric lights at home.

Across the table from me my father—I rolled the word around on my tongue—sat studying me, inch by inch and hair by hair.

I wasn't sure I'd recognize myself, if I could see what he saw. Hospitality had demanded we be given hot baths—not the showers we were accustomed to in Optica—clean clothes, and a meal before any questions were asked or answered. So there I sat, wearing the fancy pink dress after all. I was so afraid of spilling something on it, and so nervous around these strangers who were my family, that ravenous though I was, I barely tasted breakfast.

But I wasn't a mutant, a genetic blip caused by the time of the ashes; I wasn't a freak. Here were two other people with red hair, and apparently they thought it was perfectly normal. Fiona was bigger than I was, it was true, but only a bit; and yet she managed to look healthy and strong, not like someone who should be weeded out of the breeding pool. Maybe I could look like that, if I had enough to eat.

Farrell Dean sat in a carved wooden chair beside me, wearing clothes of the same style as my father's, but with a dark blue shirt. He had shaved. His hair was clean and combed, and he smelled faintly spicy. I, on the other hand, smelled thoroughly floral, thanks to the scented oils Fiona had insisted on pouring into my bath.

She also had washed my hair with scented soap and then combed it out for me, making me sit at her dressing table while she stood behind me. Her dressing table had its own matching little stool and a large oval mirror, and its surface was scattered with combs, brushes, pretty little jars, and ribbons of various colors, along with all sorts of things I'd never seen before.

As Fiona combed my hair I studied us in the mirror. My eyes were a slightly brighter green, and my coloring was a shade darker, perhaps from spending all my days outside in the fields. I was glad of the differences; though I was smaller and slighter, I didn't look completely like a pale shadow of my sister.

Now with dinner finished, she was bustling around, clearing dishes from the table. Farrell Dean and I had tried to help, but she waved us away. "Sit with Papa," she said. "There'll be plenty of time later for you to help."

The room we sat in ran the whole front length of the cottage. A fireplace and hearth covered one wall. A long table and twelve chairs—where we sat—stood between the fire and the area where Fiona moved back and forth between sink, counter, and stove.

"You have your very own kitchen," I said, and Fiona laughed.

"Things must be very different in Optica," she said.

I nodded. Here, it seemed from what I had gathered so far, people lived wherever they pleased—in what they called a *town*, which seemed to be a sort of small city, or out by themselves, like my father did. They apparently chose their own occupations and procured their own food, either by raising it themselves or by trading for it. Children lived with their parents. People chose their own breeding partners—they called these "husbands" or "wives"—and generally stayed together even after they stopped having children. This situation was called being married. Watchers, wardens, and Guardians had not been mentioned, but something called the Isle Council met now and then, though they seemed to have no real power.

And I had five brothers—*five*—whose names were Rufus, Mick, Rory, Angus and the one in the middle, age-wise, whose name I couldn't recall. Fiona went on about him less than about the others.

For I'd gathered all this from Fiona, as she laughed and chatted and rambled on about everything under the sun. I thought the constant flow might wear on me before too long, but at the moment I was glad for her chatter, which covered everyone else's silence and—yes, I had to admit it—discomfort.

Probably we were all still stunned, I thought. No one could expect us to behave as usual in a situation this bizarre.

Now my father leaned back in his chair and took a deep breath, as if preparing for something. Though his hair was red like mine, I couldn't find my features in his face, which was long with a strong jaw. He was a good-looking man in a severe sort of way, and lines of tension webbed his eyes. Perhaps it was the shock of seeing me, but he hadn't yet smiled even once. He had been welcoming, courteous, and apparently deeply moved by my arrival. But he had not smiled.

"I've been wondering where to begin," he said now, handing Fiona his empty cup, his eyes still on me. "Your beginning seems the logical place."

I nodded and sat up a little straighter in my chair. Beside me Farrell Dean shifted his chair a little closer to mine. My father's gaze fell on him for a moment, weighing, considering. He had told Farrell Dean that his name was Eric Alleyn, and I was finding it easier to think of him that way. "Papa" did not come naturally to me.

"Your mother's name was Rachel," Eric Alleyn said. "She and I married when we were not much older than you are now, and in the course of time had five sons. When she fell pregnant again, we expected yet another."

He spoke slowly, as if measuring his words. "But she was ill during that last pregnancy, and the midwife said this meant that perhaps, after all, we would have a daughter. She was right. We had Fiona. And a few minutes later, we also had you."

Strangely, I found myself listening to the sound of his words as much as to their sense. The cadences were not quite like ours in Optica. They were more rolling, melodic, rather like Ezzie's when he sang. I think, now, that it was simply too much for me, the story my father told. I was distancing myself, protecting myself, by focusing on his musical voice and letting the meaning slip in beneath it.

"I've never seen anyone as happy as your mother was then," Eric Alleyn was saying. "Worn out as she was with the delivery, hurting, still your mother was happy. She loved her boys, but she'd always wanted a girl as well, and now she had two. She laughed and cried at the same time, holding you both in her arms, with all five boys gathered around her on the bed."

"The midwife scolded her for crying," Fiona broke in from the other side of the room. "Rowena Marchrest. She said it was bad luck for a mother's tears to fall on her baby, like our mother's fell on you."

Eric Alleyn didn't turn around to look at her, but his voice was stern. "Nothing that happened was your mother's fault, Fiona. Her tears had nothing to do with anything but happiness."

Fiona didn't look a bit concerned at being rebuked. She smiled at me, picked up a pan, and slid it into a sink full of soapy water—they did their own dishes here, as well. They seemed to do everything themselves. But Fiona looked prepared. Her sleeves were rolled up and she wore long rubber gloves. She also had a big white apron tied around her waist, protecting her beautiful clothes.

"On that day we named you," Eric Alleyn continued. "And your mother nursed you and sang to you and took pictures of you, and we sent the three older boys across the island to tell your mother's folks you'd been born."

"They weren't expecting us to come so early," Fiona added. "Or else Nana would have been here already, and maybe you would have lived."

I blinked and Farrell Dean shifted in his seat, but my father merely nodded. "Eighteen hours after you were born," he said, "you died."

He gazed at me, but his brown eyes looked as if they were seeing something else. He certainly wasn't seeing a living, breathing girl sitting not three feet away from him. Although the room was warm, I shivered. It was so quiet I could hear a clock ticking. Under the table Farrell Dean's foot moved, pressed against mine, and I was grateful.

"The midwife said you were probably just too small to live," Fiona said, breaking the silence. "Too small and too early. I was a little bigger." She dried the pan she was holding, set it aside with a clang.

"Yes," our father agreed. "But you were both tiny mites. Tiny little lasses, both with red hair like mine. Rachel's hair was dark, and when she saw the two of you she said, laughing, 'No one will ever wonder who their father is.' That's what she said every time we had a redheaded baby. And this time, like every other time, I told her no one would ever wonder, not even if the child's hair was yellow, like no one of our kin."

"Because Mama and Papa were devoted to each other," Fiona explained. "Everyone knew that."

Eric Alleyn nodded, but his face was grim. "But even then," he said, "even when we were laughing together, Rachel wasn't well. She was bleeding too heavily, and she had a fever, and nothing we did helped. The midwife had antibiotics and we started her on those, and I wished I had sent one of the older boys for a doctor, but they were long gone and there was no one left to send.

"So I left the midwife to tend both the babies, and I tended my wife. And because I did, because I was sitting with your mother through the night, afraid I would lose her, I lost you as well. While your mother was dying, the midwife came and told me you were dead."

The grief and anger in his voice was as fresh as if all this had happened yesterday. I wanted my return to comfort him, give him the joy Fiona had predicted it would give, but as he sat there at the long table, looking at me as if I were still dead, a cold conviction settled in my heart. It might be that his grief was all for our mother, and my return was only a drop in the desert of his sorrow; or it might be that mourning itself had become a habit he would find hard to break. In any case, my return would not mend his wounds as easily as Fiona had hoped.

And somehow, irrationally, it felt like my failure and my loss. I felt tears prickle the backs of my eyes.

Fiona wiped her hands on a towel and sat down beside her father, across from Farrell Dean.

"The midwife lied," she said briskly, leaning toward her father.

Beside me Farrell Dean muttered, "That's a safe

conclusion."

Eric Alleyn cast a sharp glance at Farrell Dean. "Why would she lie?" he said.

"Papa—" Fiona gestured at me. "Valentina is alive. The midwife said she died. Clearly she must have lied to you."

He sighed. "Yes, Fiona," he said. "But why? Why would she tell a man that his daughter had died, if it wasn't true?"

He hadn't raised his voice, but a sharp line cut between his eyebrows. He looked around the table at the three of us, but I certainly had no answer, and Farrell Dean didn't either.

"Tell the rest," Fiona prompted.

Eric Alleyn nodded. "After your mother died," he said to me, "I wanted to bury you with her, in her arms. But Rowena had already buried you. In case you carried a contagion, she said."

"And besides," Fiona put in, "she thought you might draw my soul away. Like a drowning man trying to live, you might pull me down with you."

I opened my mouth to protest, to say I'd never do such a thing, even if it were possible, but fortunately Farrell Dean's solid presence beside me kept me from floundering into that morass.

Eric Alleyn was going on with his tale, rapidly now, as if to get it over. "I understood why she'd buried you," he said. "After all, I'd been fair out my mind with grief over Rachel. It wasn't as if Rowena could get a clear answer out of me. So, fine. She had buried you. But I wanted to know where.

"And Rowena told me. She had wrapped you in one of your grandmother's quilts, she said, and put you under one of the big willow trees. She even told me which one. She thought I would bury your mother on the other side of the tree and be done with it. But I didn't want you out in the meadow; I wanted you both to be nearer to me. So I went to dig you up."

"He couldn't find you," Fiona said, putting her hand on his. "So he dug up practically the entire meadow. Hole, after hole, after hole. He dug in the daytime, and he dug at night. He forgot to eat, to bathe, to shave. He didn't milk the cows and they went dry."

It sounded like a tale often told in this house.

"Papa was strong already," Fiona said, "but now his arms grew hard as rocks. People tried to stop him, tried to reason with him, but no one could. He dug like a man obsessed, like a man under a spell. Gabriel even came from the other side of the island and tried to stop him, but still Papa kept digging."

Eric Alleyn turned his head and spat on the pale wood floor. Fiona eyed him reprovingly, but went on without comment. "The more Papa dug," she said, "the more upset the midwife got, until finally she gave up midwifery and moved away to the other side of the island, and all the women on this side were angry at Papa because then they had to go to the clinic or risk childbirth alone, but no one said anything to Papa about it because everyone was afraid of him. They thought he'd gone mad."

"I had," Eric Alleyn said darkly. "The midwife said she must have been mistaken, that it had been dark, late … and there was more than one willow, and we'd had calves in the pasture that year, so the ground was torn up, uneven, grass and rocks and dirt, and then of course it had rained as well. And a baby's grave is very small."

"Eventually our mother's family took Mama away and buried her," Fiona said. "And the boys stayed with other people, and Granny Rose—Papa's mother—came here and took care of me, because Papa wouldn't let me leave the place."

Her father reached over and took her hand.

"Finally I realized," he said, "that I was losing the rest of my family as well as Rachel and the baby. The boys were growing unruly, especially Rory and Angus, and I was ashamed. I had neglected them. I had neglected my living for the sake of my dead." His eyes were fixed on mine. "And so I quit digging for you, Valentina. I gave up and began trying to restore our family, our home."

Eric Alleyn fell silent, watching me as if waiting for a response. Somewhere the clock ticked quietly, counting the seconds while I desperately cast around for something to say.

Should I say that it was good he stopped digging, given that I wasn't buried in the meadow at all? Should I apologize for causing all that trouble, even inadvertently? Should I say something cheery about coming back, about putting all this misery behind us now?

I didn't know. Though I'd dreamed of meeting my parents a thousand times, back in Optica, I'd never imagined anything remotely like this.

"And then Old Silas came," Fiona said.

Good—the story wasn't over yet; I didn't have to think of what to say.

But my father had an odd reaction to Fiona's words. He raised a hand—it looked as if he meant to hush her—but then he let his hand drop and didn't speak.

Fiona went on. "After all the boys came back home," she said, "about six months after the deaths, Old Silas came. He was a tinker—a traveling salesman—and not quite right in the head. He mended pots and sold odds and ends, things we could have gotten just as well at the store in Doria, but we bought from him because he meant well and he couldn't hold down a regular job. So Silas showed up late one afternoon, and when he heard our mother had died, he got all worked up—he loved our mother, everyone did—and then he went into town and got drunk. He always did drink a lot. Died of it, eventually. Pickled his liver." She leaned toward

Eric Alleyn. "Tell the rest," she said. "You tell it best."

He looked as if he didn't particularly want to, but he did. "Silas came back late that night, staggering with drink," he said. "And he banged on the door. Woke everyone up, me, all five boys, the baby, my mother. While Mother tried to settle the children I went outside to deal with Silas, and he told me that he'd just realized what he'd seen the night you died."

Eric Alleyn paused, clearly reluctant to go on.

"Silas had been sleeping near the beach that night," Fiona said. "And in the dark hours of early morning he awoke to see two lights. They came down the path to the beach, hovered at the edge of the water, and then went skimming away. A larger light, and a smaller one. Mother and child, he said. The souls of a mother and child departing this life."

Beside me Farrell Dean sat very still. Eric Alleyn made a helpless gesture with one hand.

Then Fiona spoke again, and for the first time she sounded subdued. "It's obvious, now that you've come back," she said. "Someone kidnapped you, Valentina. Old Silas saw their lights. But how could we have known? Some people say other islands were out there, but we didn't know it was true. And we don't have seaworthy boats—just coracles and such, for the tidal traps and trotlines. Who could have imagined you'd been taken off the island?"

Her voice sounded pleading. "And every single morning since then," she went on, "every single morning, someone in this family has gone to the place your souls departed. First Papa went, and then when he lost his leg, one of the boys went, and now me." She turned toward him. "It was out of respect," she said, but her voice was uncertain. "For remembrance."

Eric Alleyn didn't answer.

Finally Farrell Dean spoke. His voice, with its familiar Optica cadences, sounded solid and matter-of-fact. "You knew Red had been taken," he said to Eric Alleyn. "You were hoping somehow she would come back."

Eric Alleyn ran a hand over his eyes. "That was too much to hope," he said. "I went because I had to do something, and going to the sea was the only thing I knew to do."

Chapter 3

For a long time we sat in silence. Even Fiona stopped talking, though she fidgeted, unrolled her sleeves, straightened objects on the table. I didn't know how to feel about this story I'd been told, this painful tale of my birth and disappearance, my mother's death, my father's grief.

All this had happened to me, and I'd never known anything about it.

All those years while I was growing up in Optica, living in the children's dorm and then the girls' dorm, going to school, working in the fields, being watched by the Watchers and disciplined by the wardens; all the time I was tagging around after Meritt and his friends because there were no children my age; all the time I was pretending that Instructor Rafe was my father, searching faces, longing to see someone, anyone, with any resemblance to me—all that time, every day, someone here was going to the water to wait for me.

"The rain has stopped," Eric Alleyn said, cutting into my thoughts. "It's only misting now. Would you like to step outside and get some fresh air?"

Gratefully I pushed back my chair and stood up, and Farrell Dean and Fiona did the same.

"Fiona," said her father. "Let our guests have a moment alone. We've given your sister a lot to think about."

He turned to me. "I hope you'll forgive me, however, if I watch you from the window. You've been gone a long time. It would kill me, I think, to lose you again."

Farrell Dean and I walked across the sodden grass and stood beside the fence. It enclosed the meadow where, in the distance, black and white cows grazed. Nearby but out of sight, chickens clucked softly. I faced away from the house and took deep breaths of wet chilly air, feeling as if I had just awoken from a nightmare.

"Are you all right?" Farrell Dean said. With one hand he brushed the top fence rail free of raindrops, then leaned forward and rested his forearms on it.

"I guess so," I said. "I'm glad to have been missed. But all that grief ..." I trailed off, gazing across at the line of willows in the distance, graceful, blurred by the mist—the willows where my father had dug for my body.

"Fiona wasn't thrilled he's been misleading her all these years," Farrell Dean said, and something in his voice made me turn.

"She didn't say anything about it," I said, eyeing him.

"She wouldn't, would she? Not in front of us, and maybe not in private, either."

So Farrell Dean admired my sister's diplomacy or restraint or whatever it was. Fine. That wasn't a virtue I could claim, at least not with him.

Taking care not to snag the pink dress, I climbed up on the bottom fence rail, turning my face to the misty wet sky. "She ought to be upset," I said. "He lied to her. He taught her to mourn for someone who wasn't dead, instead of telling her the truth about why they went to the sea every day."

Farrell Dean shrugged. "It's the story about her mother's death. Lights for souls are nicer than kidnapped sisters. I can see why he'd want to soften it."

"Yeah, I can too. If he'd told her the truth, she'd have wanted him to find a way to come after me. You heard her, making excuses for why he hadn't."

Farrell Dean was silent for a long moment. I didn't look at him, but out of the corner of my eye I could see him leaning against the fence, looking unfamiliar in his borrowed clothes.

"Your father couldn't have found you," he said finally, gently. "Even bracketing off the fact that he didn't have a boat. He only learned you'd been kidnapped six months after the fact, when Silas showed up and told him about the lights. Even if he'd followed Sir Tom the very night it happened, he probably couldn't have found you. The sea is a big place."

Sir Tom.

I felt stupid. Of course it had been Sir Tom. He was Chief Guardian; he felt guilty; he'd sent us here, and sent us in his boat—the one-and-only boat, he'd said; and there was something else, too. He'd said that he owed me more than he owed anyone else.

Yeah. Like almost seventeen years with my family.

"We shouldn't have trusted him," I said, grabbing the fence rail for balance as I turned to face Farrell Dean. "I went and told everyone to trust him, and now he's got our friends—"

"Slow down," Farrell Dean said. "I've been thinking about this too, and I'm not sure we should write him off."

"He *stole me*. We should have trusted Angel instead."

"But Sir Tom sent you back, right? And we got here safely. Definitely we should be careful about him, but he's right about one thing. We can't possibly defeat the Watchers unless you and I bring back help from this island."

The Watchers had all kinds of weapons, and the wardens knew how to use them. Sir Tom had tried to teach us how to shoot, but most of us were lousy, and we didn't have time to learn to be better. And then there was the wall around Optica, which made the city easy to defend. Farrell Dean was right; we couldn't win. Not unless we found help here. People, weapons. Strategies. Food, even.

"Do you think my father will help us?" I asked, glancing back at the house, half-expecting the curtains to twitch. But they didn't move, and I wondered whether Eric Alleyn really was bothering to keep an eye on me or not.

"He might help," Farrell Dean said. "But I don't think he's who Sir Tom had in mind."

"Because he's crippled."

Farrell Dean shrugged. "Sir Tom wasn't specific about who we should look for—you know how he is—but he kept saying we'd have to get to the other side of the island. He was definite about that. He said it might be quite a walk, but that on the other side of the island there would be people who could help us."

Carefully I lifted the hem of my dress and stepped down from the fence.

"If we're going to keep listening to Sir Tom, that means we can't stay here," I said, looking at the narrow road that wound around the barn and out of sight. I wasn't sure whether to be sorry or relieved that we'd be leaving, and it suddenly occurred to me that my father had referred to me as a "guest."

"We can't stay long," Farrell Dean said. "But we can stay tonight, tomorrow even. And once we've found the people we're looking for, we can come back. There should be plenty of time for you to get to know your family, once we've done what we came to do. We'll have to wait until the currents change before we can go home, anyway."

Home.

I didn't have a home. In Optica I was a freak; here I was an extra. I didn't belong anywhere.

"Hey," Farrell Dean said softly, but I didn't look at him. "Can I still call you Red? Valentina is a pretty name, but I've been calling you Red for almost seventeen years now, and I'm not sure I can break the habit."

Tears started to my eyes. I glanced up at him, wanting to say I was sorry—though I wasn't sure for what, other than for not being calm and courteous like my sister—but Farrell Dean was looking at something beyond me.

Then, meeting my eyes, he reached up and tucked a stray strand of hair behind my ear.

"Brace yourself," he said. "I think some of your brothers are here."

Chapter 4

There were two of them—one with dark hair, one with red. They didn't stop to introduce themselves. They grabbed Farrell Dean and yanked him away from me so quickly that I didn't realize what was happening until one of them had pulled Farrell Dean's arms behind his back and the other slammed a fist into his stomach.

"Stop!" I yelled. "Leave him alone!"

They ignored me—they had to, because now they were defending themselves. Farrell Dean went slack in the dark-haired man's grip, throwing him off balance, and then twisted and shoved hard with his shoulder. The dark-haired man stumbled and fell to his knees in the mud, letting go of Farrell Dean as he fell. Farrell Dean turned just in time to duck another punch from the redhead.

The dark-haired man had gotten to his feet, and for the first time I got a clear look at his face. He didn't look particularly ferocious. In fact he lifted his hands in surrender and started to say something, but Farrell Dean swung around and punched him in the jaw, just as the redhead tackled Farrell Dean from behind. The three of them came down in a heap and then Farrell Dean and the redhead rolled free, fists flying, while the dark-haired man got to his feet and brushed himself off.

Someone was bleeding—I couldn't tell which. I saw a dark smear on Farrell Dean's face, on his hand, on the other man's neck. The dark-haired man seemed to be looking for an opening so he could kick at Farrell Dean. I shoved in front of him, between him and Farrell Dean, but he pushed me aside. "You're going to get yourself hurt," he said. "And I'm trying to break it up."

The cottage door banged open and Fiona came running toward us, holding her dress up above her knees, her legs flashing. When she reached us she plunged right into the chaos, flinging herself down on top of the redhead. He shook her off. She fell hard on one arm and cried out in pain, and I bent to help her.

That's when the brothers noticed there were two of us.

Their flabbergasted expressions would have been funny except for the fact that an already badly wounded Farrell Dean had just been attacked. He shoved the redhead off him and sat up, bracing one arm across his ribs.

"Is this how you treat guests?" I said, pointing at Farrell Dean. He was covered in mud and blood, and the sleeve of his shirt was torn. "I'm ashamed to be related to you."

The brothers stared at me; then their heads turned in unison toward Fiona, and back again to me. I felt their eyes on my face as I knelt on the muddy ground beside Farrell Dean and wiped at his bloody face with my sleeve. All I managed to do was smear the blood around.

"I'm okay," he muttered, moving my hand away and warily keeping his eyes on his attackers.

Fiona had taken up scolding where I had left off. "You complete idiots!" she said, shoving the dark-haired brother hard enough to make him stagger. "I'm ashamed to be related to you, too!"

The redheaded brother, sprawled on the ground where Farrell Dean had flung him, sat up. "But Fee," he said, looking uneasily at me, then at Fiona, then addressing the air midway between the two of us. "We didn't know she wasn't you. How could we know that?"

"You could have stopped to check before you went rushing in like fools!" Fiona said.

"Cut a guy some slack," the redhead said, still patently unsure which of us was which. "It's not like you split into two every day."

He seemed to grow more startled the longer he looked at the two of us, until his eyes were round as saucers. His hair was a lighter red than mine, more orange in color, and his face was covered with freckles.

The other brother was quicker to sort us out. Coming to where I knelt by Farrell Dean, he crouched down beside me, studying my face. He was smaller than his father and brother, more compactly built.

"Valentina?" he said.

"So they say." I spoke tersely, still angry, but at the same time I couldn't take my eyes off him. Though he had dark eyes and dark hair, I could see my own features echoed in his face.

"I'm Rory," he said. "And I'm terribly sorry—"

"As well you should be." Eric Alleyn had finally arrived, breathing hard. Fiona had said he'd lost a leg, but it looked to me like he had both. Either one of them was fake, or she'd just meant that he'd lost the use of it.

"I am," Rory said. "Truly, Valentina. Forgive me. We had no idea. We thought you were long dead."

"Farrell Dean's the one you should apologize to," I said, and Rory nodded.

"I do apologize," he said, turning to Farrell Dean. "From the bottom of my heart, I apologize. So will Angus—" he nodded in his brother's direction—"once he gets his wits about him."

Farrell Dean gave him a long level look. He was still white-faced, clearly in pain. "Apology accepted," he said after a moment. "But only because Angus pulled his first punch."

Angus got to his feet and sprang forward. "I did!" he said. "At the last second I realized I didn't know your face. Fee's got all kinds of riff raff hanging around, but most of them I at least recognize."

He held out a hand to Farrell Dean and pulled him up. Rory also stood, then cocked his head and looked down at me.

"If you'll allow," he said, extending his hand. I took it, and my brother pulled me to my feet and into his arms.

"Now you just wait one minute," Fiona said. "You mean you attacked an innocent stranger, and you're trying to blame it on me?"

"Somebody has to stand up for Tor," Angus said, but I was hardly listening. I don't think I'd ever been held like that in my life—certainly not that I could remember. Rory wrapped both arms around me and held me close, held me hard. He held me like he meant it, like he never intended to let me go, and I found myself holding him the same way.

My brother. My own brother.

From behind me Angus spoke. "Come on, Rory. Stop hogging the new sister."

He pulled me away from Rory, lifted me off my feet, and spun me around. As soon as my feet hit the ground he let out a wild whoop that nearly deafened me.

"Tor does not have dibs on me," Fiona said, clearly still angry. I wasn't sure who she was talking to, but both brothers ignored her.

Farrell Dean didn't look quite focused. I hoped he wasn't concussed.

"Tor is like another brother," Fiona said. "A better brother than you two, anyway."

Then both of the brothers were speaking at the same time, and so was Fiona, and I couldn't make a word out. Farrell Dean raised one hand to his head.

"Enough!"

Dead silence fell. Eric Alleyn looked at his sons.

"If you will try to behave like minimally civilized adults, I'll leave you to get acquainted with your sister and her friend," he said. "Don't make me come back out here to break up childish squabbles."

"Yes, sir," Rory and Angus said in unison.

Eric Alleyn looked at Fiona.

"Yes, Papa," she said.

Then he turned to me. "They're a little wound up," he said, with a glint in his eye that might have been amusement. "Angus is not quite twenty, and Rory is twenty-one. But boys mature later than girls, so they say."

Fiona laughed. When Eric Alleyn turned away and went stumping back to the cottage, Angus pinched her arm. She winced and elbowed him, but the skirmish took place silently.

"It's starting to rain again," Rory said. "Let's go to the gazebo."

He led us to a little open-sided building that had benches built around its half-height walls. I sat on one of them, sheltered, and watched my father making his slow way back to the house, the rain flattening his hair against his head. Did he move with a melancholy air, or was I imagining it?

"Don't worry about him," Rory said as Eric Alleyn disappeared from sight.

"He's actually quite perky today," Angus said. "Delirious with happiness, I expect."

Fiona gave him a reproving look. "Papa's suffered too much," she said. "You can't possibly understand."

"And you can?"

"I at least try."

Rory ignored them. He sat down and put one arm on the short wall behind me, around my shoulders, and studied my face. "I remember that night," he said quietly. "I remember you."

On my other side Farrell Dean turned, listening, and Fiona and Angus abruptly stopped bickering and scooted toward us.

"I was too young to remember," Angus said. "I was three. Excitement and then sadness, and Mama was gone. That I remember. No details."

"We don't care," Fiona told him. "Hush and let Rory talk."

"We were sitting by the fire," Rory said, his dark eyes distant, remembering. "And Fee was screaming bloody murder. Rowena tried everything but Fee wouldn't be comforted."

"An opinionated brat, even then," Angus said. Fiona pointedly ignored him, and so did Rory.

"Papa came into the room," Rory said. "He said Mama couldn't possibly rest with all that racket. It was worrying her—she wanted to take care of her babies, but hadn't the strength. So Rowena told him she would take Fee outside. Fresh air sometimes helped, she said."

His gaze narrowed, focused on me. "And I said what if the other baby started crying while she was gone? Because Papa had gone back to Mama and there was only Angus and me, and Angus was asleep on the floor, so really there was only me. And Rowena said I would be in charge of you, and she took you out of the crib and handed you to me.

"I thought she'd handed me the treasures of the earth, and was so afraid I'd drop you, but you were good as could be. We sat in Mama's rocking chair beside the fire, and you held onto my finger with your tiny little hand and stared up at me, and then you crammed your other fist in your mouth and you fell asleep."

His face grew bleak. "And I held you like that for ages, being as still as I could so as not to disturb you, until Rowena came and told me you could never be woken again."

I stared at him, horrified. "She told you I had died? While you were holding me?"

Rory nodded. "She put Fee down in the crib, and took you out of my arms. You were completely limp—your little arm fell when Rowena picked you up, just as loose as could be. I'll never forget the sight of that."

He shook his head as if to drive the image away. "Rowena said that Mama and Papa would be unhappy, so I was to not say a word about what had happened. She would handle it, she said. She would take the blame. Then Rowena took you outside."

"How terrible, Rory." What a brutal thing to tell a small child.

"I was holding you," Rory said matter-of-factly. "But somehow I had let you go."

Tears sprang to my eyes. Whoever this Rowena Marchrest was, I had a thing or two to say to her. One glance at Farrell Dean told me he felt the same. And my feelings toward Sir Tom were getting cooler by the second.

"Why'd you never tell me about that?" Angus said to Rory, and at the same moment Fiona said, "Papa will be so upset—"

Rory ignored them, focusing only on me. His dark hair was curling with the mist, just like mine did when it got damp. "Who raised you, Valentina?" he said, and then Angus let loose with a barrage of questions.

"Were they good to you?" he said. "Where were you? How long did it take you to get here? What made you come now? Will you stay?"

I couldn't answer either of them; my mind was lagging behind, asking its own question. Why had Rowena brought Fiona back inside, and sent me away instead? But nobody noticed my hesitation because Angus was still talking.

"Why are you holding your ribs?" he asked Farrell Dean. "I never hit you there. Though I did fall on you, come to think of it. Is something broken?"

That drew everyone's attention. Farrell Dean looked blank—I don't think he'd realized he was bracing his ribs—so I explained for him.

"A few days ago he was almost killed," I said. "He was flogged and beaten, and some ribs got broken, and he was chained to a wall and starved, and then they were going to shoot him but we got him away just in time. Then he had to run, and climb trees, and scale cliffs, and then he fought off a warden who was trying to drown both of us, and then he rowed across the sea to bring me here."

The brothers looked at Farrell Dean respectfully.

Fiona tutted. "You never told me he was injured!" she said to me, then bent solicitously over Farrell Dean. She smelled like her sweet-scented soap. "Is there any infection? Are you bleeding? Pull off your shirt so I can take a look."

"No thanks," Farrell Dean said, laughing. "I'm all right." He was turning a little red, I noted.

Fiona wouldn't be put off.

"You probably need more than I can do for you, anyway. We'd better get you to the clinic in town, have the doctor look at you. Do you ride? No? Never mind. It's too bad Papa won't let us keep a truck, but we can walk—it's actually shorter, walking, because we can take the foot bridge. You probably shouldn't be jolting around on a horse anyway, or even in the wagon. Not in your condition."

Angus laughed.

"In his condition?" he mimicked, gesturing at Rory's

jaw, where a dark bruise was beginning to show. "I don't think he's quite an invalid."

Fiona glared at him, her hands on her hips. "You'd better hope not, Angus bar Alleyn. Fighting a man with broken ribs—you could have punctured his lungs, you idiot, and then where would we be?"

She turned to Farrell Dean. "Your clothes are filthy," she said.

Rory and Angus cast resigned looks at each other.

"Let's go inside and get you changed. Then the boys can take you to the doctor and send messages to the rest of the family, and Valentina and I will start dinner."

"Is that one as bossy as this one?" Angus asked Farrell Dean.

Farrell Dean looked at Fiona, and then at me. "I don't think there's a safe answer to that," he said, and all three boys laughed.

Chapter 5

At the door to the cottage Farrell Dean paused. "You'll be okay?" he asked me.

I nodded.

His lower lip was swollen and he spoke carefully so as not to pull the split open again.

"Stay with Fiona," he said, lowering his voice to a murmur. "Your father's ..."

"A little scary," I finished.

Farrell Dean smiled faintly. "I was going to say 'hard to get a read on,'" he said. "But some people are like that—they don't roll with the punches, you know? And like Fiona said, he's had a lot happen. I wonder how he lost his leg?"

"At least I'll be able to outrun him," I said, only half joking.

Farrell Dean studied me. "I wouldn't let them split us up if I didn't think you'd be safe," he said. "But if you're not comfortable with it, I won't go."

"Don't be silly," I said, giving him a gentle push. "I'll be fine. And you do need to see a doctor. We'll each gather information and we can trade stories when you get back tonight. Maybe in town you can find out about the other side of the island."

Farrell Dean nodded. "It'll only be for a few hours."

He looked like he wanted to say something else, but he didn't. He reached up—I thought he was going to touch my hair—but then he let his hand drop, nodded once, and went out to join my brothers by the little gate.

I stood there watching them go, following the path in the direction opposite the way we'd come. Angus was the tallest, but he was lankier than Farrell Dean, who looked solid and broad-shouldered beside the others. Rory was the shortest and the slightest. They were all wearing dark brown pants—I wondered if all the men on the island wore those. Angus' shirt—less than clean, thanks to the fight—was tan, Rory's was dark red, and the one Farrell Dean had on now was a light blue. I wondered whose clothes he was wearing; they didn't seem the right size for any of the other men. Maybe they belonged to one of the other brothers, the ones I'd hadn't met yet. Rufus, Mick, or Sean.

My father's place sat in a slight depression, not quite a valley, and now the men were almost to the top of the rise. Both of my brothers were looking at Farrell Dean and I wondered what he was saying. Not knowing made me feel a little empty. I'd been with Farrell Dean night and day for—I started counting—more than sixty hours. My family didn't feel nearly as familiar as he did.

Fiona came up behind me and put her hand on the doorframe beside mine, and together we watched the three men vanish over the hill. "He's nice, your Farrell Dean," she said after a moment. "And quite good looking."

"He's not my Farrell Dean," I said.

Fiona's green eyes met mine. "Why ever not?"

I didn't want to talk about Meritt, or about the way breeding partners were assigned in Optica. I felt myself beginning to blush, and I tried to hide it by looking away, after the men, but Fiona wasn't fooled.

"I'll tell you about Tor," she offered. "And then you can

tell me about Farrell Dean. But let's get cleaned up first." She shut the door, linking her arm with mine, and led me toward her bedroom.

She had half a dozen dresses laid out on her bed, each a different color and each beautifully embroidered with a different pattern. A doorway off her bedroom led to a large room where her loom stood, half-filled with a fine sky-blue cloth.

The colors of the clothes here amazed me. All those colors, and they didn't even save them for special occasions; they wore them every day.

For me we picked out a dress in a pale golden color with an embroidered design of green leaves around the neck and hem, and this time Fiona also handed me knitted brown leggings to wear underneath it.

"It's getting cooler," she said. "And that dress isn't as warm as the other." We set the bloodstained pink dress to soak in cold water, and Fiona assured me it would be good as new.

"Don't worry," she said, pulling a green dress out of a drawer to replace the soiled blue one she'd been wearing. "I've got far more clothes than I can wear. The boys always tease me about it. But see? Now we need them. I must have had a premonition you'd come home. We'll need to get you some shoes, though—your feet are more dainty than mine."

Then we headed for the kitchen.

"Papa's sleeping," Fiona said, nodding toward a back room. "His missing leg hurts him and the medicine makes him sleep. He won't hear us. And I've never told anyone all about Tor because I don't have any friends I can really trust. They gossip. But a sister—" she smiled at me. "Your secrets are mine, and mine are yours. Besides, we have to pass the time somehow. We have a lot of carrots and potatoes to peel. So we'll have a good chat and get to know each other, and then the boys will be back and we'll have a nice family dinner."

We did peel a lot of carrots and potatoes. When we had finished and put them in a pot on the stove, we went outside in the misty sweet-smelling afternoon and gathered eggs. Then we cut cabbage and brussel sprouts in the garden, walking on a path of flat stones so that our feet didn't get muddy. Fiona had a cellar lined with jars and jars of summer produce she had preserved herself. She knew how to do all sorts of things I'd never tried. Fortunately she was too busy talking to notice how clumsy and slow I was, how I watched her, trying to follow her lead. Words poured off her tongue like air.

While we worked she told me about her friends and her school. She had stopped going when she was thirteen, when her father lost his leg, but most children went until they were seventeen.

She also pointed out various features of the family's farm—the cows in the meadow were milk cows, and Rory and Angus took care of them and sold milk to neighbors and to people in the towns. Sometimes they hired someone to help out, but mostly they did all the work themselves, with Fiona pitching in whenever she could get free from the kitchen garden and cottage.

"We rotate the cattle and the chickens through four separate pastures," she explained. "It's better for the soil that way. So two pastures are always planted with something, corn or alfalfa or what have you, and two are in livestock."

I wondered if that was true, that the soil did better if you rotated. We'd never rotated anything in Optica.

"I make enough from selling eggs that I can buy thread rather than spinning my own," Fiona was saying. "That frees up time for me to weave. I make most of our clothes, and sometimes clothes for friends and neighbors. They pay me, of course."

She talked without stopping for breath, without requiring anything from me besides an occasional nod. She talked until I began to hope she'd forgotten Tor and Farrell Dean, but she hadn't. She was merely biding her time.

"He's twenty," she said finally, out of the blue. "Tor is. In between Rory and Angus in age."

We were back in the kitchen by then, peeling apples to make pies. Fiona was peeling apples, that is; I was gradually gouging the red peel off one single apple and trying not to cut myself.

"He makes beautiful windows out of stained glass," she went on, her knife slipping smoothly around yet another apple, the peel sliding off in one long graceful curl. "People come from all over the island to buy fancy windows from him. He has dark blond hair and blue eyes, and a big, magnificent, crooked nose, and when he's working he doesn't hear or see anything but the glass.

"Sometimes people go out to watch him work—girls, mostly—because the glass is so beautiful, every color under the sun glinting in the light, but he ignores them because glasswork takes concentration.

"His hands are scarred from accidents—when he was eleven he almost cut off his own thumb, and more than once he burned himself with the hot lead—but he hardly ever gets hurt now."

I had stopped working to listen to her, interested despite myself. Whatever stained glass was, it must be beautiful to see.

"His father has been Council Chief for twenty years," Fiona continued. "Someday Tor will be Council Chief, everyone says. We grew up playing together because the Van Staverns live so near, about a quarter of a mile away. Their house is right beside the path to town, so every time a boy comes out to see me Tor's little sister notices and tells him about it. When I'm eighteen or nineteen," Fiona concluded, looking at me sideways, "I'm going to marry him."

She laughed at my expression.

"But then why did you say he was like a brother?" I asked, and she laughed again.

"So they'd tell Tor," she said. "So he might worry."

I eyed her warily. "And now I'm supposed to ask why you want Tor to worry?"

Fiona grew serious, setting down her paring knife and turning to face me. "Tor thinks I'm his. If I don't make him work for me a little, he'll take me for granted our whole lives long. But if he has to worry about whether he can get me, if he thinks I'm less interested in him than he is in me ... well, that's a very satisfactory beginning."

And to think Cline had accused me of toying with Farrell Dean. What would he make of Fiona? And what did the other boys think, the ones who visited her—and did they get beat up by her brothers, or had Farrell Dean had the bad luck to show up at the exact wrong moment?

Fiona was looking at me expectantly, but for the life of me I could think of nothing to say—that is, nothing diplomatic. At least being assigned to a breeding partner was simple.

"Does Tor beat up your other ... friends?" I finally asked.

Fiona laughed. "No. That is not at all Tor's way."

"But it is Angus and Rory's."

She nodded, looking at me curiously. "You sound like you disapprove. Don't men fight on your island?"

"Sometimes they do," I said. "But not over women." I hesitated, but went on. "Is this the way it always works? Marriage? With strategies, like in a game of chess?"

Fiona shook her head. "No. But I know Tor, and I know me. We both need a little adventure first, before we settle down." Then her eyes narrowed. "You're acting as if you've never heard of courting. How do people get married on this other island?"

Well, that took some explaining.

Fiona listened with growing astonishment. When I described the assigning of breeding partners, she dropped the apple she was peeling onto the counter. When I told her about relief workers, she wiped her hands on her apron and lowered herself down into one of the chairs. When I got to the part about Meritt and the blonde warden, she propped her elbows on the table and rested her chin in her hands, her eyes growing rounder and rounder.

Somehow I ended up telling her just about everything—about the city meetings, the Watchers, the Guardians, about leaving Meritt standing on the cliff above the sea while I railed at Farrell Dean. Even as I spoke, I couldn't quite believe I was telling my sister so much; but once she stopped talking, she listened so intently that I couldn't seem to help myself.

I did draw the line before I told her that all of us in Optica were an experiment; somehow that felt too humiliating, and she'd ask all sorts of questions that I wouldn't know the answers to.

Neither did I tell her about Sir Tom. I'd trusted him, and he'd betrayed me. Maybe he'd only betrayed me in the past, when he kidnapped me, but I couldn't possibly know for sure. And I'd never forgive myself, if I'd led my friends to trust the wrong person and harm came to them because of it. Despite Farrell Dean's reassurances, I had a sick feeling that I should have insisted we throw in our lot with Angel. He was unsettling, true, but he was Meritt's father. And he hadn't torn apart my family.

Even without those bits, though, I had given my sister plenty to digest.

"That is absolutely horrible," Fiona said when I'd finished my tale. That was the reaction I'd expected. Then she added something I didn't expect. "It's a good thing Farrell Dean carried you away," she said. "You've been enchanted."

"I've ... what?"

Fiona nodded grimly. "Meritt has enchanted you. Cast a spell on you."

"Why would he do that?"

"So you'll do his bidding. You said it yourself—you told Farrell Dean that you'd do anything Meritt wanted."

I stared at my sister. She wasn't joking.

"He probably learned how from his father," she said. "Angel sounds like a powerful Enchanter. Or maybe Meritt just naturally knew how—maybe the ability to cast spells is genetic."

"Um, Fiona?" I said. "I don't know if that can really happen ... enchantings. I mean ... I think I just decided, all on my own, that I like him."

"Why would you do that?" she demanded. "Do you think Meritt is good for you? Does he make you happy? Does he keep you safe? Does he love you best of all?"

"He loves me," I said. "I'm sure of it."

"Yes, but there are all sorts of love."

"He kissed me. Twice."

She snorted. "Don't be a baby, Valentina."

My cheeks flamed.

"Men are like that," she said, more gently. "They don't mean anything by kisses. At least, the ones who kiss you don't mean anything by them. The ones who don't kiss you, do mean something."

The logic of that eluded me.

"Unless they're just too timid to try anything," she added. "It can be hard to tell. Honor and timidity sometimes look a little alike. Though most boys do eventually grow out of being timid, and hopefully they don't ever grow out of being honorable."

"What makes you such an expert?" It came out sounding rude, but Fiona only laughed.

"I grew up with five older brothers, remember? And all their friends." Her smile faded. "And there were always girls wanting to be my friends because they had a crush on one of the boys. They'd ask me whether he liked them, or how to make him like them."

She shrugged, her face lighting up again. "Sometimes I'd ask the boys what to say. I got quite an education. And of course I heard all the lectures Papa and Granny Rose gave the boys, as well."

When I didn't reply she studied me carefully for a long moment. "All right," she said. "We'll put Meritt in the 'we don't know' category. Maybe he has enchanted you. Or maybe he's just a handsome boy who happened to be in the right place at the right time."

I raised an eyebrow, unsure of her meaning.

"Put in charge of you when you were young and vulnerable," she added.

I didn't think Option B was making him sound any better, and it made me sound worse.

"You said yourself that you were lonely," Fiona pointed out.

"I don't want to talk about it anymore," I said, as evenly as I could. "Tell me about the other brothers."

And that's what she did while we finished the pies. Rufus was twenty-eight and married, with four children and another on the way; apparently fertility wasn't the issue here that it was in Optica.

"He's an engineer," Fiona said, and then glanced over her shoulder and lowered her voice. "And he's a little too much like Papa. They're always either in perfect agreement and driving everyone else crazy, or at complete loggerheads and driving everyone else crazy."

The next oldest, Sean, was twenty-six and recently married, with an infant son. "He's a schoolteacher," Fiona said. "But he was never mine, thank goodness."

I waited for an explanation, but my sister merely smiled. "Just wait," she said. "You'll understand when you meet him. Now the next one, Mick, you'll love. Everyone loves Mick."

"Is he married?"

"No," Fiona said dryly. "And I'm not holding my breath. He's one of the ones who kisses."

Mick was a construction worker who built buildings. He recently had helped Rory and Angus build their own cottages; Rory was courting, and Angus insisted that he'd surely be courting soon, just as soon as he met a girl who laughed at his jokes. Angus had just started to breed peacocks. Fiona described their feathers, but I couldn't quite believe what she said. Peacocks sounded as unlikely as Enchanters.

In addition to running the family dairy farm, Rory also wrote stories, took them to town and had copies printed, and sold them to people who paid to read them.

About this time Eric Alleyn finally came out of his room. I wished then I'd remembered to ask about his leg, but I didn't want to mention it in front of him. He sat down in one of the rocking chairs by the fire and watched us sweep the floor, season the stew, and fold clean laundry.

It made me self-conscious, having Eric Alleyn in the room, but I tried to act natural. He spoke to Fiona occasionally, but mostly watched us—me in particular—from his chair across the room. It was as if he couldn't take his eyes off me, but couldn't bear to speak to me. I told myself that Fiona was right; he had suffered.

At six o'clock Fiona looked at the clock, which hung on the wall near the door.

"They should be here any time now," she said. We set the table and Fiona sliced a loaf of bread. Eric Alleyn said nothing, and under his watchful gaze our conversation faltered.

Half an hour later, Fiona looked at the clock. "Any minute," she said.

I wandered over to look at the books on the low shelf beneath one of the windows. Most of them were farm-oriented—veterinary information about cattle disorders, books about textiles and weaving, a few cookbooks. Then there was one that seemed out of place: *Your Self, Your Dreams*, it was called.

I flipped through it. Some of it was about interpreting dreams, but a lot of it was about thinking about yourself while you were awake. There were chapters on recognizing your own motives, articulating your emotions, assessing your desires and your goals, considering where others fit with your "personal profile," and managing "counter-indicated" thoughts. Was this where Fiona got all that business about Meritt enchanting me?

Fiona walked up as I was putting the book back on the shelf. "Oh, look at that old thing," she said, picking it up and turning it over in her hand. "That's one of our introductory textbooks. We were tested over it in school. Did you have psychology classes?"

I shook my head. "We just sort of … get on with things," I said. "Optica's more about being practical than about—" I groped for a phrase from the book—"dreaming your desires and living your dreams."

Fiona looked at me seriously. "But you aren't in Optica now," she said, handing me the book. "When you have to make your own decisions, it helps to know who you are. Otherwise your decisions aren't your own, are they? They're someone else's."

I didn't know what to say to that.

"Leave her be, Fiona," Eric Alleyn said from across the room. "Not everybody likes to take her heart apart like a broken clock."

It was almost enough to make me glad he was in the room. But I'd be far more glad to see Farrell Dean. The unfamiliarity of this place was getting to me.

Was that a "counter-indicated thought?" Or was that an "accurate articulation of emotion?"

Fiona, obviously trying to distract me from worries about what might be delaying Farrell Dean, took me into the back room and showed me how her loom worked. It was interesting, but I kept wishing I could see the clock.

At seven-thirty we went back into the front room to stir the stew. Eric Alleyn watched us gravely, then heaved himself up and went to the front door. He bolted it and reached up, and for the first time I noticed the long gun resting on hooks up above.

Fiona looked distressed, but without a word she went to the kitchen door and bolted it as well.

"They're probably just running a little late," she said, coming back. "They had errands, and we don't know how long they had to wait to see the doctor."

Eric Alleyn didn't answer. He stumped out of the living room and into the room where he slept, and I heard him trying the window there. Then he went to the other two ground floor bedrooms and the bathroom, and did the same thing.

Fiona watched his progress silently, but I couldn't stand the suspense.

"What is he locking out?" I asked. All day she had never said a word about wild men or wardens, or about anything fearful.

"We always bolt the doors at night," she said vaguely. "Especially now that it's only Papa and me."

"Stay away from the windows," Eric Alleyn said, coming back into the room. "And turn out those lights."

In the flickering firelight I watched my father's face, the lines that ran from his nose to the corners of his mouth, the wave of dark red hair that fell across his forehead. I wanted to like him. I wanted to love him. But all I felt right then was puzzlement—puzzlement, and a painful longing for Rafe. He'd only been a pretend father, true, but he'd been a good one. Maybe that's the way it always was when you chose your own.

Silently we sat and listened to the clock tick. At eight o'clock Fiona got up and dipped out three bowls of stew. The smell of meat and potatoes made my stomach growl, but I didn't feel hungry; I was too worried about Farrell Dean. We all ate without speaking, taking care not to knock our spoons against the bowls, listening for any movement outside, any noise.

"Where's Rex?" I said suddenly.

Fiona nodded. "He's guarding the barn," she said. "He'll let us know if anyone or anything bothers the cows or the horses. But the henhouse is still open—" she spoke now to Eric Alleyn. "I was going to close it while the boys washed up for supper."

Eric Alleyn nodded. "Leave it be," he said. "Better lose a few chickens than risk losing you."

Good grief—what were they expecting?

The next hour was very long. The clock ticking was the only sound, though I strained my ears to hear whatever it was that Fiona and her father feared. I wanted to ask questions but they both seemed walled off in their own thoughts, shutting me out. Fiona pulled out some yarn and knitted; Eric Alleyn gazed watchfully at the door.

At almost nine o'clock, I heard voices.

Eric Alleyn got up and took the gun down from above

the door. The voices outside grew louder. They seemed to be arguing, but I could make out no words. Fiona was on her feet now, and so was I.

I thought Eric Alleyn was preparing to defend the house, preparing to keep out whomever it was who was speaking outside. To my surprise, however, he unbolted the door and swung it wide open, then moved back to let a man step inside. The man was medium height and his hair was so dark it was almost black. He was very handsome in a dangerous sort of way, and a glint in his green eyes made me think that he knew it. Like my father, he held a gun in the crook of his arm.

"Mick," Fiona said, gesturing at me. "Did Angus and Rory find you? They were supposed to tell you—this is—"

"I've got eyes, Fee," the man said, coming closer. "And I got their message."

He set his gun down beside the fireplace and turned to me. "Welcome home, baby girl," he said, pulling me to him and kissing me on the cheek. His chin was rough with stubble. He smelled of smoke and rain, and something that made me think of the city meetings, of death and chaos. After a moment I identified it. Gunpowder.

My throat was tight—what had happened, where was Farrell Dean?—and I couldn't speak. As Mick held me at shoulder length, studying me, I nodded at him in what I hoped was sufficient greeting.

"Where'd you come from?" he said. "Where have you been? How'd you get here?"

"Another island," I began, but the door was opening again.

This time it was a tall man with dark red hair like Eric Alleyn's. Before glancing our way he shut and bolted the door. Then he turned, broke into a smile, and hurried forward.

"Welcome home," he said, setting his gun down next to

Mick's. "Welcome home, Valentina. I'm Rufus."

He held out his hands and, when I gave him mine, held them and looked me over. Except for the smile he reminded me of Eric Alleyn, not just because he looked very much like him, but because he approached me in the same almost formal way, less impulsively than the others, and he stood very straight and dignified, like his father.

Then the smile on Rufus' face faded and he looked even more like his father, grim, strong jawed, inexorable.

"So it's true," he said, shooting a look over his shoulder at Eric Alleyn, who was returning his gun to its place above the door. "You didn't die. Someone stole you away from us."

I nodded.

"We'll find out who it was." His tone was severe. "And he'll pay. I promise you that. No matter who he is, he'll answer for what he's done."

Eric Alleyn snorted.

"Sure he will," Mick said. "Once we're sure of our facts. Not before."

Rufus threw him an impatient look; over by the door Eric Alleyn gave a low humorless chuckle.

I didn't know what was going on, and Fiona ignored the dark tensions. "Valentina didn't even know her name," she said. "They called her Red. And whoever took her didn't raise her—he gave her to the city. She was brought up like an orphan, without any family at all."

I wanted to clarify—that I did know my name, at least one of my names, and that everyone in Optica was raised like that—but there was some undercurrent here I didn't understand, and it made me cautious.

Then Mick put a hand on his brother's shoulder. "Will you look at the two of them," he said. "They're as much alike as Martin's little boys. Prettier, though." He winked at us.

Rufus' expression eased a little. "Makes our girls the first doubles on the island, doesn't it?" he said. "Martin's boys are only four."

Mick looked at me. "We've seen twins before," he said, explaining. "Babies born at the same time, but who don't look more alike than any other brothers or sisters. But nobody had ever seen a double person before, not until Martin's boys."

I wasn't sure I liked being called a double person. Fiona was herself, and I was myself.

Fiona sniffed, indignant, but for a different reason. "If people think they're going to accuse us of sorcery, they've got another thing coming," she said.

"Now, Fee—" Mick put an arm around her shoulders. "That's calmed down. Nobody thinks anything of it, any more. It was hard for people to get their minds around, that's all. They were alarming, Martin's boys, because we'd never seen anything like it before. But the doctor explained it, and now everything is fine."

Fiona didn't look mollified. "I'm taking Valentina to town to buy shoes tomorrow," she said. "And if a single person says one hateful word to us, I'll ... I'll ...." She apparently didn't know what she'd do.

Mick and Rufus glanced at each other. "You might better hold off on those shoes," Mick said. "Just for a day or two, until things settle down. No need to attract Drewblood's attention."

A heavy thud made me jump. It was Eric Alleyn, slamming the end of his cane against the floor. "We are not afraid of Gabriel Drewblood!" he roared.

Wide-eyed, Fiona rushed to his side. She didn't touch him, but her hands hovered near him, making calming gestures.

"We are not afraid of Gabriel Drewblood, or his sycophant sidekick Tristan Oldfamily, or any of his men,"

Eric Alleyn muttered, more quietly but no more calmly.

Rufus eyed his father with disapproval. "Of course not," he said shortly. "But there's no point in bringing Valentina to his notice sooner than we must."

"Who is Gabriel Drewblood?" I asked quietly, directing the question to Mick, who was nearest me and who seemed less explosive than the other two.

"Just a name we try not to say around here," Mick answered. He spoke in an undertone, but Eric Alleyn heard him.

"Gabriel Drewblood is nothing but a well-dressed thug," he said loudly, his face turning a dangerous red. "An overbearing scoundrel who thinks his money gives him a right to run other people's lives."

"Rufus," Fiona said. "What happened tonight? Has there been another raid?"

"Drewblood burned Lee Doormouse out," he said. "His house, his outbuildings. They got him out first, him and the cat, and then held Lee down while they set the fires."

"We got there in time, though," Mick put in. "About ten of us went out together. We shot four of them—killed one, sent the others back with Martin to be held until the Isle Council meets—and we're pretty sure we winged the fifth. May be able to track him come daylight, unless this rain keeps up."

"Tristan?" Eric Alleyn said only the one word, and looked disappointed when Rufus said, shortly, "No."

"But Rory and Angus weren't with you?" Fiona broke in. "And another man, a stranger?"

The two men glanced at each other. Then Mick looked at Fiona and shook his head.

"We haven't seen them," he said. "We heard about them, though. The doctor came out with us—and it was a good thing he did, because Rufus was voting we let

Drewblood's men bleed."

Fiona made an exasperated sound. Rufus met her eyes levelly but said nothing.

"The doctor said he'd treated a stranger that Rory and Angus brought in," Mick went on. "Asked us who he was, but we didn't know. Asked us who'd beaten him within an inch of his life, but we didn't know that either."

"He's Valentina's friend," Fiona said. "He's the one who brought her back to us. I can't imagine what's keeping them so long …"

The siblings began discussing what to do if Rory and Angus weren't back by morning. I sat quietly as they argued about whether Fiona and I could handle the milking alone, or whether Rufus and Mick ought to stop on the way back to town and speak to someone named Trevor about helping out. Eric Alleyn stood listening for a bit, then without a word stumped off toward his room.

"Take care of her this time," Rufus said to his father's departing back, his voice too loud in the quiet room. "If you can't do that, I'm taking her home with me."

Eric Alleyn froze, his back still to us.

Startled by my brother's harsh words, I glanced at Fiona; she was glaring at Rufus, her lips in a tight disapproving line.

Eric Alleyn turned, his face hard, and I thought he'd start yelling again, pounding on the floor with his cane. Instead he merely gave a curt nod.

"She's well nigh a woman grown," he said. "If she wants to go with you, so be it. But no harm will come to my daughter while she's under my roof. I swear it. Though not to you, Rufus. I swear it to her and to myself."

His eyes met mine. "Goodnight, Valentina," he said. "I'm glad you've come home."

When his door closed, the room was silent for a long uncomfortable moment. I had no intention of going off somewhere with Rufus, and I hoped he wouldn't try to make me. This was where Farrell Dean expected me to be, and this was where I'd stay until he returned.

Rufus didn't say anything to me; he didn't say anything at all. Instead, Mick turned to Fiona. "Sean was talking to Drewblood in town today," he said. "He's intending to head back to the other side of the island soon, so you won't have to stay out of Doria for long."

Rufus snorted. "Sean should stay out of this."

"Sean tries to keep on good terms with both Papa and Gabriel," Fiona said to me. "He says there are always two sides to every story."

"Which is just plain ignorant," Rufus said. "Sometimes black is black, and white is white."

"But we don't always know which is which," Mick said. "And that's the problem."

Rufus glowered at his brother. He opened his mouth to speak, but I spoke first.

"Why did Gabriel Drewblood burn that man's house?" I said, looking at Mick.

Mick shot a glance at Rufus. "We don't know that he did."

I blinked. "But you said—"

Mick nodded, his green eyes scanning my face. "Here's the thing, Valentina. When people get wind that Gabriel's around, they take advantage. Pay off grudges, try to get a leg up on the competition, whatever. They know Papa will blame it all on Gabe, and most everybody on this side of the island follows Papa's lead."

Rufus was still glaring steadily at Mick. "Even if Tristan wasn't at Doormouse's place tonight, his fingerprints are all over that fire," he said. "And if he's hanging around here, it's at Gabriel's orders."

"And if Gabe isn't to blame tonight, he's to blame for

other nights," Mick said, throwing up his hands as if in surrender. "I'm not disagreeing with you there, Rufus. He's trouble. No doubt about it. I'm only saying the man can't possibly be behind every blame thing that goes wrong on this side of the island. It's humanly impossible."

"He cost Papa a leg," Rufus said. "We don't have to give that man the benefit of the doubt."

Mick gave a nod of grudging agreement. "In any case, Fee, stay out of town until we know Drewblood's gone," he said, reaching out and tugging gently on a strand of her hair. "We'll check around and let you know when it's clear."

"And now we'd better get going," Rufus said, moving toward the door. "We wanted to meet Valentina, but now we have to get back. Martin's half inclined to let the vandals go."

"And Sherman's half inclined to finish them off," Mick said.

I was lost again, and the tension was back again between the brothers.

"Not the best night for a homecoming, is it?" Mick said wryly, pulling me into his arms once more, then taking my hand and twirling me around as if we were beginning a dance. "We'll make it up to you, though. Have a grand big party soon, introduce you around. And don't be worrying about the boys. Angus always talks too much when he goes to town, slows Rory down. They're sure to be fine."

And Farrell Dean, I added silently. Surely he was fine, too.

Chapter 6

I slept restlessly that night. Fiona and I shared her bed, and though she fell quickly into stillness, I tossed and turned, worried that I'd wake her but unable to lie still.

It felt strange to be sharing a bed, strange to be in a house and not a dormitory, and of course I was worried about Farrell Dean. More than once I got up and padded into the dark front room, peering at the clock, listening in hopes that the boys had come back during one of my brief fitful spells of unconsciousness.

I tried to reassure myself by repeating Fiona's words: They didn't actually live here, Rory and Angus—they had built their own houses nearby. Perhaps they'd gotten back too late to come here, and were simply sleeping in their own beds, and Farrell Dean with them.

But though I repeated that explanation to myself again and again, I didn't believe it. Farrell Dean would have come back to me, no matter how late. He would know I'd be worried, and he'd want to check that I was fine.

When Fiona woke me, light was streaming in the windows.

"Good morning," she said, sitting on the side of the bed. She was already dressed.

Blearily I sat up and rubbed my eyes. "What time is it?"

"Gone nine," she said. "I knew you'd been up in the night, so I didn't like to wake you. But Tor is here, and I want you to meet him."

"Is Farrell Dean back?" I asked, adding belatedly, "And Rory and Angus?"

Fiona's face darkened. "Rory and Angus were here," she said. "They came and did the morning milking, but now they've gone off again."

"And Farrell Dean?"

Fiona hesitated. "He's why they're off. It seems they lost track of him yesterday. They've gone to try to find him."

I was struck speechless. My brothers had *lost* Farrell Dean?

"I'm sure there's no need to worry," Fiona said, and then sighed. "Actually, that's not so. You can worry. I'm worried about him too."

This was a nightmare. Maybe I was still asleep. But when I swung my legs over the edge of the bed, the cold floor seemed hard and real.

"How did they lose him?"

Fiona shook her head. "I don't know. *They* don't know. They were about to head home yesterday evening when they saw Gabriel Drewblood outside the gunsmith's shop. They crossed the street to avoid him, and told Farrell Dean—well, the same sort of thing Rufus and Mick told you. Then a little later they turned around and Farrell Dean was gone. The boys looked for him for ages and ages, but they couldn't find him. They searched a long time and talked to some people, and—" she hesitated—"Well, it sounds very much as if Farrell Dean disappeared right about the same time as Gabriel Drewblood."

"What does that mean? That Gabriel Drewblood *took* him?"

Fiona shifted uneasily from foot to foot. "I don't know."

"But what would this Gabriel Drewblood want with Farrell Dean?"

Fiona shook her head. "I don't know that, either. But Valentina, we'll find him. It'll be okay. Tor will help."

Before I could say another word, she stood up and pulled her pale blue dress over her head.

"Here," she said, handing it to me. "See if Tor knows it's you and not me. I told him my sister had come home, but he doesn't know we look alike."

I blinked. "Farrell Dean's missing, Fiona—"

She cut me off. "Yes, I know," she said. "I'm so sorry. And we'll take care of it. We will. We'll find him. But this will only take a second, and Tor—" She stopped. "I need to know, Valentina. I need to know if he really sees me. And there can only be one first time for him to meet you."

So I dressed in Fiona's clothes. Then I washed my face, brushed my hair, and went out into the big front room, where a man with dark blond hair stood with his back to me, facing the front window. He was the first man I'd seen here who wasn't wearing dark brown pants; his were a dark charcoal gray, and his shirt was blue.

Fiona had warned me not to talk—my accent would give me away, she said—so I went to the kitchen and picked up the kettle. I felt a little sorry for the man; surely Fiona wouldn't hold it against him, if he failed her test. And then I wondered—if Farrell Dean had come upon Fiona unexpectedly, without knowing of her existence, would he have known the difference? Would Meritt?

Tor came into the kitchen area before I followed these thoughts any further, talking as he came.

"If she's not up, I can stop by again before—" I looked up and he stopped short, blinking at me.

Just as Fiona had said, he had a distinctive face with an

enormous nose that should have been silly but was, some-how, dignified instead. His eyes were not a clear blue, but a dark sleepy blue, like the sea.

"You look—you have—" he broke off again, glancing at the gas lamps as if making sure the light in the room was good. Then he looked at me again. "You've gotten unac-countably tan in the last few minutes," he said.

I smiled at him, but didn't say anything. He studied me seriously for a long moment. Then he smiled, too—a little wryly—and said, "You must be Fiona's sister."

There was almost a question in his voice; I nodded, and he looked relieved. "She didn't tell me about the rather un-canny resemblance," he said. "It's … unexpected."

"Fiona," I called. "You can come out now."

Fiona came dancing into the room, now dressed in pale green. She stopped beside Tor and looked at me expectantly.

"He wasn't fooled," I said, and a smug look crossed her face but was quickly hidden as she turned to Tor.

"You must have the artist's eye," she said.

I knew she wanted him to be gallant and say no, he had an eye for *her*, but he merely gave a deprecating shake of his head and said nothing.

"He always says he's not an artist, just a craftsman," Fio-na told me. "He says it's plain hard work and that a muse would get in the way. But I know better. He has an incredible eye for detail—"

I didn't have time to figure out what she was talking about, because Tor turned to me.

"I hope you had a pleasant journey?" he said.

I knew I should be courteous and make small talk, but I couldn't stand it anymore. I made some sort of apologetic gesture and turned to Fiona.

"I have to find Farrell Dean," I said. "I have to go after him."

To my surprise Fiona nodded in agreement. "Of course," she said. "You must leave at once. That's why I woke you."

Tor turned to her, startled.

"You'd send your sister chasing after Gabriel Drewblood?" he said. "Fiona, that's—he'll—it would be like setting a match to a keg of gunpowder. I told you—"

Fiona smiled innocently. "Oh, I wouldn't send Valentina," she said. "But can't 'Fiona' go?" She made little quotation marks with her fingers.

Tor looked at her blankly.

"She could be visiting her grandparents," Fiona said. "She hasn't seen them for a long time. So she'd simply happen to be visiting Ionia, unconnected to Farrell Dean. And if Gabriel sees her, well, he's always liked Fiona better than he likes the rest of the Alleyns, so he won't get all upset."

It was more than a little weird, hearing Fiona talk about herself in third person, knowing she meant me.

"And anyway it isn't like we're forbidden to cross the island," Fiona said. "He doesn't own Aislin."

Tor was nodding, though slowly. "It might be all right." He looked at Fiona, and back at me. "Unless Farrell Dean has already given the game away."

Fiona shook her head. "Why would he mention the Alleyns? Rory told him the Drewbloods aren't exactly our friends." She shot me an apologetic glance. "That's surely why Farrell Dean went after Gabriel alone."

"You think Farrell Dean left *intentionally*?" I said. "He wouldn't do that, not without telling me."

Fiona gave an odd little shrug and tucked a strand of hair behind her ear. "No one could have grabbed him while he was standing right there beside Angus and Rory. Even they would notice something like that. So maybe Farrell Dean slipped away from them, only for a moment, to talk to Gabriel. And then—well, who knows."

"But why would he want to talk to Gabriel Drewblood?" I said. "Especially if he knows your family doesn't trust him?"

Fiona gave me an encouraging look, as if she was sure I'd catch on if I thought about it. "You're supposed to find help on the other side of the island, aren't you? That's what you told me."

Then I did get it. "And Gabriel's from the other side."

Tor looked incredulous. "You think Farrell Dean's trying to get help from *Gabriel Drewblood*?"

"It's possible," Fiona said. "At least, Farrell Dean might think it's possible."

"Then what?" I said, my voice rising. "He talked to this Drewblood person, and then what happened? He wouldn't go off somewhere without telling me. Absolutely, he wouldn't. So what happened to him?"

Fiona put an arm around me and pushed me toward her bedroom. "You'll find him. I know you will. Let's go get you packed. If we hurry we can be ready by the time Tor gets back for you."

"Tor's going with me?" I was relieved, but surprised. I glanced over my shoulder; the big room was empty and the front door was swinging closed.

"I asked him to catch up with Rory and Angus," Fiona said. "To be a calming influence. They don't need to go showing up and accusing Gabriel of abducting anyone, and they absolutely shouldn't tell him there are two of us again. I shouldn't have let them go—and I did try to get them to wait—and then Tor—"

She broke off, cramming a dress in a bag, stuffing stockings in after it.

"Tor what?"

"He said he'd go after them. He'll stop them from telling Gabriel about you, and he'll look for Farrell Dean, but of course he'll need you for that, because he won't recognize Farrell Dean. He's never met him. I'd recognize him, of course, but if I went then that would leave you here to take care of Papa, and—" she waved a hand.

She was talking about the chores I didn't know how to do, the difficulty of managing Eric Alleyn. But all that was irrelevant; no way would I sit around here waiting for someone to bring me news about what had happened to Farrell Dean.

"I'm going," I said. "But I don't understand—why should Gabriel Drewblood be upset that I've come back?"

Fiona shoved the bag into my arms and headed for the kitchen. "You'll need food," she said. "But you'll be fine for water. There are wells along the way."

"But – "

"I'll explain to Papa. He won't be happy, but it's his sons who lost our guest, so ..." She paused, a block of cheese in her hand, but she didn't pause long enough for me to get a word in. "Papa doesn't go very far—walking hurts him and he says the horses are too much trouble—and he sleeps a lot. If he gets too upset I can add some extra medicine to his dinner."

"Don't overdo and poison him," Tor warned from the doorway. He was carrying a bag slung over one shoulder. "Though I suppose that would make life easier."

Fiona cast a reproving look in his direction. "Not funny," she said, putting the cheese in the bag, along with a loaf of bread and some apples. "Are you ready? Good. She's ready too."

So, just like that, I found myself walking along the path toward town with a man I'd met less than half an hour before. As soon as we were out of sight of the house, I glanced at Tor.

"Why do I have to pretend I'm Fiona?" I said. "Why would Gabriel Drewblood be upset to know I'm back?"

Tor shook his head, a wry expression on his face. "Fiona did this on purpose," he said. "Left it to me."

I waited.

He sighed. "She can't stand to hear a word said against her father. Look, there's my house."

Up ahead was a house built of white-painted boards, with brightly lit windows shining cheerfully against the gloomy day, and a neat white waist-high fence. A little girl was outside swinging on the gate.

"You're getting too big for that," Tor said as we drew near. "You'll bend the hinges."

She merely smiled and waved at me, and I waved back. I guess she thought I was Fiona, and Tor didn't tell her otherwise.

"You don't have to be tactful," I said, as soon as we were out of earshot. "I barely know Eric Alleyn."

Tor shot me a sideways glance. "Yes," he said. "Well."

I raised my eyebrows.

He grimaced. "Blast Fiona," he said. "All right. There's a sort of feud between the two of them, between your father and Gabriel. It started back when you supposedly died, and Gabriel wanted your body."

"He *what*?"

Tor half smiled. "Sorry," he said. "That did sound a bit gruesome." His smile faded. "What happened was that Gabriel blamed your father for your death and your mother's. He's very progressive, is Gabriel, and he didn't approve of your father's 'backward' ways. If Eric Alleyn had at least agreed to keep a truck, Gabriel said, he would have been able to get you and your mother into town, to the clinic, when trouble hit. As it was, your father was living way out here alone—my parents were away at the time, buying sheep—and so your father attempted to handle the birth by himself, with no one but a superstitious midwife for support. It was … Gabriel said it was …well …"

"Irresponsible?"

Tor looked relieved. "Among other things. So Gabriel wanted to take your mother's body, and yours, and bury you both on the other side of Aislin, near your mother's side of the family. Sort of returning their child and grandchild to them, as best as he could."

"But Eric Alleyn couldn't find my body," I said.

Tor nodded. "And Gabriel was not amused," he said. "He had the Council remove all the children from your father's care. He said Eric Alleyn wasn't competent to care for them—and truly, for awhile, he wasn't." Tor looked over at me, his face serious. "Your father has never forgiven him for that. For taking his children away."

"No," I said. "I can see that he wouldn't. But now that I'm back, it seems like Eric Alleyn would want this man to know it. Because I'm alive, and that sort of vindicates my father, doesn't it? He couldn't very well find a body when there wasn't one to find."

Tor was shaking his head. "If Gabriel learns you've returned, it will re-open all manner of old wounds—and worse. Because now, as it turns out, Eric Alleyn didn't just lose a baby's body; he lost a living baby."

If Gabriel learned of my return?

Maybe Tor had simply misspoken, but I wasn't sure. Eric Alleyn, after all, had referred to me as a visitor.

It was a big adjustment for them all, I told myself. They'd thought I was dead, or at least gone forever. Still, as I thought about the implication of Tor's *if*, a hollow place formed inside my chest. If I looked at matters in the worse possible light, one home was trying to kill me, and the other was trying to hide me until I went away again.

"It would be easier if we didn't have to go through town," Tor was saying. "But Fiona made me promise to get you some shoes." A faint smile touched his lips. "Though I guess I'd better stop talking about Fiona. As of now you are Fiona, for all intents and purposes."

Huh. Not exactly. I liked my sister, but didn't much relish the thought of answering to her name—especially when I still didn't fully understand why this whole charade was necessary.

"I'm sorry," Tor said. He stopped and turned toward me. "That was a stupid thing to say. You aren't Fiona, of course. It's only that this won't be easy for me, remembering to call you by her name."

He was more alert than those sleepy sea-blue eyes suggested. And even though he was about the same age as Rory and Angus, he seemed older, less puppy-ish.

"While we're in town," Tor went on, "it would be better if you didn't talk. If anyone speaks to you, point at your throat and I'll say you've lost your voice. That way you won't have to answer questions."

"Will I have to play mute at Gabriel Drewblood's town, too?" I asked. How was I going to find Farrell Dean, if I couldn't speak?

Tor started walking again. "We can start with reticent, and go to mute if we have to," he said. "Fiona hasn't been there for more than three years. Some people will recognize her—she's fairly noticeable—but they won't be surprised if she doesn't recognize them. And as for any questions they might ask, I'll be right there with you."

Suddenly he laughed.

"What?" I said.

"People in Doria would certainly find it odd if I suddenly started speaking for Fiona," he said. "But people in Ionia don't know us nearly as well. Just to be safe, though, you could try to imitate her tone. You sound … more matter-of-fact, I suppose. Fiona—most of the Alleyns, come to that—taste their words. They don't spit them out whole like you do."

Though I studied him from the corner of my eye, I couldn't tell if he meant that to be as insulting as it sounded.

The rest of the way to town Tor coached me, and by the time the roofs of the town rose before us in the distance, he declared that I sounded, if not exactly like Fiona, at least close enough to avoid raising suspicions in Ionia. It seemed to be mostly a matter of cadences—I did best when I pretended to be singing without singing.

"What towns are there, besides Doria?" I asked then.

"Well, there's really only one—Ionia, to the northwest, way on the other side of Aislin. Where Gabriel Drewblood lives. That's the oldest and biggest town, where the original settlers built. Then to the north of us is Locria, but it's quite small and probably doesn't even count as a town. Basically people who can't get along with anyone else move up there, and then have to try to get along with other prickly sorts."

"Aislin? What's that?"

Tor gestured broadly. "All of us," he said. "This land. This island."

"And how old is Ionia?"

"That's something of a mystery," Tor said. "There was a plague, an epidemic, about fifty years ago. It killed a lot of people and affected the brains of those who survived. Amnesia. There are letters and books and so forth from earlier, of course, but nobody really remembers anything before the plague. And none of the written records mention specific years."

A cold chill was running down my spine.

"They don't remember anything at all before the

plague?"

Tor shook his head. "Daily things. Names, relationships, how to do their jobs, functional things like that. But as for long term memory, nothing."

I tried to read Tor's face, but it didn't seem like he was keeping anything back.

Optica hadn't suffered a plague, but we had suffered some sort of devastating event that left our city in ruins and our people without memories of what had come before. Had it been the same thing that caused the plague here?

And was all this before, or after, Optica became an experiment? Or —

My head began to hurt. I wished Farrell Dean were with me to talk this through.

As we reached the edge of town, Tor took our bags and stashed them under a hedge. "No one will take any notice of Fiona and me in town," he said. "But Fiona and me with baggage—well, by nightfall the whole island would be saying we've eloped."

I guess I looked baffled, because he explained. "To elope means to run away and get married in secret," he said. "Some people do that, though mostly only if their families don't get along."

It seemed wisest to say nothing. I didn't want to give Fiona's game away, and I couldn't tell if Tor was suggesting anything about a future with Fiona or not. Nor had I been able to tell how he felt about her when they were together. He was just ... Tor.

Maybe that was Fiona's problem.

Finally we drew in among the buildings of Doria. I don't know what I'd expected—something more like Optica, I suppose—but this town was nothing like my city. My first impression was one of disorder, even chaos. Houses and stores were mixed in with one another, and the streets ran crookedly in all directions, crossing one another, doubling back on themselves. The buildings didn't match—some were brick, some stone, some wood, some metal siding. Some were well maintained, while some were so ramshackle that they looked dangerous. Some had high fences built around them; others had dogs tied beside the doors. Chickens pecked here and there, unrestrained. I had to watch where I stepped.

Unlike Eric Alleyn's house, the town had electricity. On this overcast day I could see the whitish blue light inside stores and houses. A few buildings, however, seemed to be lit by gaslight or even candlelight.

Some of the shops had displays set out on the pavement, and people browsed among brooms, wheelbarrows, bins of tools, racks of clothes. At one shop a woman was wheeling a rolling bar of clothes back inside, looking up at the sky as if checking for rain.

Most of the women wore dresses more or less like mine. A few women wore pants like the men wore—not many, though, and even those women wore pretty, brightly colored shirts far fancier than the men's.

Twice I saw someone with red hair farther down the street; both were women. The first time, Tor saw the direction of my gaze and muttered, "I don't think you're related, though you might be distant cousins or something. If you were, it would be through Eric Alleyn's mother. She had red hair."

He glanced at me as if something had occurred to him.

"Have you heard about her?" he said.

I shook my head.

"She was a good woman. I liked her. We called her Granny Rose." He looked around to make sure we weren't within anyone's earshot, then continued.

"After your mother died, Granny Rose moved back here to help Eric Alleyn with the children. She would have come back anyway because her husband had died shortly before, and they'd been living way out in the woods in an isolated area. It wasn't a good situation for an older woman alone. So she came back here and lived with your family until you were eleven. That's when she died."

I wanted to know more, but a woman and several children were getting close, so Tor had to stop explaining my family history.

When people spoke to me I followed our plan, pointing at my throat and smiling apologetically. Most people made sympathetic noises and went on, but one woman looked me over and said, "Yes, dear, I can see you look peaked. Are you getting enough iron?"

My feelings were a little hurt, but when she was gone Tor glanced at me sideways and said, "She thinks everyone looks peaked. She's the doctor's wife. *And* she sells vitamin supplements."

A shop sign caught my eye: Dream Recorder, it said. I pulled on Tor's sleeve and raised my eyebrows questioningly.

"It's our research facility," he said. "Don't you have dreams, where you come from?"

What a bizarre question; of course we did.

But Tor seemed to be waiting for a reply, so I nodded.

"Then you know that sometimes dreams are just stories, but sometimes they're more than that. They're memories. That's how we've pieced together information about the days before the plague—through dream memories."

That made a little sense. After all, when I'd been desperately trying to remember what Rafe had said to me just before he died, I'd had strange dreams, and the message he'd been trying to tell me was in those dreams, though I didn't realize it until I finally remembered his words with my waking mind. And I'd always dreamed of the sea, though I thought I'd never seen it and certainly had no idea that I'd traveled across it as a baby.

"The Dream Recorders write down any interesting dreams, and then try to sort through them to see if they're anything important," Tor was saying. "Sometimes one person has dreams that match up with dreams someone else has had, and that's an indication that they're real—not just made-up stories, you understand, but somehow connected to the waking world. There are other things to consider, as well—" But now we were at the shoemaker's.

In fact, there were two shoemakers, right across the street from each other. Tor led me into the smaller of the two shops, where the shoemaker measured my foot and brought out a beautiful pair of soft brown leather boots that came up to my ankles.

While I walked around in them, testing them, Tor chatted idly with the shoemaker. He did it very well, moving easily from random conversation to a remark about the raid the night before, which caused the shoemaker to mention Gabriel Drewblood.

"I hear he's gone now," Tor said.

"Good riddance," the shoemaker agreed. "Gone back to plague his own neighbors instead of us."

"Or else to bother Locria," Tor said, but the shoemaker shook his head.

"No, they're to be spared this time around. Drewblood told Maudie Evensong that he had to get back and tend to some sort of problem at home. Sounded serious, whatever it was. She said he left out without even finishing his dinner."

Anxiously I darted a look at Tor, but he was giving the man some silver pieces and wouldn't meet my eyes. Was Farrell Dean the reason Drewblood left so suddenly?

When we finally left the shop I walked quickly, anxious to get out of town so I could talk. But as we passed the Dream Recorder shop the door opened and an elderly woman waddled out. Her clothes were a stained and yellowed white, as if she'd laundered them improperly, and her pallid face was almost the same color. She was quite fat, her little black eyes embedded deep in a floury face.

When she saw us she smiled widely. She didn't say anything, and I was glad. She looked unpleasant, and as if she might be carrying some illness.

At first I thought it was a coincidence that she just happened to be headed the same way we were going, but though we made turn after turn, she stayed behind us. I looked a question at Tor; he kept his eyes straight ahead and kept walking, not hurriedly, but as if we were simply out for a stroll. I wished he'd speed up. We could easily have outdistanced the woman.

When we reached the edge of town and the place Tor had stashed our bags, he didn't pause, but continued down the road that led to Eric Alleyn's. This was maddening—I was anxious to go after Farrell Dean, find him, make sure he was all right, but the old woman was still waddling along behind us. It was disconcerting, and I was surprised Tor hadn't confronted her.

Finally we rounded a curve and Tor stopped, glancing back the way we'd come. Putting a finger to his lips he sat down on a large stone and began fiddling with a shoelace. He tied and untied it for several minutes, but the Dream Recorder never appeared.

"Presumably she has tired of her game and gone back to town," he said finally, standing back up.

"What was that about?"

He gave a short laugh. "Who knows? She likes discomfiting people. If you challenge her over it, you'll be dealing with the repercussions for weeks."

"What sort of repercussions?"

Tor shrugged and started back on the path toward town,

toward our bags. "Little things, generally, but irritating. Your garden fence develops a hole and rabbits eat all your cabbages. Your dog gets mange, your child ends up with lice. Your well water begins to smell sulphuric."

"She does those things?"

He smiled a little wryly. "Some, no doubt. Enough to encourage the superstitious to blame everything bad on their run-ins with her."

"But why?"

He shrugged. "People make themselves important any way they can," he said.

After retrieving our bags we cut through the woods and circled around, finally reaching a path that led northwest. The sky was still overcast, but the air was pleasantly crisp—a good day for walking fast, as we were doing.

"How far is it to Ionia?" I asked, remembering this time to practice Fiona's voice, Fiona's rhythm.

Tor noticed. "You're improving," he said. "It's a full day's fast walk to Ionia, and more. Usually we stop for the night at the Grateful Fields. We'll stop there tonight, assuming we catch Rory and Angus by then. If they've gone on, we'll have to as well. We can't stop if we're alone."

"What are Grateful Fields?" I was imagining some sort of crop, one that people especially liked, but that wasn't it at all.

"Every September people from all over the island meet there," Tor said. "It's centrally located and big enough for crowds, and it usually isn't raining that time of year. We come for Grateful Day. We talk about the good in the previous year and we trade gifts. Lots of people bring produce, a bushel of corn or a basket of wheat, what have you. I bring stained glass, Fiona brings fabric she's woven and dyed. Rory brings a story or poem. People from the other side of the island bring whatever they do best—radios, binoculars, they tend toward mechanical and electronic things. Or people give services—they'll teach someone how to knit, or they'll agree to plumb a house, or they'll offer to take care of the little ones while the mother goes visiting, things like that."

"What does Eric Alleyn bring?"

Tor hesitated. "He used to bring fancy cheeses. Angus brings those now." I waited, and after a moment Tor went on. "Eric Alleyn doesn't go anymore."

"Because of his leg?"

"That, too. But he stopped going long before then." Tor didn't look at me. "He never went after your mother died."

He gestured back toward town. "The gifting was one of the earliest Dream Memories," he said, and I knew he was steering the conversation away from Eric Alleyn's grief. "So many people dreamed of giving presents that we decided to start it up again. Then the Dream Recorders had to sort through conflicting bits and advise the Council on how to implement the whole thing, because nobody's dreams are identical."

"There's more than one Dream Recorder?" I asked.

"That's right. There used to be four or five, but the others have died. This one ought to be training someone to take her place. Maybe she is and I just don't know about it, or maybe she enjoys her role too much to give it up in a timely fashion. If that's the case I don't know who'll take over when she's gone. Someone will have to, because the Dream Drops have to be monitored."

"Dream Drops?"

Tor nodded. "They have some other name, something scientific, but everyone calls them Dream Drops. You know how sometimes you'll know you've had a dream, but you can't quite remember it? Supposedly the Dream Drops make it stay with you longer. The Dream Recorder keeps the drops and some people stop by regularly each evening to take a dose, while others, like your father, are opposed to them entirely. The people who dislike them say they aren't natural, that they have strange effects, that they create dreams rather than just preserving them. In that case, you see, dreams would be more like self-fulfilling prophecies. We dream something, and then because we think it's true, we make it come true."

For a few minutes we walked along silently while I thought this over. The trees towered above us—surely they were taller than the trees in our woods—and a dense dark shrub that Tor called salal crowded between them and leaned out into the path and caught at the skirt of my dress.

No matter how I looked at Tor's words, I didn't know what to make of Dream Drops and dream memories—the whole idea made me feel uneasy, as if the world inside people's heads was bigger than I could handle.

We rounded a curve in the path and saw, up ahead, three men sitting on a fallen tree. As we neared them, one stood up and stepped into the middle of the path. He was none too clean—I could smell something rancid—and his eyes were bloodshot. He had a large stick in his hand.

"Here we go again," Tor said under his breath. "Good morning," he said aloud to the man.

"Fine day for a walk," the man said, grinning. "Ready to pay a little toll?"

"For the privilege of using this lovely footpath," said one of the two on the log, waving a bottle expansively.

"Finest in the land," said the other, nodding so vigorously he seemed to make himself dizzy.

Tor stood looking at the three men, saying nothing. The man in the path stopped grinning and shifted uneasily. "Come on, now," he said. "Nice path like this? It's cheap at twice the price."

"No one owns this land," Tor said. "Step aside."

The man blocking our way shook his head. "No, now, that's not fair," he said. His face twisted as if he were about to cry.

One on the log spoke up. "Seems to me there's three of us, and only one of you," he said.

"Not counting the little missy," said the other, nodding politely at me.

Tor nodded. "But I have an advantage. I know your names. Warren and Kenny Stubblefield, aren't you?" He looked at the man in our way. "And you're Len Whitespoon. I don't suppose you recognize me."

"We're not here to meet people," one on the log said. "We're here to earn a living."

I couldn't quite see what Tor was doing—moving his shirt collar, it seemed.

"Aw, now, it's the Council Chief's son," one of the men said in tones of disgust. "You're a good bit older than you were last time I saw you. I didn't recognize you." He clearly blamed Tor for this.

"We were just joshing," said the one in the path, looking alarmed. "Having a little fun. Say hello to your old man for us—tell him we're making sure this path is safe for travelers."

He moved off the path and sat back down on the log with the others. Without a word, Tor put a hand on my lower back and nudged me forward, and we set off down the path again.

We walked in silence for quite some time.

"Who were those men?" I asked finally.

"Your general run-of-the-mill thieves. Too lazy to work, so they coerce people into paying to travel the path."

"Do they ever do more than that? Do they ever hurt people?" I was thinking about Farrell Dean.

Tor shrugged. "If they're too lazy to work, they're generally too lazy to fight as well. And they don't want to attract attention and get in trouble with the Council, so they rely mostly on intimidation. The key is to not be intimidated. If you give into them once, from then on they know you're an easy target."

"What did you show them?"

Tor pulled his collar aside to reveal a silver chain with an oddly shaped pendant hanging from it.

"My family wears them," he said. "Once they knew I was a Van Stavern, they knew they'd either have to leave us alone, or take what they wanted by force. Van Staverns pay what we owe, but we won't be cheated out of what we don't owe."

"We should have asked if they'd seen Farrell Dean," I said, but Tor shook his head.

"If he came this way, it was at night. They're too lazy to be out after suppertime. And it's better not to make your business known to such as those."

The narrow patch of sky up above us seemed hazier now, a darker gray. A pattering sound above told me rain had begun to fall, but the trees were so dense only a drop or two hit me. We were walking briskly, striding through the dimness of the trees, and it felt good to be active, to be doing something instead of sitting around moping and brooding.

Eric Alleyn seemed to do that all the time. Though Fiona was right—he'd had a lot of bad luck. He was crippled, and his wife had died, and his baby's corpse had mysteriously gone missing, and his other children were taken away. Even now he didn't even have his wife's grave there near him, where he'd wanted it to be.

Tor squeezed past a half-fallen tree that blocked the path, shoving at it to make sure it was stable before gesturing for me to follow.

"There's something I don't understand," I said, ducking past it. "What gave Gabriel Drewblood the right to take my mother and bury her somewhere else? I thought your father ruled the island."

Tor's look was unreadable, some baffling mixture of annoyance and amusement. Was it directed at me? I'd probably once again demonstrated my utter ignorance somehow.

Feeling myself begin to blush, I looked away, walking a bit more quickly through the increasingly uncomfortable drizzle. The wet woods felt completely remote and uninhabited—there was no sound of human occupation, no smell of wood smoke or cooking. It was just rocks and mud and trees and, above, a small patch of overcast sky.

"Your sister," Tor said from behind me. "I'm sorry, Valentina. It's no wonder you're confused. I assumed Fiona had explained."

I was beginning to think Fiona talked nonstop to hide all the things she didn't say.

Tor went on without waiting for me to press him. "First of all," he said, "I wouldn't exactly say my father is in charge. There's a Council. He's the head. But he doesn't rule the island; no one rules Aislin."

He paused.

"And second of all?" I turned to face him.

Tor grimaced. "Second of all, Gabriel Drewblood is your uncle. Your mother's younger brother."

Something constricted in my chest.

"Fiona has a way of avoiding unpleasant topics," Tor said, brushing a scattering of raindrops off his sleeve. Then his eyes met mine. "Don't take it too much to heart," he said. "Most every family has a black sheep."

He misunderstood my discomfiture. It wasn't so much that Drewblood sounded like a horrid person, though he did. What bothered me was the realization that I knew so little about my own family. I was completely dependent on others to tell me what they thought I should know.

And even if they told me everything, it would take years.

How could I ever catch up after a lifetime away?

The thought took root. Fiona had grown up with so much, and I had grown up a freak. An outsider. Why had the midwife sent me away, and not my sister? And now that I was back, I seemed to be more trouble than I was worth. There were two identical girls, after all—maybe one was expendable.

Such thoughts were probably "counter-indicated," and if I'd read Fiona's book I'd have known how to manage them. As things stood, all I could do was tell myself that the dark woods were getting to me. Dark stories, dark woods, dreary half-hearted rain.

At least that changed before too long. Soon the trees began to thin a little, and the path grew wider and less claustrophobic, until finally it joined a broad road laid with white gravel.

"This is the road for trucks and horses," Tor said, his footsteps crunching as he stepped onto the gravel. "We'll only be on it a little while. It's longer than the footpath because it skirts the densest woods and some steep spots, so if we stayed on it we'd have to walk about ten extra miles."

It also was less protected from the rain, so I opened my pack and pulled out a midnight blue hooded cloak belonging to Fiona. It was beautiful, and she hadn't hesitated so much as a second before pressing it on me. "It's the warmest one," she'd said. "And you'll look pretty for Farrell Dean, if you care about that."

I might be bitterly jealous of my sister, but I couldn't help but like her.

"There's a truck coming," Tor said, pulling me over to the side of the road, and sure enough, within a few moments a blue truck appeared in the distance in front of us.

"They're quieter out here in the woods than they are in Optica," I said.

Tor gave me an amused look.

"What's so funny?" I said.

"Just that your father hates trucks because of the noise," he said. "Pretty much everyone on our side of the island has given up on keeping them, because Eric Alleyn kept sneaking into people's yards and disabling the things. Now that he can't get around as well, one or two people have bought trucks. But most people on this side are content to let people from Ionia ferry goods back and forth. That's probably what this is—someone coming to buy or sell."

The truck slowed to a stop beside us, its whirring fading to a barely audible hum. One of the windows slid down and a man leaned out, holding his hand over his eyes to shield his face from the rain.

"You folks heading to Ionia?" he asked.

Tor nodded. "That's the plan," he said.

The man cast a cautious glance past us, into the dense woods.

"Might want to rethink that," he said. "There's a lunatic out here somewhere—tore up Ionia and then got away into the woods before we could stop him."

"He's violent?" Tor asked. Like the man in the truck, he too was scanning the woods.

The man shrugged. "Violent enough to bust up some shops. They'll find him eventually, get him back to Locria. In the meantime, though—" he gestured to the back of his truck—"I can give you a ride back to town."

I opened my mouth to protest, but Tor was ahead of me.

"Thank you, but no," he said. "We can't turn back."

The man looked unhappy. "I'd offer to drive you this evening when I go home," he said. "But I'll have a full load of goods then. Cheeses. No room for passengers."

"We'll be fine," Tor said. "Thank you for stopping to warn us."

The man looked as if he wanted to argue, but after a moment's hesitation he merely nodded and, with a wave, pulled away. Within seconds the engine noise faded into the distance.

"How long does the journey from Doria to Ionia take in a truck?" I asked.

"It's fifty miles by this road," Tor said. "Trucks can do that in an hour, but most drivers take about two. It's better to go more slowly in case a person or a deer is in the road."

"Even two hours is fast," I said. "That really would be convenient."

Tor laughed.

"Don't let Eric Alleyn hear you say that," he said, and then produced a fair imitation of my father's loud, decisive voice: "Today's convenience is tomorrow's necessity. Catering to convenience results in weakness and dependence!"

I looked at him curiously. "So he didn't sabotage trucks just because of the noise?"

Tor shook his head and dropped back to his normal voice. "He considered it a public service—protecting other people's independence even if they were too weak to protect it themselves. And he has the courage of his convictions, I do have to give him that. Won't even let anyone run electricity out to his place." He slid back into Eric Alleyn's voice. "Luxury is slavery in disguise. Slavery isn't only the selling of others; it's the selling of yourself."

"But he has gas lights," I said.

Tor nodded. "He only has those because, years ago, my father showed him it could be done without becoming tied to anyone else, once the drilling was done and the lines laid. Eric Alleyn was worried, even so—what if the gas failed and Rachel had forgotten how to cook on a wood-burning stove? But he didn't want your mother to work herself to death, either, trying to keep the household going with all those little children underfoot."

Our discussion of trucks had led us away from the issue of a lunatic loose in the woods, and I decided not to bring it up. I was worried for Farrell Dean, if he was on foot and alone; I didn't want Tor to have second thoughts about going on.

We had been on the larger road for about ten minutes when Tor pointed off in the distance to a break in the trees near the top of a long sloping hill. "See way up there?" he said. "That's where the footpath leaves the main road again. It's quite narrow for awhile, because the trees are so thick. We'll have to go single file. Horses can't even manage it."

Lovely. More dark claustrophobic woods, and with a lunatic loose somewhere.

A few yellow leaves drifted through the misty grayness, spangling the path with color. The rain had slowed to a weak drizzle and I pulled back my hood, wanting to feel as unconfined as possible. At least we still had a little while left on the bigger road. Maybe I'd feel better by the time we reached the footpath.

A pounding noise behind us made me look around.

"Look!" I said, completely distracted from the dark woods ahead. Two beautiful dark brown creatures were running toward us, carrying men on their backs.

"Are those horses?" I asked.

Tor looked startled, but not by the creatures. "Of course," he said, giving me an odd look. "Haven't you ever seen a horse?"

I shook my head, feeling once again like an uneducated barbarian.

The horses' hooves were flying fast, their long tails swinging with their strides. Though I'd only just seen them, they were almost to us already. Their riders' jackets were flapping open in the wind of their passage.

Tor turned toward the riders as they pounded up and slowed to a walk beside us, the horses tossing their heads and snorting. They were beautiful animals, their coats smooth and gleaming, their muscles rippling as they moved. Did being the same color mean they were related, I wondered. How many colors of horses were there?

"Van Stavern," one rider said. He looked at me and pulled on the brim of his hat.

"Lester," Tor replied, and nodded at the other. "Cobb."

The one called Lester was thin and wiry, and very tan, as if he spent a lot of time outdoors.

The other, Cobb, was larger, heavier, with a barrel chest, powerful hairy forearms, and tiny eyes. Both men had long guns on their backs, hanging from straps across their bodies. Both looked about the same age as Rufus, maybe in their late twenties or early thirties. The larger man was on the smaller horse. I felt sorry for it.

"Heading toward Ionia?" Lester said. He wasn't unpleasant, but his tone was cool and business-like.

"That's right." Tor started walking again and I followed. The horses kept pace alongside us, their hooves making a soft clopping noise on the hard gravel path. Lester's horse was right beside me. It was quite big, and it was breathing hard. Its hooves looked large and dangerous. I edged a bit away.

Lester took off his hat and shook the rain off of it. His hair was short and dark, and a red line ran across his forehead where the hat band had rested.

"Any news from out your way?" he said. He kept his eyes on his hat, shaking it, shaping it.

"Not really," Tor said, and I thought he sounded a bit too casual. "You heard about Doormouse's place burning last night, I suppose. Other than that it's been a quiet few weeks."

"He's been asking for trouble," Lester said, settling his hat on his head and pulling it forward, obscuring his eyes. "A burn, though. Some might say that's a bit too much."

Tor didn't answer. His lips were pressed firmly together, his face unreadable.

We walked in silence for a few minutes. I glanced over at the heavy man and looked quickly away when I met his eyes. He still hadn't said a word, but the redness of his face reminded me of Garry, the bullying field worker back in Optica.

"Do you have business in Ionia?" Tor said, clearly attempting to leave the subject of the fire for a less sensitive one.

"Maybe," Lester said. "If we find what we're after in Ionia, then that's where our business is."

Out of the corner of my eye I saw Cobb shift on his horse. He was watching me. The narrow claustrophobic footpath, unsuitable for horses, was beginning to sound more appealing by the moment.

"I take it you've heard about the trouble," Lester said. "The stranger."

"The lunatic? We've heard."

Lester eyed Tor skeptically. "Not him," he said, as if Tor knew that quite well. "The other one."

"Another Locrian?"

Lester looked at me. "A stranger going around with the Alleyn boys," he said.

"I haven't seen the Alleyn boys since yesterday morning," Tor said. "No one was with them then."

Lester was still looking at me.

"Rory and Angus came by this morning to do the milking," I said, being very careful with my cadences. "But they were alone."

Lester didn't answer.

I met Tor's eyes. He was ready to reach the footpath, too.

We climbed the low sloping hill, finally nearing the place where we could split away from the riders. Just before we reached the dark mouth of the footpath leading into the woods, however, Lester turned his horse across our path. From beneath the brim of his hat, he gave me a hard look.

"Tell your brothers to stay clear of strangers," he said. "I don't have anything against your father, so I'm warning you. Not everybody would."

Beside me Tor shifted.

"What's this all about?" he said. "Since when does Edgeling care what the Locrians do?"

Lester started to speak but Cobb cut him off. "Edgeling doesn't want trouble with the Alleyns," he said, and his voice was disturbing, strangely soft and high for a man his size. "But if that's what it takes to handle this little problem for the Dream Recorder, so be it. Tell your brothers to stay out of the way. Unless your father's in the mood for more digging."

He reached around and adjusted the long gun on his back, caressing it, looking at me pointedly. Then, digging his heels into his horse's side, he took off down the road.

Lester nodded once, sharply, and followed, his own long gun swaying on its strap in time with the horse's strides.

Chapter 7

"They're looking for Farrell Dean," I said as the horses disappeared around the curve.

Tor didn't answer; he was watching me assessingly, as if he thought I might fly into a panic. It irritated me and made my next words come out even and calm.

"Why are they after him? What will they do to him if they find him? And who's Edgeling?"

"I've no idea why they're after your friend," Tor said. "As for Edgeling, he's a man who likes power of any sort. He blackmails people, for one thing. At a guess, that's how Lester and Cobb ended up working for him."

"What does Edgeling have to do with the Dream Recorder?"

"She has her own brand of power, so I suppose Edgeling thinks an alliance is to his benefit. I don't really know. All I know is that when the Dream Recorder runs foul of the Council—as she regularly does by invading people's privacy, badgering them to talk to her, pulling her irritating tricks when they don't—then Edgeling comes to her defense."

"With men and guns? Or just by talking?"

"Whatever it takes to get his point across. Or hers."

Tor was looking thoughtful. "Strange though it seems, perhaps your friend actually will be safer if he's with Gabriel."

"But what does the Dream Recorder want with Farrell Dean?"

Tor shrugged.

My chest felt tight. I took a deep breath and made myself concentrate on the path ahead, the overhanging trees, the scattered pine needles. Either Farrell Dean was okay, or he wasn't. I couldn't do anything about it until I found him.

We pressed on through the dark woods, single file on the narrow footpath, and I couldn't help but wonder where the lunatic was. For a while I kept hearing noises everywhere—a snapping twig, a rustling of the dense undergrowth—but as time passed and no one leapt out at us, I began to relax a little.

How much of the day was gone already? I didn't know. The heavy clouds, the darkness of the trees pressing against us made it very hard to tell how much time had passed.

Behind me Tor was whistling softly under his breath. It was irritating—Farrell Dean was in trouble. This was no time for music.

"Did you make up that tune?" I said, making Tor talk so he'd stop whistling.

"No. It's an old one. A Sunday song."

"Today isn't Sunday."

"That's just the name." When I glanced back at him, he shrugged. "There are quite a few Sunday songs. It's what we call them."

"It can't be very useful, to call them all by the same name."

"No. But names are funny things—sometimes they just happen, and they're hard to change. Here's another one."

He started whistling again. This time I didn't try to stop him; he was whistling a song Ezzie used to hum, a song his older relatives had taught him—at least I assumed they were his relatives, because they were the only people who had dark skin like his. What did it mean, that Tor knew the same tune?

We walked on, Tor whistling one oddly familiar song after another, until we reached a large fallen log that blocked the path. Tor edged around me, climbed up on the log, then reached down and took my hand to pull me up. I saw the old scars Fiona had mentioned, and the crescent-shaped one at the base of his thumb.

"Those men," I said, as we clambered down on the other side. "They seemed to think you had something to do with the fire."

Tor looked uncomfortable. "I imagine they think the Council was behind it."

"Instead of Gabriel Drewblood?"

"Not exactly," Tor said, starting off down the path. It was wider now, so we could walk side by side. At least theoretically we could; Tor was walking very fast, as if he could outpace my questions.

"You can't just leave it at that," I said, panting a little in my effort to keep up.

Tor shot me a look that wasn't particularly friendly. "I'm not trying to leave it," he said. "But it's complicated. It's not like on your island."

I opened my mouth to snap back at him, but then it occurred to me that starting an argument would be a good way for him to avoid explanations. So I shut my mouth without saying another word. Instead I raised my eyebrows, pointedly waiting for him to go on.

"The Council has certain steps they follow when someone's a persistent troublemaker," Tor said. "It's important to have protocols for these things. Otherwise you're open to the charge of favoritism. You have to have written rules, and follow them to the letter, applying the rules equally to everyone. If you don't apply them equally to everyone, you aren't being fair. It's hard, though, because sometimes there are mitigating circumstances that mean bending the rules might be more fair than sticking to them. You can't do that, though, because you can't be sure you're actually being more fair rather than less fair."

Great. Now he was going to try to bore me into forgetting my question.

"Get to the point, Tor," I said.

His expression definitely wasn't friendly now.

"How am I supposed to know how much background you need?" he said. "You'd never seen a horse. You didn't even know what the word Papa meant."

So Fiona had told him that. What else had she said, I wondered, about her ignorant sister?

I bit back an angry retort. "What steps does the Council follow with troublemakers?" I said, my tone carefully even.

Tor's jaw tightened, but he answered. "First they go as a group and tell the person to behave. If he doesn't, then the Council suggests that people stop doing business with him. To boycott him, in effect, for a given period of time."

He stopped.

"That's it?"

He shrugged.

I looked at him doubtfully. "Does it work?"

"Sometimes." The tone of his voice told me it didn't work often enough.

"And when it doesn't?"

"Sometimes it doesn't work because people want milk or cheese more than they want to discipline the person selling it. To use your father as an example. Which is why the Council was never able to persuade him to stop disabling trucks."

So Tor considered Eric Alleyn a chronic troublemaker.

"Go on," I said.

"Sometimes the troublemakers aren't doing business

anyway. Like those petty thieves back on the path earlier."

"Spit it out, Tor," I said. He was rambling again. "What does the Council do when people won't boycott the trouble-makers?"

Tor threw a resentful glance in my general direction. "Then Gabriel Drewblood or one of his men steps in," he said. "Unofficially, of course, because the Council doesn't officially condone the use of force."

Huh? No wonder Tor was embarrassed. His precious Council didn't want to get their hands dirty, so they used bad guys to keep other bad guys in check. It sounded to me like the Council needed to step up and officially condone at least a little force. Though if they did, where would they draw the line?

I edged around a thorn bush, carefully keeping it away from Fiona's pretty clothes. "So *was* the Council behind that fire last night? Was Gabriel Drewblood acting on their behalf?"

Tor looked unhappy, but he answered readily enough. "I'm not sure. The Council isn't sure. They don't exactly give point-blank instructions, you know."

Right. Because then they'd be culpable.

"What had Doormouse done wrong?"

"He promised to supply hay to someone last year. And he took payment for it. But then he sold it again to someone else. It's the third time he's pulled that trick."

"Why do people keep falling for it?"

Tor shrugged. "They're either stupid, or they haven't heard, or they just plain need the hay and hope this time it'll be different."

"So because of that, Gabriel Drewblood burned his house?" It seemed a little excessive.

Tor frowned. "Maybe it was Drewblood. Or maybe the man who didn't get the hay he'd paid for decided to take matters into his own hands. Or maybe it was someone wanting to make Gabriel Drewblood look bad. That happens more often than your father wants to admit, especially on our side of the island. Make Drewblood look overbearing, get Eric Alleyn all upset—it's like a game. At least, that's what my father suspects. We don't know for certain, and we don't know who's behind all that. It could even be just one person, someone who likes mischief and doesn't care if people get hurt."

"But Gabriel Drewblood really does do things like burn people's houses when the Council is upset with them."

"Drewblood is behind many unofficial disciplinary actions," Tor said diplomatically. "But not everything that happens is down to him."

It sounded to me like people on this island could never be sure whether the Council was "unofficially" disciplining them for something wrong they'd done, or whether they were being targeted by random vandals, or by the Dream Recorder and her supporters. What a way to live.

"Look," Tor said, running a hand through his hair. "My father knows it isn't the best way to do things. But it's far better than nothing.

"Take your father, for instance, back when he was sabotaging trucks. We don't have an unlimited number of trucks, and it was just a matter of time until Eric Alleyn did something that ruined one altogether, and he simply would not listen to reason. When something like that is going on, everyone looks to Drewblood to do something. Not just the Council. Everyone. And if Drewblood thinks it's necessary, he does. That's why he's both useful and dangerous. Now, here's my question."

He stopped walking and faced me directly. "Why do you want to help your city, when they kidnapped you?"

I blinked. "That's quite a change of subject," I said. I

kept walking, and Tor followed.

"You're not the only one allowed to ask questions, are you?" he said. "Fiona told me about your city, and it sounds like a very strange place. For one thing, why would they steal you if all they intended to do was put you in the general holdings, so to speak? If some woman didn't have a child of her own, and she wanted one to raise, to love—well, that I could understand. It would still be wrong, to kidnap you, but it would make sense. But your situation makes no sense, at least not to me."

I shrugged. It was starting to make perfect sense to me, but I had no intention of explaining it to Tor.

The Watchers had said they'd let me live because "subjects" were hard to come by. Why were they hard to come by? Because no babies were being born on Optica in those days, during the time of the ashes. So the Watchers stole me to fill the gap, the empty place in their test tubes.

Because I was extra. There were two baby girls—surely the family could spare one. That's probably what Sir Tom thought.

But I wasn't going to say this to Tor. I already felt small and worthless compared to my sister; I had no intention of admitting I'd been stolen because I was redundant. I had no intention of admitting I'd been stolen so I could be experimented on like a rat.

Instead I answered Tor's first question. "I have friends in Optica," I said. "They're the ones I want to help. They didn't have anything to do with me being stolen. They all thought I was born there in the city, just like they were."

Tor's eyes were on my face. His scrutiny made me uneasy and I used the steepness of the path as an excuse to look away, fixing my eyes on the ground ahead.

"Everyone else was warehoused, just like you were," he said. "Put in those dormitories, kept from their parents. And this system, everyone accepted it? Everyone took orders about ... breeding?" He said it as if it were a dirty word. "And they gave up their children? They don't care about flesh and blood?"

"It's the only way we've ever known," I said, feeling defensive. "We didn't know things could be different."

"But didn't you imagine they could? Didn't you wish for another way?"

Hot anger rose in my chest. What did he think? That we enjoyed being ordered around, assigned breeding partners, kept apart from our parents? Who could possibly want a life like that?

I wanted to say so, but the words wouldn't come. They were drowned by my dreams of the sea, my dreams of freedom—dreams of a life with Meritt, a real life with him—and all I could do was shut my mouth tight and try not to cry.

Tor was still watching my face. He didn't say anything more, just nodded, as if satisfied by what he saw. It irritated me—Tor irritated me—and I focused on that, on being annoyed with him, until the urge to weep had passed.

The path was wide enough for us to walk side-by-side now, though just barely. On this uphill stretch the ground was less densely covered with pine needles and leaves, the bare earth exposed. The air smelled heavy with moisture, fecund. Fronds of ferns reached into the path and spattered my legs with raindrops when I brushed past them.

We rounded a bend, a hill rising ahead of us, and saw footprints climbing its muddy slope. Two sets, at least. Rory and Angus?

"Is it them?"

"I don't know," Tor said, but like me he had perked up at the sight.

Hurrying, we scrambled up the steep hill to the top. There the trees suddenly opened out and the land dropped gently away, sloping through a long open meadow, its grass still green. The path stretched out ahead of us through this wide open vista, first straight, then winding and climbing a distant hill, growing thinner and thinner as it spooled away from my feet to vanish into the distance. In all that long winding way, I saw no one.

The disappointment made me suddenly weary and I lowered my pack to the ground. The path ahead was so very long, its ending vanishing in distant mist, and it had been a long time since I'd had a full night's sleep, a restful night. How many miles would I have to travel before we caught up to Rory and Angus, and then found Farrell Dean, and then gathered help for our friends back in Optica?

The wind shifted, blew my hair back from my face. I reached to pull Fiona's cloak more firmly around my neck, and as I did, a sound reached us, faint but sinister. Gunshots. They drifted to us from across that wide expanse, distant but distinct. Two, three. Then several too close together to count.

I looked at Tor.

He said nothing. He simply reached down and picked up my pack, swung it onto his free shoulder, and started down the winding path.

Chapter 8

The sun had set by the time we reached the edge of the Grateful Fields.

In the long blue-gray twilight the empty meadows and long open-sided buildings looked forlorn, abandoned. Here and there I saw evidences of the previous month's celebration—a crumpled handkerchief caught beneath a bramble, a torn scrap of paper, a cup sitting on the low stone wall that circled the fields, its contents dried to a brown crust in the bottom.

Tor touched my arm and nodded. There, at the farther end of the meadows, a fire sparked, sprang to life.

"Is that them?"

"If it isn't, it might be someone we know. Someone we could camp with tonight."

I didn't know what to hope for. I was tired, and the thought of walking all night was a miserable one; but if we kept walking, we'd find Farrell Dean sooner.

We crossed the meadow, the grass springy and damp beneath our feet. When we reached the open-sided buildings Tor didn't go around but cut straight through. He was walking faster now, was several steps ahead of me, and I had to hurry to keep up. There was something unnerving about these empty buildings, so obviously meant to be filled with hordes of people. I imagined them dancing, singing, exchanging gifts—then vanishing, leaving nothing here but the memory of happiness long past and the knowledge of winter coming on.

It felt colder under the roofs, on the concrete floors, and I was glad Fiona had insisted I have shoes. I glanced up to say something to Tor about it, but what I saw drove all other thoughts away. Tor was carrying both our packs over his left shoulder. His right arm was relaxed, hanging down by his side, and his right hand held something. As I watched, he moved his thumb. A blade flicked out, thin and bright in the growing gloom.

Fiona had said fighting wasn't Tor's way. Did he even know how to fight? We were so isolated out here—what if Tor got hurt and I was left alone? Was there anywhere I could go for help? Was it faster to go back the way we'd come, or forward to the other side of the island?

As I reached to grab Tor's sleeve, to whisper these questions, the shadows around the fire moved, separated into more than one person. Definitely not the lone lunatic, then. It was two people. As I watched one of them shifted again, and the firelight gleamed in his bright orange hair.

Tor turned toward me with a smile—he'd seen as well—but before either of us could speak, the snap of a branch ahead and to the right, in the thick woods beyond the open fields, made us freeze. Someone or something was in the undergrowth.

Another branch broke, and leaves rustled. Someone coughed and then cleared his throat. Whoever it was didn't seem to be trying to be silent.

Whoever it was seemed to be moving steadily toward my brothers.

They were oblivious—I heard Angus laugh, and then a quieter response that must have been Rory.

"Wait here," Tor murmured.

"Who is it? Is it the lunatic?"

"I don't know."

"What if it's Farrell Dean?"

"I won't hurt him. Now *stay put*." I didn't like his tone, but I also didn't want to tangle with a lunatic, and that was probably who it was. I couldn't be certain, of course, but that cough somehow hadn't sounded like Farrell Dean.

Tor slid our packs from his shoulder and dropped them quietly on the ground, then moved quickly and silently toward the noise, his knife at the ready.

Just as he reached the tree line a dark figure came out of the thicker darkness, and Tor sprang.

I couldn't see what was happening—it was too dark. The man let out a strangled shout and Angus and Rory leapt to their feet and began running toward the disturbance, and I ran, too.

My brothers got there first, and Angus's voice rang out. "Ease up, Tor," he said. "He might be a lunatic, but he's our lunatic."

And then the captured man said, quite clearly, "Don't cut me—you'll get contaminated."

I sprang forward with a cry.

"Fiona?" Angus looked shocked.

"Valentina?" That was Rory.

"Red!"

I flung myself at Ezzie, shoving Tor aside, and wrapped my arms around his neck. "You're alive!" I said. He smelled terrible, of sweat and dirt and salt, but he was whole and upright, not crumpled on the ground as I'd last seen him, curled at the feet of armed and angry wardens on the beach outside Optica.

Laughing, he loosened my grip on his neck. "Won't be alive for long, not with you choking me like that."

I let go of his neck but caught a bit of his sleeve instead.

"Just look at you all dressed up like that," he said, smiling. "Like one of those fairies old Louie used to talk about." In the flickering firelight I could see that his clothes were tattered and his eyes looked tired, but there didn't seem to be any new wounds, and he didn't seem to be favoring the leg the wild man had clawed. "So you made it—that's good, Red. I sure was hoping that you and Farrell Dean made it."

"Have you seen him?" I asked. "Have you seen Farrell Dean?" I looked at Ezzie, then at Rory and Angus, but they all shook their heads no.

"How did you get here?" I said to Ezzie, at the same time that Tor said, "Who *is* this?"

"It isn't the lunatic," I said. "It's Ezzie—he's from home, from Optica." I turned back to Ezzie. "How did you get here?" I said again.

"I was collecting more firewood to cook that rabbit," he said, pointing at the meat on the spit over the fire, "and this guy jumped me."

"No, I mean to this island—"

"Oh, that," he said, and I saw he was teasing me. "Got here the same way you did. In a boat."

"But Sir Tom said there was only one boat."

Ezzie nodded. "The thing I came in probably doesn't deserve the name," he said. "For all I know, it wasn't even supposed to be a boat. But I could fit in it, and it floated. Mostly. I felt like I swam here, I was sitting in so much water."

That didn't sound safe at all. "Why did you do that?" I asked. "Why would you set out in something that barely floats? You could have been killed."

"I know it," Ezzie said, looking uncomfortable. I didn't know why, but I could see that he wanted me to change the subject, so I did.

"Where did you get it?" I asked.

"I found it in the stockade. Nobody else was around—they were checking the main supply rooms."

"So we got the stockade?"

Ezzie nodded.

"I'll go find our packs," Tor said, casting one more wary look at Ezzie. He went out into the darkness, which now was very dark, as black as could be—there was no moon, and clouds obscured the stars, and the brightness of the fire made it seem darker still. I looked at that fire and the smoke rose up and carried with it the scent of meat, and suddenly I was so hungry I felt faint.

Ezzie apparently was familiar with that particular look of mine. "Somebody feed the girl," he said, leading me over to one of the tree stumps that ringed the fire. Rory bent over and rummaged in a bag, handed me a piece of bread.

"But Ezzie," I began.

"Eat and then talk, Red," he said. "You know how you get." He looked at Rory. "She doesn't have any reserves," he said. "If she gets too hungry, she gets lightheaded and staggers around like a drunk person."

Tor walked back into the circle of light, carrying our bags.

"Rabbit's about done," Angus told him. "What food did you bring?"

Tor started unloading his pack, but I wasn't going to be put off. "What happened to Farrell Dean?" I said, looking at Rory. "How did you lose him?"

Rory took the piece of rabbit Angus offered him, but didn't delay in answering me. "After we saw the doctor, we were walking down the street, when suddenly Farrell Dean stopped dead in his tracks," he began.

"He stopped so fast I ran right into him," Angus interrupted. "Smack! And he said, 'who's that?' and we looked and said it was Gabriel Drewblood, and that if Drewblood knew what was good for him he'd go straight back to the other side of the island. And Farrell Dean said he wanted to talk to him, and we said sure, we always liked to introduce our new friends to our old enemies, but that with his damaged ribs it might not be smart to start another fight."

Tor handed me a piece of cheese and I bit into it as Rory took over the story again. "Farrell Dean said since he was all fought out, he'd pass on the introduction."

"So we went on," Angus said. "And we started telling him about how Drewblood was bad news, especially for anyone named Alleyn. We told him how Drewblood booby trapped that truck so that Papa lost his leg, and we told him about the lowlifes Drewblood keeps on his payroll, like Tristan Oldfamily, and then I said that was a depressing subject and we should talk about something else and maybe Fiona would like us to pick up some store candy, to celebrate Valentina coming home, and Rory said we should get her a welcome-home present, a necklace or something, and somewhere in there we turned around and Farrell Dean was gone."

He paused and took an enormous bite of bread.

"Gone?" Tor prompted, as Rory handed me a piece of rabbit.

"Just flat-out gave us the slip," Angus said around the bread.

"We searched for him, Valentina," Rory said, his dark eyes apologetic in the firelight. "We looked everywhere. And then we heard that he'd been asking after Gabriel Drewblood. So we tried to find Drewblood ourselves, but he was gone. People said he left town in a hurry."

"Why do you call her those other names?" Ezzie interjected, leaning forward with his elbows on his knees. "Her name's Red. It's not Fiona or Valentina or Esmerelda or Marianna or anything else. Just Red."

Tor met my eyes and smiled. In the firelight his big nose looked even more dramatic than usual. He held out an apple to me and I took it and held it in my hands, turning it round and round, while I explained my family to Ezzie.

"So this other girl looks just exactly like you?" he asked when I was finished.

"Dead ringer," Angus said around a bite of rabbit.

"Not quite," Tor amended. "But very close."

"And these two are your brothers?"

I nodded and took a bite out of the apple.

Ezzie looked at Angus. "I guess that explains the hair," he said. Then he gestured at both men. "They got me out of a fix. Somebody was shooting at me from inside a truck, and these two brothers of yours came out of nowhere and shot at the truck until it went away and left me alone. You come from good blood, Red."

Rory and Angus looked uncomfortable. "Well, you see …" Angus began, scratching his head. He cast an imploring look at Rory, who sighed but took up the explanation.

"It was Gabriel Drewblood's truck," he said. "He was shooting at someone running through the woods. We couldn't see who."

"But we knew it didn't seem sporting," Angus said, and took a big bite of cheese.

"The enemy of my enemy is my friend," Tor said.

My brothers nodded. "So we thought we'd interrupt the game," Rory concluded. "We weren't exactly trying to rescue Ezzie. Though we're glad we did."

"I still say thank you," Ezzie said. "It worked out good for me."

"But why was Gabriel Drewblood shooting at you?" I asked.

"Well, I don't exactly know," Ezzie said, shifting on his tree stump. "But I figure maybe because of the illness."

"What illness? What do you mean?"

Ezzie sighed. "Okay, Red, here's the thing." He cast a cautious glance at the other men, but continued, his voice low. "You know those wild men that came after us, out there in the wilderland?"

I nodded.

"You heard what Sir Tom said about them?"

"That they used to be Guardians…"

Ezzie made a rolling "keep talking" gesture with one hand.

"Then they got infected or contaminated by something during the time of the ashes …" I broke off. Tor and my brothers were watching me curiously—even Angus seemed to have forgotten his dinner—but I couldn't bring myself to say the rest.

"Ezzie," I said, jumping up and going to him. "That won't happen to you."

He looked at me but said nothing.

"It won't happen to you," I repeated, putting my hands on his shoulders and looking him straight in the eye. "It can't."

"And exactly why not?" Ezzie was perfectly calm. "You saw my leg. That was no normal infection—to get that bad, that fast? It only took ten minutes to go from a little scratch to oozing pus, and then I was delirious for hours. All that, just from one little scratch from that thing."

Tor looked a little sick.

"But being delirious doesn't mean anything. You were treated right away. Sir Tom had special medicine, and Shawna sat up all night drawing the infection out, and those other men might never have been treated at all. And however they caught that illness, Ezzie, it wasn't on our island, it was on the mainland, wherever that is, and it was way back during the time of the ashes. Maybe by the time they got back to our island it had gone too far for Sir Tom to treat it—and maybe it doesn't even spread by cuts or blood. Maybe they ate something bad, or breathed something." I was gabbling, and I knew I was. I so much wanted to be right about this.

Ezzie didn't look convinced; he just sat there waiting for me to wind down.

Then I thought of one other thing. "And Sir Tom's been dealing with those men all these years," I added. "He's probably been clawed or bitten himself, and that's why he knew to treat you right away—and he's perfectly fine."

Ezzie raised his eyebrows but I held my ground. Sir Tom might be a little eccentric, but he was nothing at all like the wild men. Compared to them, he *was* perfectly fine.

Except, of course, for the fact that he was a kidnapper who had ripped my family apart.

I turned to the others for support. "You don't think Ezzie's crazy, do you?" I said. When no one answered immediately, I looked directly at Tor.

"I've only been around him an hour or so," Tor said, noncommittal. I glared at him, but he merely turned his hands palm up.

Rory and Angus were studying Ezzie.

"We've been with him three or four hours," Rory said finally. "He told us he was sick and wanted us to tie him up, but I didn't see the point. He seems sane enough to me."

"Me, too," Angus echoed. "Besides, if we ran into any of Drewblood's crew, it'd be good to have an extra pair of hands on our side. Untied hands, that is." He had been running his own hands through his red curls and now they were standing on end. If anyone looked crazy, it was Angus.

Grateful for his support, feeling sisterly, I walked over and smoothed his unruly hair.

"Thanks, Fee," he said vaguely, his attention still on Ezzie.

"Thing is, I had a bad spell, there on the island," Ezzie said. "On the cliff when the wardens showed up and went after you? I felt like I could tear them apart with my teeth. Not just fight them—I wanted to rip their throats out, pull their arms out of their sockets, gouge their eyes out of their heads. That's not like me, Red. You know it's not. I've never been a fighter. And it freaked me out. So I just sat myself down and held as still as I could, until it passed, but I knew then that I had to get away. So I wouldn't hurt anyone, especially not one of us."

He nodded to the other men apologetically. "I didn't mean to end up here," he said. "Didn't mean to make myself your problem. Thought I'd probably get lost at sea or drown or something. But I hit land, and even though it was the middle of the night there were all these people there, like they were waiting for me."

"He came close to missing the island," Angus put in. He had returned to his meal and was gnawing at a piece of rabbit. "There's one bit of land that sticks out a little, and they've built a pier out from it. He snagged on that, and some fishermen who were out there spotlighting for squid hauled him in."

Ezzie nodded. "They were all excited, helping me out of the boat and giving me food and water, even though I told them to stay back. And I just felt so bad, Red—leaving our island because I was too cowardly to straight out do away with myself, and then there I was, putting all these other people's lives at risk, and they were all being so kind to me even though I told them I was going crazy and it was contagious, and so I started yelling some stuff that didn't make sense, to try to make them believe me, and busted up some things, and then I ran."

Angus took over. "He's been hanging out in the woods and following the road away from town," he said. "Then

Drewblood showed up, and he didn't stop to ask questions. Not a single question." Angus shook the rabbit leg in emphasis. "Not a one. Just started shooting."

Ezzie's laugh rang out, startling me. "Don't worry, Red, I'm not being crazy," he said. "It's funny, is all. Why'd I run? I wanted to die. Somebody was willing to kill me. I should've stood still and let him shoot me and thanked him for it."

I didn't think it was funny. I turned to the crackling fire and leaned over it, feeling its heat on my face, wishing its warmth could thaw the cold foreboding feeling in the pit of my stomach.

"Was Drewblood headed toward town or away?" Tor asked.

"Away, like I was," Ezzie said.

Tor nodded. "So he'd been home and was leaving again. Was anybody in the truck with him?"

"Didn't see anyone," Angus said, and Ezzie and Rory nodded in agreement.

"But his truck has tinted windows, so someone could have been there," Rory added.

I saw where Tor was going and shook my head. "If you're thinking of Farrell Dean, he wouldn't have sat there and let someone shoot at Ezzie," I said.

"Might not have known it was me," Ezzie said.

"Farrell Dean wouldn't just randomly shoot at anyone!" I said. "He wouldn't shoot at someone who wasn't an immediate threat, someone who was running away—"

"Calm down," Tor said, not very patiently. "I'm just trying to figure out where your friend is." He turned toward Rory and Angus. "Cobb and Lester are out looking for him, on behalf of Edgeling and the Dream Recorder. Seriously looking for him, if you know what I mean. They're well armed."

Rory looked startled.

"I know," Tor said, shaking his head. "It makes no sense. Did Farrell Dean speak to the Dream Recorder while you were in town?"

"Not a word," Angus said. "At least, not while we were with him. We never even saw the Dream Recorder, and we sure didn't see Edgeling. But maybe Farrell Dean talked to one of them after he left us."

Tor looked at Ezzie. "And you're sure you haven't seen him?"

Ezzie shook his head. "Wish I had," he said. Then his face changed. "Unless I did see him and just don't remember it, because of the sickness."

"Stop it, Ezzie," I said.

"No, I don't think I did see him," he went on. "I don't have a mark on me, and he could take me out in a fight, pretty sure. Unless—unless I took him by surprise, which I could have done, because he wouldn't have been expecting me to attack."

"Ezzie, *stop!*"

Ezzie spread his hands helplessly, but he stopped talking.

"You didn't hurt Farrell Dean," I said firmly.

Nobody else commented. Tor gazed off into the distance. I don't know what he was staring at; it was so dark I could see nothing beyond the range of the firelight. Anything could be out there, or nothing. The thought made me shiver.

"What did the doctor say about Farrell Dean?" I asked, turning toward Rory, who was tossing another stick on the fire, but it was Angus who answered.

"Have you seen his back?" he said.

I nodded.

"What's wrong with his back?" Tor wanted to know.

Angus's eyebrows drew together. "Somebody beat him like they meant it." He turned to me. "When I saw how bad it was, I felt like a real jerk for tackling him yesterday."

I pulled Fiona's cloak more tightly around me.

"But the doctor said he was healing well," Rory put in. "There wasn't any infection. Farrell Dean said he'd been dunked in salt water, and the doctor said that probably helped."

"Also said it must have hurt like the dickens," Angus added.

Rory ignored him and kept talking. "And his ribs aren't broken, just cracked. The doctor didn't even tape them because he said it was more important for him to be able to take deep breaths. So all in all, it was good news."

"Yeah," Angus agreed. "But the doctor also said it would have been better if the bigger cuts had been sutured. Too late for that, now, so the scarring will be worse. He was kinda freaked out by the whole thing, the doctor was. Kept looking out the window like he thought whoever had done it might come after him next. Can't really blame him—I sure wouldn't want to get whipped like that. Looked like somebody peeled entire strips of skin off him."

"Angus," said Tor quietly. "Time to shut up."

"I'm just telling her what the doctor said," Angus protested. "She asked."

He turned back to me. "He also said Farrell Dean must be one tough customer, to be up and moving around. Farrell Dean said yeah, whatever, you did what you had to do, and the doctor said in any case he'd better take it easy for a few days, give his body a chance to recover."

But instead, Farrell Dean had vanished. Was he with Gabriel Drewblood? Or someone else? Was he warm and safe, or was he alone in the dark somewhere?

Rory was watching me, looking sympathetic. "I assume you came after us because you're worried about him?" he said. I nodded.

"And she's pretending to be Fiona because we didn't think it was a good idea for Gabriel to know Valentina is alive," Tor put in. "There's no need to exacerbate the family feud." His face darkened. "I don't know what we should do if Farrell Dean has already mentioned Valentina to Drewblood. If he has, and she goes in there pretending to be Fiona ..."

Ezzie commented before I could. "Farrell Dean's careful," he said. "Always has been. Keeps his own counsel. He won't be making small talk, if that's what you're asking."

Then he turned to me.

"But given all this about family feuds and secret sisters, wouldn't it be better if you stayed out of it? I get that someone needs to find Farrell Dean and make sure he's okay. And someone needs to warn him about those men on horseback, and tell him not to trust this Drewblood man. But does it have to be you?"

I took a deep breath and tried to consider his question, but it felt monumentally unfair—Farrell Dean was my friend, and we were here to get help for our friends back in Optica, and we had nothing to do with whatever feud the Alleyns and Drewbloods had going.

Tor cleared his throat before I could speak. "As long as Farrell Dean hasn't given the game away, it should be safe for 'Fiona' to show up," he said. "Angus and Rory are far more likely to cause problems than she is."

Angus looked indignant, but Rory nodded. "Right. Drewblood likes Fee—she's never been anything but sweet to him—but he thinks we're Rufus and Mick in miniature."

"I'm not a miniature anybody," Angus protested.

"You know what I mean," Rory said.

Tor jumped in before Angus could argue. "So here's the plan. 'Fiona' and I will go and visit your Nana and Grandfather in Ionia. We'll locate Farrell Dean and make sure he's okay, and we'll warn him to be careful, and if he happens to call Valentina 'Red' and Drewblood hears it, he'll just think that's Fiona's nickname. He won't know Farrell Dean thinks she's a different girl."

"I *am* a different girl," I said faintly, but they all ignored me.

Angus gave a snort of disgust and got to his feet. "We've been walking all day and now you're telling us to go home?" he said, picking up a handful of pinecones and flinging them onto the fire.

"Stop it—they spark," Tor said.

Angus ignored him and threw another cone, which did indeed spark wildly as the flames caught it. Rory stamped at a few, but Angus merely crossed his arms over his chest and looked bullheaded.

Ezzie spoke. "I get that all three of us are liable to cause problems in town," he said. "But I can't say I much like the thought of leaving altogether. Farrell Dean might need backup. More backup than just one guy," he added, nodding at Tor.

"And one girl," I added irritably, but nobody answered.

"Can we stay nearby, out in the woods?" Ezzie went on. "Keep out of sight unless somebody sends for us?"

Tor and Rory exchanged glances. "Nana and Grandfather have that fishing cabin at the edge of the river," Rory said. "Nobody uses it, now that Grandfather's gotten so frail. We could camp out there."

"That would work," Tor said, and Angus seemed appeased.

"What's the river?" The words were out before I could call them back. I could feel Tor staring at me in disbelief, and I carefully avoided his eyes.

Angus was the first to answer. "The river's the river," he said, unhelpfully.

I wanted to change the subject, but everybody was staring at me, and now Ezzie chimed in. "Okay, got it," he said. "The river's the river. And did you know the loop-wrangler is the loop-wrangler?"

This was actually an improvement. Now Tor and Angus were staring at both of us as if we were unhinged.

"Do you have streams?" Rory asked.

Ezzie and I nodded.

"A river's like a big stream. Streams flow into rivers, and rivers flow into the sea."

Ezzie nodded, satisfied.

And what does the sea flow into? I wanted to ask the question, but of course, nobody here would know the answer.

"So the three of us will wait beside this river," Ezzie said. "And if you two need help, Red, all you have to do is get word to us and we'll come."

And so it was decided. Then Tor arranged watches for the night, and all of us but Rory lay down to sleep, huddled in our cloaks around the fire.

Ezzie was nearest me. Since someone was needed to stand watch against outside trouble, there was no reason to tie him up, though he had said more than once that we should.

I chose to believe he was wrong. Whatever had happened on the cliff could have been normal anger and outrage, couldn't it? It didn't mean Ezzie was becoming a wild man.

I watched him settle, stretching his wounded leg out carefully, and wished I could have taken him aside for a private conversation. I desperately wanted to know what had happened there on the cliff, whether he'd spoken with Meritt, whether the wardens had captured or hurt anyone, but it seemed awkward somehow to discuss these things in front of the others.

In particular, I admitted to myself, it felt awkward to ask about Meritt. I wasn't sure how my brothers would react.

They might scold me, or tease me, or ask questions I didn't want to answer. Families—at least my family—seemed quite involved in each other's business.

Angus was snoring. Rory got up from his tree stump and rolled Angus onto his side, and the snoring subsided.

I tried to find a comfortable position. Fiona's cloak was warm but the ground was hard and damp, and I wished Farrell Dean were here; it would have been easier to sleep, not fretting about his whereabouts. As I watched the flames and the thin curl of white smoke that rose and faded into the blackness, trying not to think of the darkness all around us, I wondered whether Nana and Grandfather would realize I wasn't the granddaughter they knew. Tor thought they wouldn't. They were quite old now, he said, and very nearly blind.

That seemed so sad—and more sad for Fiona than for me. To think these people, her own mother's parents, might not realize that she had been replaced by someone else …

Tor turned over and sighed deeply. Tomorrow he would pretend I was Fiona, the girl he had known all his life.

In the dying glow of the firelight I studied my hands, the ends of my flaming red hair. I wished I had a mirror and could see my own face, make sure I recognized myself.

Perhaps I truly was a fairy child, replacing a real girl.

Chapter 9

The bridge over the river was charming—lovely curved wood and carved posts arching from one bank to the other. I paused at its peak and stood looking down at the flowing water below. Streams, I could step over. This was nothing like a stream. The water rushed along with a force that would knock a person off his feet, even assuming he could touch bottom. It was smoother than the sea except where it swept around rocks, eddying and foaming.

"The river divides our side of the island from the other side," Tor said, stopping beside me. "Our side is larger and tends toward agriculture and cattle; this side is older and more technology oriented."

"Except for fishing," Angus put in. "One beach up here even has a gooey duck farm." He laughed at my expression. "Also called elephant clams. They're delicious."

Tor ignored his interruption. "The older side of the island is also more prosperous, or at least more progressive. They have more advanced medical care, and they also run the hydroelectric dam, which provides the entire island with electricity."

Meritt and Farrell Dean would be full of questions about that, I thought, a sharp pang of loneliness shooting through me. And Rafe—he would have been fascinated.

Mostly, now, Rafe's death was a sort of dull ache in the back of my mind, like a nightmare you can't quite shake no matter how sunny the day. But being on this island, with all its different ways of doing things, kept getting to me. Rafe would have been so interested in it all. He especially would have been interested in a world without Watchers, without experimenters—though, I reminded myself, Rafe probably hadn't known about the experiment part. None of us had.

Thinking about that—thinking of Rafe—ruined my enjoyment of the river. I suddenly realized that my feet were tired and that, despite our long walk, I was chilled. Mostly, though, I was homesick—not for a place, but for a time that was gone. I wanted to be a child again, happy that Meritt took an interest in me, conniving to spend extra minutes with Rafe, blissfully unaware that we were rats in a lab and that death was coming.

Rory's eyes were on me. "Do you suppose our names are still carved on the other end?" he said to Angus, who grinned and started walking. Rory followed, talking to Tor as he went, so that Tor followed too.

"We were quite small," he said. "We were visiting Grandfather and one day ..."

His voice faded, covered by the sound of flowing water.

I dropped a leaf into the river and watched it twist and swirl away.

"You up for this, Red?" Ezzie asked, leaning against the bridge railing beside me. In the daylight he looked a little haggard, but not ill. I remembered the strange feverish energy he'd had right after he'd been wounded; maybe being tired was a good sign, a sign that whatever swam in his blood was working its way out again.

"Of course I'm up for it," I said, watching the willow trees dipping their fingers in the running river. "I can't leave Farrell Dean hanging out there on a limb."

"So you're going out on that limb with him. Got it." Ezzie smiled at me, but his eyes were thoughtful. "I don't blame you, though. We've got to stick together."

Tor and my brothers had reached the other side of the bridge. They stepped off it and over to one side, peering at something under the first few planks.

"Red," Ezzie said, his voice low. "I saw Meritt. He's alive. He's okay."

"I saw him as we were rowing away," I said, turning toward Ezzie. "What happened?"

"Well, first of all the wardens arrested us. Cline, Judd, and me."

So the extra figure had in fact been Judd, my twelve-year-old friend—the one who had killed the warden I'd been blamed for killing. Why had he been out there? He was supposed to be helping take the stockade, not hanging around fighting wardens.

Ezzie was gazing down at the river. "The wardens cuffed our hands and linked our legs together so we could barely walk. Then they fished up that one warden who'd gone chasing after you down the cliff. They asked him all sorts of questions but he couldn't remember much of anything."

"Farrell Dean hit him in the head with a rock after he tried to drown me."

"Ah," Ezzie said, nodding. "That would explain it. Well, that warden was pretty woozy and another warden was having to help him along, so we were moving pretty slowly. But we were moving all right, toward Optica. So I thought we'd had it—thought we'd be center stage at the city meeting that night."

I screwed my eyes shut tight, trying to block out images of past city meetings—Rafe falling at my feet in a pool of blood, Lavinia's hair streaming like oil across the ground, Farrell Dean facing a gun held by his mother.

"Then here comes Meritt out of the trees," Ezzie said. "And it was the strangest thing, Red. Meritt barely even glanced at Cline and Judd and me, just started talking to the wardens. He said it was a good thing they'd managed to catch a few of the troublemakers, though they hadn't caught the one who mattered."

Ezzie scratched one arm and kept scratching it, absently, as if not realizing what he was doing.

"The Watchers sure must be furious Farrell Dean escaped the city meeting. Not good, is it? People hunting him there, people hunting him here. But anyway, the wardens kind of snarled at Meritt, but it was an apologetic sort of snarling, if you get me. It was like Meritt was in charge. Makes no sense, but that's sure how it seemed."

Ezzie didn't know Meritt was negotiating with the Watchers, working his way into their trust, and I didn't want to explain it. Not then.

Fortunately Ezzie was too involved in his story to realize I couldn't meet his eyes.

"So Meritt was talking with the wardens, and we were still walking toward the city, and then all of a sudden here came Angel and Jensen. And they set about disabling those wardens, but they left Meritt alone, and us too. Then once the wardens were all down, Meritt took a key from one of them and unlocked our cuffs, and told us to get going before the wardens came to."

He put a hand on my arm. "So you see? You were right about Angel. He and Sir Tom, they might not get along. But Angel's helping us anyway."

"Angel is Meritt's father," I said. "I saw them standing on the cliff together—it's obvious when you see them side by side."

Ezzie's eyes widened. "They do favor, now that I think about it," he said, and then he shook his head. "I will say it's a

AMANDA WITT

real good thing Angel's on our side. He sure can fight. I'd hate to have that man against us."

"Sir Tom told me once that Angel unarmed was more dangerous than an armed warden," I said.

"That about says it," Ezzie said. "And Jensen, crazy as he is—he knows some moves, too. Makes me think he wasn't really trying, that night we took him down. So anyway, once those two took out the wardens, Meritt got down on the ground pretending like he'd been hit too, and Cline and Judd and I headed off to the stockade. There's some food there, Red, enough to last awhile, but most of the weapons were gone. Angel must have stashed them somewhere else. But that'll be okay, since Angel's helping us. He'll tell Cline and them where the guns are, I bet. It'll all be okay. Right, Red?"

Ezzie was looking at me, his face baffled. Obviously he thought he was giving me good news, and was wondering why I was struggling not to cry.

And maybe it was good news. I didn't know. It was bad news for my judgment sense, that was certain. I should have trusted Angel, not Sir Tom, who'd stolen me from my family. I'd led everyone astray, and who knew how deadly that mistake would be? I should have trusted Angel.

But what about Meritt? I didn't know what to think. I was the one bargaining chip he couldn't do without. I was the only one the Watchers had demanded, and they had demanded me because they were convinced I was the one Meritt cared about most. If the wardens had caught me that day, would Meritt have set me free along with Ezzie and the others? Or would he have kept me, turned me in for the sake of Optica?

It was all too complicated.

To hide the tears that threatened to spill over, I kept my gaze fixed on the river flowing beneath us, watching it carry twigs and autumn leaves, spinning and drowning, around the

116

bend. Sunlight unexpectedly broke through the clouds and glittered on the flowing water, setting fire to the autumn leaves along the bank, sparkling in the water droplets along the wet grass.

"Meritt's okay, Red," Ezzie said. His voice was gentle and almost apologetic, as if he thought he might be treading on something too personal to mention. "He's got some sort of inside track, that's what I think. And with him working on the inside, and Sir Tom and all them working on the outside, and Angel helping too, Optica will be okay. You'll see."

The tears I'd been fighting spilled down my cheeks.

Ezzie patted my arm awkwardly. My head began to throb. I wiped my tears on the sleeve of Fiona's pretty pale blue dress, wishing I were at home wearing my plain grey uniform, and tried not to look at the men at the end of the bridge who were now murmuring to each other, casting glances our way and looking concerned.

Then Tor said something to Angus and Rory, and started back up the bridge toward us. The wooden planks moved under his feet, so that even with my eyes shut I felt him coming. Couldn't he give me just a few minutes to myself—just a moment or two to talk with Ezzie, to think of our friends back home?

"Best be off, Red," Ezzie said, throwing an arm lightly around my shoulders. "Let's go find Farrell Dean."

Chapter 10

We followed the path along the river as it wound west, passing every now and then little cottages, most of which looked abandoned.

Eventually the path rejoined the wider road, and then we had to be more careful. Tor didn't want Gabriel Drewblood to see my brothers—he acted as if the bare sight of them would cause the man to instantly begin frothing at the mouth—and of course we didn't want anyone seeing dangerous lunatic Ezzie. So, on the two occasions when we heard the distant growl of a truck, Tor sent my brothers and Ezzie into the woods and he and I stayed on the road alone. We did the same thing once for a man on a horse, though he almost caught us unawares.

About an hour after the horse incident, we came to a little house that sat almost on the very brink of the river, so close that it was built up on stacked cinder blocks to keep its foundation dry. A set of concrete steps led up to a covered porch that circled the house and hung over the river. At the top of the steps was a door.

"Here's where we say goodbye," Tor said, turning to the others. "Stay out of sight. We'll send word if we need you."

"Yes, sir!" Angus said smartly.

Tor glared at him. It probably was a good thing the two

of them were about to be separated. Frankly, I was ready to be separated from Tor, too. He seemed to be getting bossier by the minute.

Angus smiled innocently at Tor and turned to me. "If Nana asks you a question and you don't know the answer, make something up," he said. "She's so dotty now she won't know any better."

"Or just say you don't remember, or change the subject," Rory said. "And don't worry. They're nice people, Nana and Grandfather. Even if they do seem to be living in their memories more than in the real world, these days."

I turned to Ezzie, not wanting to say goodbye—he was, at the moment, my only link to home—but the look on his face distracted me.

"What is it?" I asked.

"Tell you later," he said, patting my shoulder. His eyes seemed a little unfocused. "Nothing to worry about. Just thinking. You go on, and be careful." He was scratching at his arm again, hard enough to draw blood.

Angus and Rory exchanged glances. When Angus saw that I'd seen them, he flushed and waved a hand awkwardly in my direction. "See you later, Fee," he said. I was beginning to think Angus either was seriously absentminded, or simply couldn't be bothered to keep his sisters straight.

Rory, however, called me by my birth name. "Good luck, Valentina," he said, pulling me into a hug.

"Don't hurt Ezzie," I murmured. "Please—even if he acts crazy, don't hurt him."

"We won't," he said against my hair. "We'll take care of him."

"And don't let him hurt you," I added as he released me. He met my eyes and gave a reassuring nod as he turned away, and I felt a little better. I wasn't entirely sure about my other brothers, but I knew I liked Rory.

"Time to go, Fiona," Tor said, jerking his head toward the path. Reluctantly I followed him as the three others climbed the steps to the river cabin.

Tor walked briskly and at first I had to hurry to keep up. Then, as I drew further away from Ezzie, my worries shifted from him to Farrell Dean, who could be in all sorts of trouble. Soon Tor was having to hurry to keep up with me.

The river flowed on our left, golden in the sunlight. On our right the trees hung over us, dropping their red and gold leaves at our feet. It was very beautiful, but somehow its beauty only made me feel more anxious. The world didn't care what happened to Farrell Dean; in all its beauty it was indifferent to human hopes and fears.

Without warning Tor stopped and turned to face me, catching my arm to make me stop, too. "We're almost there," he said, looking down at me. "Ionia is just around that bend. So before we go any further, we'd better get a few things straight."

Really, he was unbearable this morning.

"Fiona?" he said, and I flinched and dropped my pack.

He smiled without humor. "That's exactly the problem," he said. "You can't look annoyed every time someone says your name."

"It isn't—"

He cut me off. "I know it isn't your name. But we have to pretend it is."

Did he think I was stupid? I wouldn't do it once we were around the people we had to fool. And hadn't I been practicing their silly accent?

Tor looked as irritable as I felt. "Let me explain exactly how serious this is," he said, dropping his pack on the ground next to mine and crossing his arms over his chest. "If Drewblood finds out who you really are, he won't just be angry. He won't just go and yell at your father a bit."

I gave him a bored look. "What will he do? Kill him?"

"That well might be the end result."

"My uncle would kill my father because I turned out to be alive? You can't be serious."

Tor eyed me coldly. "I am completely serious. They have a long history, and an ugly one, and you'd do well to take it seriously. But whether you do or not, I expect you to be convincing. No one can suspect that you're the missing sister."

"Who's going to suspect?" I said, flinging my arms out in frustration. "They think I'm dead. And even if they do think 'hey, maybe the dead girl is back,' why is that so dangerous? Yes, I got kidnapped. But that was a long time ago, and it wasn't Eric Alleyn's fault, and if I'm not mad at my father about it then why on earth should Gabriel Drewblood go into some murderous rage because of it?"

"Maybe because he's murderous, as you so aptly put it, about Eric Alleyn in general!" Tor looked around and lowered his voice. "Frankly I can't really blame him. I don't mean to be rude, but your father is a very difficult man. He has to know that Gabriel isn't behind half the trouble he's blamed for, but he lays every problem, large or small, at Gabriel's feet. And he's highly opinionated, and wants everyone else to do things his way."

I opened my mouth and Tor held up a finger, stopping me from interrupting. "Yes, he accuses Gabriel Drewblood of that exact same thing, but it's a case of the pot and the kettle."

"But Gabriel Drewblood burns down people's houses."

"And you think your father is above that sort of thing? If he can't persuade someone over to his perspective, he feels perfectly justified in moving on to bullying, browbeating, blackmailing, staging accidents, destroying property—and if he hasn't personally laid a hand on anyone lately, it's only because of his leg, and he's got plenty of sons willing to do the dirty work for him."

"And yet he's the one who lost his leg. Not Drewblood."

Tor was flushed with exasperation. "I've heard people say that accident was the best thing that ever happened to our side of the island. It keeps Eric Alleyn close to home, prevents him from going around rabble rousing, coercing, stirring up mischief. Mischief my father, as the Council Chief, had to deal with for too many years."

I half shrugged and started to turn away. Tor caught my arm and stopped me.

"Eric Alleyn has enemies," he said. "Deservedly so. And one of them is a prominent member of the community we're about to enter as outsiders. As guests. Would Gabriel Drewblood go after Eric Alleyn for not taking care of you, for losing you—his niece—his dead sister's child? Absolutely. And would your father retaliate, exacerbating the situation until one of them ended up dead? Without a doubt. Their history is a keg of gunpowder and you are a match. So I am dead serious when I say you can't just go barreling recklessly around—I mean, look at you. You were practically running. You must slow down and be careful."

"All right," I said, picking up my pack. "So I'll be careful. Let's get on with it."

"You'll be more than careful," Tor said. "You'll be *Fiona*."

As he spoke a breeze kicked up. It stirred the fallen leaves around our feet and blew my hair into my eyes, blinding me. I reached up to shove it back but Tor caught my wrist and pulled my hand away. I thought for a second that he was going to shake me, trying to get my attention, trying to make me mind him. But instead he dropped my wrist and, with both his hands, stroked my hair away from my face, tucking it behind my ears. It was so unexpected that I froze.

"Before we go any further, we also need to talk about this," he said, his hands still on my hair.

My face flushed hot. I knocked his hands away and stepped back, out of arm's reach.

Tor breathed out a harsh breath of exasperation, but then the corners of his eyes crinkled in a reluctant smile.

"You don't have to hang all over me," he said, and his face grew serious again. "Fiona doesn't. But don't blow your cover by greeting this Farrell Dean like your long lost lover, either."

"He isn't," I said stiffly.

Tor shrugged. "That should make things easier, then," he said. "Because whatever you might do in Optica, in Aislin young women don't go heading off across the island, un-chaperoned, with young men who aren't related to them. So if we're successful and everyone believes you're Fiona, then everyone also will assume that you and I will shortly be an-nouncing our wedding. That means you must at least act pleasant towards me. And vice versa. There's no way around that." His face was grim.

"But—"

I stopped myself. Was he implying that Fiona had set him up? Trapped him? But I thought she was playing a dif-ferent game. I thought she wanted to make him jealous—wasn't that why Rory and Angus jumped Farrell Dean, be-cause Fiona had been seeing different boys?

Tor cocked his head, his gray-blue eyes unreadable. "What's so confusing?"

I waved one hand helplessly.

"You don't know Fiona very well yet," he said, and though he was still flushed with annoyance he began to look faintly amused. "But surely she's told you she wants to marry me?"

What could I say that wouldn't give my sister away?

"You don't have to commit yourself," I said finally. "You can go back home now. Or you can wait with the others at the fishing cabin. I can find Farrell Dean on my own, and I'll be very careful. I won't let anyone know I'm not Fiona."

Tor was shaking his head. "You'll never succeed on your own," he said. "You'll have to talk to people, to get a lead on Farrell Dean, and that means you'll have to answer whatever questions people put to you. You'd give yourself away in a heartbeat, but I can jump in and direct the conversation and so forth. And besides, Fiona's family would never have let her travel all this way alone."

"I wasn't alone. Come to that, *we* weren't alone."

"Nobody knows that. We left Doria alone, we're arriving in Ionia alone. So we have to be credible."

"And if we aren't?" I said, as a bizarre thought hit me. "If people figure out that I'm not Fiona, will they expect *me* to marry you?" Whatever was done or not done on this island, I had no intention of spending my life with Tor.

"If that happened," Tor said, looking torn between amusement and disgust, "the Alleyns would blame me for any harm that befell their father. And if, heaven forbid, he managed to get himself killed? Then they wouldn't let Fiona or you either one marry me, even if you wanted to, which you clearly don't, and if I may respectfully say so, the feeling is mutual."

I ignored that. "I can't imagine Fiona letting her brothers tell her who to marry or not marry," I said.

Tor made a gesture as if he were swatting away a fly. "She wouldn't," he said. "But as irritating as her father can be, he's her life. If I let anything happen to him, she'll have nothing to do with me. So you can see why you have to be believable. I have a lot at stake."

I stared at him for a long moment, sorting through it all.

"So you do want to marry Fiona," I said.

Tor looked at me as if I were very slow. "Of course I do," he said. "We've planned to marry since we were knee high. And Fiona wants to marry me, though lately she's been entertaining herself pretending otherwise."

That sounded really arrogant, but since it was pretty much the truth, I let it pass.

"Can we go now?" I said.

Tor picked up his pack and took my hand, inserting it in the crook of his arm. "We can go."

I pulled my hand away and started toward town and, after a moment, Tor followed.

Gold and orange leaves lay several inches deep along the path, rustling and swirling around my feet as I walked. I kicked through them irritably, not caring whether I soiled my pretty shoes. I hated this stupid island with all its complicated relationships. I hated that Ezzie might be sick. I hated that Farrell Dean had gone off and left me to worry about him. I hated that I didn't know what was happening back home, that the Guardian I'd trusted was unreliable, to say the least. I hated not knowing what Meritt was thinking.

I hated that I was going to have to pretend I liked Tor—and soon. Already, there in the distance, I could see the roofs of town.

Abruptly I stopped, there on the path. I wasn't ready. I wouldn't fool anyone, feeling like I did just then. Unless I could pretend to be Fiona being angry at Tor?

When I stopped, Tor stopped too, looking at me as if expecting me to say something. When I didn't, when I just stood there taking deep breaths, trying to prepare myself for whatever lay ahead, his expression began to soften.

No doubt he was thinking about Fiona. It was creepy, having people look at me and see her. Tor probably had kissed her; or maybe he was remembering their childhood, when he'd comforted her over a scraped knee, or commiserated with her after Angus had been mean. Whatever he was thinking, though, whatever memories he was reliving, they were of Fiona and not of me. I was a completely separate person. This was my face, not hers; behind it lay my memories, my thoughts and feelings, my life. Not hers.

After a moment, Tor spoke. "You look so much like her," he said, touching my elbow. "This probably will be easier for me than for you."

That was certain.

But if it kept Farrell Dean safe—and my father—I could do harder things than this. I could pretend to be my sister, and pretend to like the man she liked. Cynda did harder things than this every night, when she smiled and made nice to wardens. And Tor wasn't a warden; he was helping me find Farrell Dean. He was helping, and I was acting like a pouty child.

"I'm sorry," I said, turning toward him. "I'll try my hardest. So don't worry."

Tor studied me gravely. "Thank you," he said.

Chapter 11

The first thing I noticed about Ionia was the smell of flowers. Even this late in the year, the air was sweet with them, and great bushes of red, pink, or purple blossoms grew beside every doorway. I'd never seen anything like it.

Then I noticed the music that drifted out of various buildings as we passed. Sometimes it was a person singing, but other times it was wordless, lovely sounds, like those Meritt and I had heard coming from the Watchers' compound when we sneaked past late at night.

Tor put a hand on the small of my back, and I was proud that I didn't flinch.

The buildings here were similar to those in Doria in that they weren't uniform at all, but were a mixture of materials and styles. And the people were dressed in similar fashion. But this town seemed less chaotic. The streets weren't ruler-straight like Optica's, but neither were they Doria's rambling jumble, and the buildings were neat and clean. A few looked old, and many were quite simple, but they were all in good repair. And although I saw some chickens and even a goat or two, all the animals were fenced away from the street.

"It's tidier than Doria," I remarked.

Tor nodded. "That's Gabriel Drewblood's doing."

"He threatened people?"

"No. He persuaded the shopkeepers that it would be good for business if the downtown was a pleasant place for shoppers. Drewblood is well-versed in the use of carrots as well as sticks."

We passed a produce stand of eggplant, carrots, lettuce, and apples, their vibrant colors contained in neat piles. Then came a dressmaker's shop, with a shape in the window like that of a woman. The fabric of her dress was pretty, but nothing compared to Fiona's work.

A faded sort of man coming toward us on the sidewalk slowed and stared at me. He was unremarkable in every way—even his clothes were a nondescript tan, not the bright colors I'd come to expect on this island—but his eyes stood out starkly in his face, a vivid but cold blue.

I glanced at Tor; he was looking straight past the man as if he didn't know him, so I tried to ignore him as well. I let my eyes slide past him and pretended that my attention was fixed on a furniture display in the next store window.

It really was pretty furniture, chairs and tables with beautiful curved legs. Carvings of leaves and flowers ran along the wood, and some of the chairs had colored cushions on the seats. In the reflection of the shop window I saw the faded man pass on by, his head turning to keep me in sight for longer than I liked. Then he went into a building that said "Radio Studio" on the door.

"Your Nana and Grandfather live on the other side of town," Tor said, glancing around to make sure no one was in earshot. "Out a bit, but not too far. How have your new shoes been? Are they rubbing blisters?"

He was trying to be nice.

"They're fine," I said. We had walked a very long way, but the shoe leather was soft, and Fiona's stockings were good and thick.

I left the furniture window. The building next to it sold

dry goods—pots and pans, rakes, barrels, all sorts of useful things.

The one after was a cheese shop. Big round cheeses dipped in red wax were stacked in the window, and inside the store wedges were laid out behind a glass counter. A man in a white apron was weighing a slab on a scale and listening to something a small gray-haired woman was telling him.

We passed two men who were replacing a window in a shop front. A woman was sweeping up piles of broken glass from the sidewalk. A few stores down we passed a similar scene—broken glass, irritated faces—and then a third.

I looked up at Tor; he nodded but said nothing. This must be the damage Ezzie caused as he was escaping the well-meaning people of Ionia, convincing them he was crazy.

Next came a hardware store that seemed to be mostly nails and wires. Beside it was a glass-blower's shop, with beautiful extravagant bowls and vases in every color of the rainbow. I was glad Ezzie hadn't smashed this window, destroying all those beautiful pieces.

At the next shop a wonderful warm smell drifted out to the sidewalk; a bakery, the sign said. Some of the cakes in the window were amazingly fancy, rimmed with wreaths of colored icing flowers, and topped with pools of jam. Beside them were rows and rows of muffins, folded pastries, and piles of breads. I didn't recognize most of the baked goods I saw there, but they all looked delicious.

"Makes your mouth water, doesn't it?" Tor said. My stomach growled loudly as if in answer, and Tor laughed, and the remains of my bad mood faded. The town was simply too perfect to be believed. Everyone who lived here should be happy, I thought, at least on a day like today with sunshine and music, and the smell of flowers and warm sugary cake.

And yet there was a decided tension in the air. As Tor and I had walked along, a few people cast worried glances our way. One or two seemed to recognize us and nodded or waved, but most hurried about their business, their faces tight and closed. Was it all because of Ezzie?

Turning away from the delicious smells of the bakery, I saw that across the street from us was a shop with a blue door and a Dream Recorder sign, similar to the one in Doria but freshly painted. It reminded me unpleasantly of the unsettling woman who had followed us, who was some sort of danger to Farrell Dean, and so I looked away.

The next building had a sign in the window: "Musical Instruments." Surrounding the sign were many objects I didn't recognize. Were they all for making music, those things in the window, all gleaming silver and rich warm wood? What did the strings do?

"Fiona!" someone called. "Tor Van Stavern!"

"Dang it," Tor muttered, but he smiled and lifted his hand in greeting, and then, without warning, the whole street seemed to tilt. For a heartbeat everything looked very bright and sharply defined—the cobblestones of the street, the indigo door of the Dream Recorder shop, the red shirt of the dark-haired man moving towards us—and then the world went blurry and dark and I felt myself falling and heard, distantly, Tor's alarmed shout.

When I opened my eyes I didn't know where I was. I tried to look around but the sun was too bright and all I gathered was that I was half-lying, half-sitting on a damp sidewalk.

Then I heard a voice—one I knew, but not well. It reminded me of being annoyed.

Cautiously I opened my eyes just a slit. A man was supporting my head and shoulders with one arm; when he saw that my eyes were open, he reached up with his free hand and stroked my hair off my forehead. Instinctively I started to jerk away, but he gripped my shoulder warningly and I looked into his gray-blue eyes and everything came back in a jumbled sort of flash—I was searching for Farrell Dean, Optica was far away, someone named Gabriel was dangerous, this man was Tor, there was a girl who looked exactly like me, my sister, and I had to be very careful.

Buying a few precious seconds to gather my wits, I lay still against Tor's shoulder, irritated with him without quite remembering why, but grateful that he'd kept me from shoving him away and ruining everything. Somewhere out of my line of sight, another man was talking.

"You walked? That's an odd choice for this time of year. Couldn't either of your fathers spare a horse?"

"Fiona preferred to walk," Tor said, very politely. "The footpath is picturesque this time of year, and she doesn't like sharing the road with trucks."

"And you didn't bring enough supplies to keep her on her feet?" The man's tone wasn't aggressive, but his words were pointed enough.

Tor didn't react. "We brought plenty," he said. "But you know Fiona. One minute she's fine, and the next she's light-headed. I suppose the smell from the bakery did her in."

"My new place is right across the street," the man said. "Let's get her over there so she can rest and eat something."

Tor nodded. "All right. Thank you, Mr. Drewblood."

Drewblood—it was Gabriel Drewblood. I struggled to sit up, meeting Tor's worried eyes as I did so.

"Feeling better?" he said gently. "You fainted."

I nodded, afraid to trust my voice—afraid, that is, to attempt Fiona's rhythms. I knew exactly why I'd fainted, and it wasn't because I was hungry.

I also knew that the acting job required of me had just

gotten far more difficult than any of us could possibly have imagined.

"You were only out a few seconds," Tor went on. "Next time, find another way to test my reflexes, all right? If I'd missed, you'd have a whopping headache right about now."

Irritating though he'd been earlier, I had to admit that his calm meaningless talk was comforting, and so was his arm around me. I needed some sort of anchor at the moment, and Tor was all I had.

"Can you stand up?" Tor said. His gaze was questioning and I knew he was asking about more than my physical strength; he was afraid I'd be confused, forget to be Fiona.

I gave him what I hoped was a reassuring smile—to me it felt more like a grimace—and then I nodded. He got to his feet and helped me stand, keeping one supportive arm around my waist.

I smoothed my clothes and my hair—surely only a second or two passed while I readied myself, but maybe it was longer. Time had slowed, stretched, become unreliable.

But it had not folded, I told myself firmly. This was not the past strolling up to greet me. The past was dead and gone, and this was now.

I took one last steadying breath and lifted my chin. Then I turned to greet Gabriel Drewblood.

Gabriel Drewblood, my uncle. Gabriel Drewblood, dangerous, feared and hated.

Gabriel Drewblood, who looked exactly like my beloved Rafe.

Chapter 12

Fortunately for me, Gabriel Drewblood didn't expect me to talk much at first. He chatted to Tor and led us across the street, into the shop with the blue door, while I did my best to look at him without staring.

That surreptitious scrutiny did nothing to change my first impression. Gabriel and Rafe were identical, every bit as identical as Fiona and me. They had the same dark short hair, though Gabriel's still had only a few silver strands, while Rafe's had gone heavily silver in the preceding couple of years. They had the same brown eyes and the same expression in those eyes, carefully pleasant but watchful, alert.

Gabriel Drewblood was a tiny bit heavier than Rafe; Gabriel Drewblood had a close-cropped beard and mustache circling his mouth while Rafe had been clean shaven. The physical differences were all small ones, strictly cosmetic.

No wonder Farrell Dean had come to a dead stop when he saw this man. No wonder he'd slipped away from my brothers to go after him the second he could. How could he stand to let Rafe's image out of his sight? I would have followed him across the island myself, with never a thought of anything else.

Kindly but without fuss my uncle settled me in a big overstuffed chair upholstered in a deep blue fabric, brought me a hot drink and a tray of food—cheese, crackers, sausage, and a bowl of berries—and then left the room again.

Tor gestured at the tray. "Go ahead—we don't want you fainting again."

Of course he didn't know the real reason I'd fainted, and I couldn't tell him now, so I went ahead and took a bite of cheese. And it was true that I was ravenous. After all, we'd walked for two days to get here.

Gabriel Drewblood came back with a tray for Tor, and then sat down across from me in another stuffed chair, watching us eat, making casual conversation.

"Did you have any trouble on the way?" he said.

"You mean did we get ambushed by a dangerous lunatic?" Tor said. "No. Someone stopped on the road to warn us and we kept an eye out, but we never had any trouble. Who exactly is this person?"

Gabriel Drewblood shook his head and his eyes took on the same half-amused, self-deprecatory look I'd seen so often in Rafe's eyes.

"We're pretty thoroughly baffled," he said. "He showed up at the pier in a leaky little boat and started shouting all kinds of wild tales, then tore up the town and took off."

"Is he from Locria?" Tor asked. "I've heard they've been working on boats up there. Maybe he skirted the island, came around the coast."

"The Locrians do keep to themselves," Gabriel Drewblood said.

Uncle Gabriel—I had to remember to call him that. Uncle Gabriel, or at least Gabriel. That's what Rory had told me. That's what Fiona called him, not "Drewblood" like the rest of them did.

"No doubt there are plenty of Locrians whom I wouldn't recognize," he was saying. "And his boat certainly doesn't look as if it would make it any farther than that.

But—" he looked at me—"He claimed to be from another island entirely."

I plastered a surprised expression on my face.

"An island rife with some vicious contagion," Gabriel said.

"If there's any chance of that being true, we can't have him roaming around," Tor said.

Gabriel nodded. "Exactly. That's why we've been looking for him. One of my men spotted him yesterday and almost got him with a tranquilizer dart, but the lunatic had real bullets, so my man backed off and lost him."

A knot in my chest unwound just a bit. Rafe's lookalike—Rafe's brother—hadn't been trying to kill Ezzie.

"Any other interesting happenings?" Tor asked.

Gabriel shook his head. "Business as usual. How's your father?"

He didn't ask about mine, not then or later.

While he and Tor talked I let myself study Gabriel some more, taking care to seem casual. He and Rafe had the same wrinkles at the corners of their eyes, the same laugh, the same way of always looking at you straight on. Their voices were the same, except for the accents. Gabriel even had Rafe's calm tone, the one that had always made me feel that somehow everything would be all right in the end.

If Gabriel Drewblood—Uncle Gabriel—was half as sharp as Rafe, I had my job cut out for me.

Uncle Gabriel.

That was the really important thing. Gabriel was my uncle.

And that meant Rafe was my uncle.

I'd pretended Rafe was my father; I knew he'd loved me. But now it seemed he'd truly been mine. We were related by blood, though we looked nothing alike. My red hair came from my father, and Gabriel and Rafe were dark-haired like my mother, their sister. I was small like she'd been, though, and no one would call Rafe and Gabriel small, although they weren't as tall as some men. They weren't as tall as Eric Alleyn and Rufus—but now that I thought of Rufus, I could see something of him in Gabriel. Rufus looked so much like Eric Alleyn, but the little part that didn't, looked like Gabriel. Like Rafe. My uncle.

The strange thing was, I couldn't decide whether I felt happier or sadder, now that I knew. I was thrilled that Rafe was my uncle, but I wished I'd known before he died. I wished he had known. And suddenly, too, I was replaying the moment of his murder, and feeling it even more personally than before, if that was possible. They were killing my beloved instructor. They were killing my pretend father. They were killing my real uncle, my own flesh and blood.

While I was pondering these things, and eating as slowly as I reasonably could in order to buy myself time to think, I gradually realized that Gabriel was studying me as carefully as I was studying him. He didn't stare, or look at me too often, but when he did glance my way, his attention was completely on me.

Surely that was nothing to worry about—it had been, Tor had said, at least three years since Fiona had spoken to Gabriel or done more than wave to him from down the street. He was bound to want to take a good look at his sister's daughter.

Tor set down his cup. "This is a nice place," he said. "Why did you move over to this part of town?"

Gabriel looked around the room as if assessing it from our eyes. The shop—or office or whatever it was—was cozy. The windows were hung with pale blue curtains sheer enough to let in light, and the floor was covered with a large dark green rug. Paintings hung on the walls—beautiful drawings in rich, vibrant colors—and soft music played. The focus of the room was the group of comfortable chairs, but a desk stacked high with papers and books stood in one corner.

"The older area of town has shifted to a more industrial focus," Gabriel said. "I wasn't getting the foot traffic a Dream Recorder needs."

Tor nodded. "You need impulsive stops," he said. "Men waiting on their wives to finish shopping. Women who can spare five minutes, but only if they don't have to go out of their way."

"Exactly," Gabriel said, leaning forward, his elbows on his knees. "And there's more to it than that. People think dreams are something supernatural, and anything supernatural is embarrassing. At least on this side of the island. So people might wander in if they can do it casually, but they won't be seen deliberately going out of their way to seek me out."

"And you don't see dreams as supernatural?" Tor asked.

Gabe shook his head. "Natural, supernatural," he said. "It's an artificial distinction. Dreams aren't scientific in the same way chemistry is, but they're perfectly natural phenomena. Everything in existence is by definition a natural phenomenon. It might not be visible, it might not be material. Emotions aren't. Thoughts aren't. But they're all natural."

"On our side of the island the problem isn't the definition of natural," Tor said. "The problem is that dreams aren't all true, and it's hard to sort out the ones that are—harder than it is to see which medicines work for which illnesses, for instance. And that makes people doubt the whole Dream Recorder process. Makes them throw out the baby with the bathwater."

Gabe looked at him with interest. "You've thought about this," he said.

Tor nodded. "My grandfather talked about it a lot. He had dreams about drilling for natural gas to power his furnace, and the dreams were right. And he hadn't even taken any Dream Drops—they just came on their own, those dreams. I don't know whether they were memories or visions, but they were as practical, as real-world, as you can get. Nothing airy-fairy about them."

"And nothing like a dream where Angus eats the cake I was saving for Papa and then turns into a giant pink pig," I said, and they both looked at me with surprise. What? Was that too silly for Fiona? I thought I'd pegged her.

Then I realized it was the first thing I'd said at all.

Tor was talking again, carrying us through. "Right," he said. "Sometimes it's obvious your mind is sorting through a ragbag of things you're too polite or too scared to think about when you're awake. Other times, well … there's something bigger than you there. Something wiser and older that wants out."

"The past seeps through," I said, and then shivered, realizing I was echoing something the Watchers had said the night Meritt and I spied on them.

"That's right," Gabriel said, his dark eyes fixed on me.

Now I'd done it—I'd drawn Gabriel's attention too firmly to myself.

Hurriedly I put a spoonful of berries in my mouth, but it was too late. He leaned forward and shifted a lamp so that the light shone more directly on my face, and my heart began to pound. There, in the cozy colorful room, I felt as if I'd returned to the cold bare interrogation room in Optica's prison.

But this was my uncle, I told myself, and Tor was here to help me. And there was no way that Gabriel could possibly suspect the truth. Even if I made a misstep in my imitation of Fiona, Gabriel wouldn't jump to the wild conclusion that I wasn't her; he'd merely put it down to the fact that he hadn't seen her recently, or to her light-headedness and fainting spell.

Thus reassured, I was able to act normal. I scraped my bowl and put the last bit in my mouth.

"I've been wanting to ask, Fiona," Gabriel said. "Do you ever have dreams about your lost sister?"

I choked on the berries.

Tor patted me on the back, and Gabriel gave me a strange look. "I'll get some more water," he said, standing and reaching for my empty cup.

When he returned seconds later, I was hoping the interruption had distracted him; but one look at his face told me he was still waiting for my answer. If I tried to change the subject it might seem suspicious, so instead I turned the question back on him, avoiding Tor's eyes for fear we'd somehow give ourselves away.

"Dreams about my sister?" I said. "Why would you ask something like that?"

Gabriel's eyes were very dark, intense. "Because I was a twin as well."

"A twin," I echoed, genuinely surprised. Of course I knew he was a twin—but it surprised me that he knew it.

"That's right," Gabriel said. "A double birth. Like you."

"A double birth like me." Oh, that was brilliant. I sounded like a complete idiot. Or rather I was making Fiona sound like one.

"I don't expect you to know about him," Gabriel said, watching me steadily. "Eric Alleyn never let you spend much time with your mother's side of the family."

I settled for looking sober, and kept my mouth shut.

"But I did have a twin brother," Gabriel said. "He was stillborn. And through the years I've had dreams that, as Tor says, could merely be ragbag odds and ends." His expression turned thoughtful. "But if so, it was as if I was sorting through ... well, through someone else's ragbag."

Despite the need for care, I couldn't hide my interest. I

leaned forward. "What sort of things did you dream?" I asked.

Gabriel leaned forward as well, his eyes fixed on mine. "Different things at different times," he said. "Some were pleasant, but many were terrible dreams. I was flogged, my children were stolen away from me, my wife murdered. Recently I've had a recurring dream that there are walls all around me, walls I can't escape. And more than once, over the years, I dreamed I was reading to a little redheaded girl. I called her Lost Child as if that were her name."

My breath caught in my throat. He had dreamed of me, this uncle whom I'd never before met. Not of Fiona, but of me. He had caught glimpses of life in Optica through Rafe's eyes. He had actually seen us.

And had Rafe caught glimpses of this island? Was that why he questioned so much, why he could imagine a world that wasn't bound in a tight circle?

"Those dreams sound like manifestations of your own subconscious fears," Tor said. "Worries about your children, about your wife. About the limitations we all face. And of course you knew about Fiona's dead sister as well. Death is typically referred to as *loss*, and in your dream it became *lost*."

Gabriel eyed him steadily. "If I were a fearful person, then yes, those emotions could have been mine," he said. "But I'm not a worrier. And besides that, I always awoke associating those dreams with my brother. My long-dead baby brother."

"Fiona," Tor said uneasily, coming to stand behind me, his hands on my shoulders. Only then did I notice the tears streaming down my cheeks.

"I've come up with various theories," Gabriel said, reaching into his pocket and handing me a handkerchief, completely ignoring Tor. "Perhaps it begins with the biological basis: half of what began as me in the womb has gone missing, so in a very real way I am lost to myself. Lonely for something foundational. And maybe I try to work through this in my dreams—my brother has been walled off from me, metaphorically speaking. He's lost to me, as your sister is lost to you. I've suffered a psychological flogging, so to speak. That sort of thing. Or perhaps when I dream I construct a brother, make up the life he lost, tell myself stories of what might have happened had he lived. I've had a good life, a happy one. Maybe my dead brother is something of a scape-goat in my mind, the bad-luck child to offset my good luck."

Unable to speak, and anyway unsure of what to say, I merely nodded and hid my face by patting at my cheeks with his handkerchief. I couldn't tell Gabriel he had dreamed about a reality playing itself out across the sea, but I felt like anything I said would lead to that, would lead to the truth. To Rafe, and to me.

"You've had similar dreams?" Gabriel said. "You've felt incomplete, alone?"

After a moment's hesitation, I nodded.

"You're upsetting her," Tor said sharply. Then, more po-litely, he added, "Fiona might feel more like talking about this some other time, when she isn't so tired already."

Gabriel sat back. "You're right," he said, his eyes still fixed on mine. I began to be afraid he could read my mind. "I'm sorry if I tired you." He didn't sound particularly sorry, though, and he didn't leave the topic.

"If we can't talk now," he said, "we must talk later. Soon. You're my best hope. Of course there have been other twins born—and as you know, only recently have there been cases where both survived, thanks to modern medicine." His face darkened and I knew he was thinking of Eric Alleyn, blaming his backward ways for my mother's death and my own. "But dreams of lost twins are troubling, and very personal. Not many surviving siblings have been willing to speak freely to me. We secretly all feel guilty, I suspect. Guilty that we lived, while our identical twins died."

His eyes were hypnotic—so dark, so like Rafe's—and he was watching me, silently compelling me to make some response. But Tor was hurting me, standing behind me with his hands on my shoulders, gripping me too hard.

Finally I found my voice. "Is that why you became a Dream Recorder? Because of your dreams?" At this more general question, Tor's grip on my shoulders relaxed a little.

Gabriel shook his head. "No. I was trying to make Carol happy. I'd sold off a couple of businesses, trying to make more time for her, but then she said I was underfoot too much." There was something odd in his tone—fondness, I thought, but also concern. And he seemed to think we'd understand some implication in his words.

But I didn't understand. I didn't even know who Carol was. His wife? His daughter? Tor should have prepared me better; but then, Tor had probably been hoping we could somehow avoid Gabriel Drewblood entirely.

"When the last of our old Dream Recorders died last year," Gabriel said, "I took over his shop because it seemed like something to do that was different. A challenge. And I liked the idea of reading his private notebooks. That old buzzard had been driving us crazy since time began, poking and prodding, always at the most inopportune moments."

Tor laughed. "Ours is like that, too," he said. "We only have one left, and she smells bad, and is about as nosy as can be. Nobody ever voluntarily goes to talk to her anymore, so she comes knocking on doors, prying into people's lives, asking questions."

For someone who usually chose his words with great care, he was speaking quite eagerly with Gabriel—trying, I knew, to steer the conversation away from dangerous territory. "Some people tell her what she wants to know, but some of us—" he glanced down at me—"invent stories just to wind her up."

Who was he talking about, I wondered. Eric Alleyn? My brothers?

Gabriel didn't immediately answer. "No one has actively lied to me about their dreams," he said finally. "Although there's a first time for everything. Someone might well come along and think he can make a fool out of me." He spoke lightly enough, but there was a sharp edge beneath his words.

Tor was silent just a fraction of a second too long. "I doubt anyone would be foolish enough to try that," he said. "In any case, I hope you enjoy your new hobby." His tone was final, formal, drawing a line under the talk of dreams.

"Are you feeling better now?" he asked me.

I nodded, but couldn't take my eyes off my uncle. He was sitting very still, looking at me. I had the impression that all his attention was focused entirely on this moment, this conversation—that only if he allowed it would we be able to change the subject, much less get up and walk away. I wasn't even sure I wanted to get away. It was dangerous, I knew, but this was Rafe's brother, and he was talking—though he didn't know it—about Rafe's life.

I wondered whether he had dreamt anything the night Rafe died.

Gabriel was caught back on Tor's last words. "It started as a hobby," he said quietly. He was answering Tor, but looking at me. "Now I'm finding it important. In a way I can't quite explain, even to myself. All those old records"—he jerked his head toward the desk, where the lamp cast a pool of light over stacks of papers—"There's something going on there. Like a pattern I can't quite see, a song I can't quite recognize. Something underlying everything else. I've even begun to wonder whether our old Dream Recorder left certain things out—there are gaps here and there, pages torn out of the record books, as if perhaps when he was declining he decided to edit what posterity saw."

His gaze shifted to Tor. "I went over to your side of the island this week. I wanted to see the dream records there, see if they were more complete. But your Dream Recorder refused to let me in the door. There I was, ready to do business with her, and she stood blocking the doorway with her body as if she expected me to manhandle my way in, smiling this knowing sort of smile at me. Her mouth is too wide for her face, have you noticed that?"

Tor nodded.

"And she does have a distinctive odor, as you say. Some sort of endocrine problem, at a guess. In any case, all I wanted was a glimpse of her books, which is perfectly within my rights as a fellow Dream Recorder. She probably has records going back to before the plague."

"I suppose there are privacy issues," Tor said vaguely. Then he leaned over me. "Ready to go to your grandparents' house?"

He wanted me out of there, away from Gabriel, and he wanted it now.

But I turned my face toward him, so Gabriel couldn't see, and shot him a look of protest. We hadn't found out anything about Farrell Dean.

"There's a time for everything," Tor said firmly. "And now that you're rested, it's time for us to go."

Chapter 13

Once we left the town and were walking on a narrow gravel causeway between two bodies of water—inlets from the sea, I suppose—Tor finally let me talk. He had been shushing me, and walking very fast so I'd be too out of breath to speak, ever since we'd left my Uncle Gabriel.

"You didn't find out about Farrell Dean," I said. "He's why we're here."

"How could we ask?" Tor kept a tight grip on my arm. "We aren't supposed to know anything about him. And I did ask whether anything interesting had happened other than the lunatic invader, and Gabriel said no. I think he'd count yet another mysterious stranger as interesting."

"Then where's Farrell Dean?" I said. "How are we going to find him? What if he's injured, sick, lost? What if those men found him?" I tried to pull my arm out of Tor's grasp. "Let go. You're hurting me."

Tor let go. "Maybe he's here but hasn't found Gabriel yet," he said. "We can ask your grandparents if they've heard anything—we can ask them things we can't ask Gabriel. They won't notice if our questions are odd, and if they do they'll forget soon enough."

"We have to find him," I said again, fighting down panic. Where was he? What would I do if we never found him, if the riders got to him first and took him, killed him? I might not even know what had happened. He could vanish and leave me here on this island alone. Yes, Ezzie was here, but Ezzie was sick, and I didn't know how to take care of him. I needed Farrell Dean.

"We have to make sure Farrell Dean is okay," I said.

Tor gave me an exasperated look. "*We will.* As you said, that's why we're here. We'll find him, warn him not to mention you, and then we'll get out of town before Gabriel smells a rat. I do *not* want to get on that man's bad side."

Gabriel Drewblood did seem a little intense—like Rafe—but I couldn't see that he was anyone to be feared. Then again, perhaps I was expecting him to be too much like Rafe. I of all people should know that Gabriel had his own personality, his own character.

"Tor, there's something I need to tell you," I said. He kept walking, fast, as if determined to put as much space as possible between us and Gabriel.

"*Tor!*" I said, hurrying to keep up.

He kept walking, but this time he at least looked over at me.

"You know how Fiona and I look alike?" I said.

Exasperation flooded back into Tor's face. "Of course I know. And I know you aren't her but I fully intend to persuade everyone here that you are. Don't keep revisiting this, *Fiona.*"

"No, it's not that. It's just …" I took a deep breath. "Gabriel Drewblood looks exactly like a man I knew in Optica. A good man. A man who got killed last week trying to save our city."

Tor stopped in his tracks. He stared at me for a long moment. We were all alone, out there on that narrow stretch of gray gravel, with water to our left and water to our right. We were alone, and for the first time all day Tor actually seemed to be seeing me. Me, and not some inconvenient and unsatisfactory imitation of Fiona.

Then, "Gabriel's lost brother," he said softly. "The still-born."

I nodded, a lump in my throat.

Tor stepped closer. "That's why you fainted," he said. "It was the shock of seeing a man you knew to be dead."

I nodded.

"And you didn't tell Gabriel. You must have wanted to tell him."

That was an understatement.

"Thank you for keeping quiet," Tor said.

I made a helpless gesture. "I suppose you're welcome," I said. "But Tor, this changes things. I need to tell him. He deserves to know the truth—and when he knows, he'll help us."

Tor didn't answer; he was staring vaguely at the air in front of him, lost in thought.

"Tor, listen to me. All those dreams he was telling us about—those were things that really happened. The floggings, the stolen children. Those things actually happened to his brother, to the man I knew."

Tor faced me, his expression aghast—but not for the reason I thought. "Valentina," he said, which told me exactly how distracted he was. "What if Gabriel didn't really dream those dreams?"

"Of course he dreamed them," I said. "What on earth do you mean?"

"Maybe Farrell Dean has already told Gabriel about his brother. Maybe Farrell Dean told him those stories, and for some reason Gabriel presented them to us as his dreams."

"Why would he do that?"

"To trick us—to catch us lying to him." Tor pressed both hands to his head, as if he were fighting off a headache. "You heard what he said, about people playing him for a fool.

He might look like the man you knew, but he isn't. He's Gabriel Drewblood, and Gabriel Drewblood is shrewd and cunning. If Farrell Dean has already told him about you, then he knows I'm lying to him ..."

"You're being paranoid," I said, tugging at his arm to get him to look at me. "Gabriel doesn't know. And Farrell Dean wouldn't go barreling in and blurt everything out, not when he knows that Gabriel is my family's enemy."

I really didn't think he would. If I could manage to keep my mouth shut when faced unexpectedly with Rafe's ghost—if I could think clearly enough to see that I'd better consider my next step carefully—then of course Farrell Dean could do the same. He was cautious, and had learned how to spy in circumstances where making a mistake meant death. And he'd been good at it. Even I hadn't known what he'd been up to, and I'd been living side by side with him all that time, while he and Meritt and Rafe quietly went around gathering information and cutting camera wires and planning a rebellion against a powerful collection of Watchers and wardens. And I hadn't known anything. I'd thought Farrell Dean was just a nice boy who shared his food with me.

Tor was looking at me expectantly, hopefully, clearly wanting to be persuaded. I started walking again, thinking it would steady him—and me, for that matter. We were both worked up, and standing here staring at each other made everything seem so dire.

"For two days Farrell Dean has known who Gabriel is," I said. "Ever since he saw him in Doria. That's why he wanted to talk to him. And he sneaked away from Rory and Angus to do it because he knows the Alleyns are on bad terms with Gabriel." A thought hit me. "And that's probably why he didn't come back to Eric Alleyn's. He was protecting me until he saw which way the wind blew—keeping us out of it. He isn't going to go blurting something out."

Yes, that was true. Farrell Dean would want to check out Gabriel first, without me, so that he could soften the blow if Gabriel turned out to be nothing like Rafe. Plus he probably figured I'd get all emotional and be more trouble than help. I was paying for those hysterics in the boat.

The causeway beneath our feet had grown thinner as we went, until now it was only three or four feet wide, with water lapping at its edges.

"Does this ever get covered with water?" I asked, nodding at the path.

Tor nodded. "Twice a day, at high tide. Then your grandparents are cut off by foot, but they have a coracle."

Well, that was just dandy. I'd been telling myself that if worst came to worst, I could slip away on my own and look for Farrell Dean, but I wasn't sure I wanted to try my hand at a coracle. Not until I learned to swim, anyway. Why did my grandparents want to live in such a remote place?

Tor was walking more briskly now and seemed to have fully recovered himself.

Leaving the narrow causeway, we rounded a stand of tall evergreens, and I stopped short. Across yet another inlet gentle blue hills rose up, their tops covered with low-lying white clouds that looked painted on the bright blue sky. Maybe this was why my grandparents lived out here.

Tor, too, was looking at the view. "I always forget how striking it is," he said. "That's their house." He pointed across the inlet to a brown cottage, barely visible among the green and brown evergreen trees.

"And up there," he said, pointing farther away, up the hills, to a large elaborate building made of something pale and gleaming. "That's your Uncle Gabriel's house."

So Tor wasn't managing to get us completely away from Gabriel.

"Who else lives there with him?" I asked.

"His wife, Carol, and their youngest child," Tor said. "A girl. Her name is Rain. The boys are grown and live in town. Their names are Miles and Galloway. They're married, but you've never met their wives."

"Only three people live in that whole big place?"

"Three people and their gardeners, security guards, servants, housekeepers, and so forth. Probably fifteen all together."

Tor turned to face me. "Despite the fact that he's playing around as Dream Recorder, your Uncle Gabriel is very wealthy."

I looked at the house on the hill. It wasn't as big as the Watchers' compound back home, but it was far bigger than Rafe's tiny house that he'd shared with Lonna.

I wondered whether Gabriel had ever dreamed about that, about having only one room and a small bathroom to call his own. It seemed strange for Gabriel to live so far out here—an inconvenient distance, for a busy man like him.

"How did Gabriel get to be so wealthy?" I asked.

Tor shrugged. "Various things. He has a knack for figuring out what people need—or think they need—and managing to supply it. Guns. Medicines. Transportation. He came up with a more efficient way to recharge truck batteries, and made a load of money before other people began copying his method and cut into his sales."

"Did that make him angry?"

Tor shook his head. "He's always one step ahead of everyone else anyway, making his own products obsolete by the time other people are copying them."

Tor was sounding glum again, and I knew why. "He's really smart," I said softly.

"Yes," Tor said. "He is. He's smart, and he gets his way. That's why the less time we spend with him, the better. Especially now that he's fixated on lost siblings."

Unfortunately, that was exactly why I needed to spend more time with my uncle.

We skirted the inlet, walking on the pebble-covered beach, and soon reached my grandparents' house. Up close it looked comfortable but a little run down. It had brown wood shingle siding and a few scraggly bushes beside the door, but there were also rose bushes that looked full and lush, a couple of them still bearing a few late blooms.

As we approached, the front door flew open and a plump elderly woman trotted down the path to meet us. "Fiona!" she cried, flinging her arms around my neck. She was very soft and smelled like baby powder, and was shorter than I was. Her gray hair was caught in a bun on the back of her head, and little tendrils curled around her face.

"What a lovely surprise! Let me look at you," she said, holding me at arm's length. Then she shrieked at the top of her lungs. "Frederick!"

I almost jumped out of my skin.

"Frederick!" she shrieked again. "Come see Fiona!"

The door, which had swung shut, swung open again and a large balding man came shambling out. His shirt was buttoned crooked and his shaving job was splotchy, but his eyes were bright with delight.

"My dear!" He enfolded me gently in a hug.

"You look so grown up," Nana said, hooking her arm fondly through mine. "And just like your mama, but with that lovely red hair. Can you stay long?"

She began leading me to the house, Grandfather puttering slowly along behind us. I cast a desperate look over my shoulder at Tor. He was standing where we'd left him, smiling—probably at my discomfort.

"Nana," I said, "did you see that Tor came with me?"

She froze. "Someone came with—" Releasing my arm she peered down the path.

"Oh!" She trotted off toward him. "Frederick! Look! It's Tor Van Stavern! Why, we haven't seen you since…" She stopped just a few inches in front of him. Her words stopped, her movement stopped. For ten seconds or so she stood there, then spun around and hurried back to me.

"Fiona!" she hissed in a loud whisper. "Tor has grown up!"

"Yes, Nana," I said.

She cast a surreptitious glance over her shoulder. "He's better looking now," she said. "He's almost grown into that nose." Tor became very interested in the activity of some birds in a nearby tree.

Getting right up in my face, she whispered, "When is the date?"

I didn't know what she meant, so I shook my head.

"You haven't set a date?"

"Not yet," I said, hoping that was a sufficient answer.

Nana looked baffled for a moment, then brightened. "In the spring, no doubt. Or the summer. Who would want a winter wedding?"

Oh. Despite myself, I began to blush.

Grandfather had been talking to Tor. Now he turned and began wandering off toward the beach from where we'd come. "Frederick!" Nana screeched again. "Don't fall in!"

Then she took my arm and led me into the house, and this time Tor followed.

The inside of the house was clean enough, but things were in odd places. A box of cleaning powder sat on the mantle; a bowl of flour was half-hidden behind a cushion on the couch; a dying houseplant sat in the darkest corner of the room, with a row of knives sticking, dagger-like, from the soil around its withered roots. Having grown up in a dormitory I didn't know much about people's homes, but surely that was not a normal arrangement.

Nana bustled around, chattering about people and places I knew nothing about, darting back every now and then to peer into my face. She must be quite nearsighted, I finally realized; and Grandfather must be going deaf. They were older than I'd expected.

Tor moved the bowl of flour to the floor and sat down on the couch. I wanted to sit down—I felt like I'd been walking for years—but it seemed rude to sit while the older woman scurried around. I think she meant to be straightening up, but mostly she was moving things from one random spot to another while she caught "Fiona" up on various happenings.

"Lorraine was heartbroken," Nana was saying, picking up the bowl of flour and dumping it into the soil of the dying plant. "This silly plant," she said. "I think it has bugs. But Lorraine—you probably don't remember her—poor thing had had that dog for fifteen years. Loved him like a son."

I had no idea what she was talking about, of course, but I tried to look receptive.

"A very small and hairy son," she said, "who never learned to speak properly. But he was potty trained much earlier than Gabriel was. And then of course he wasn't there to bark at the lunatic—how could he bark, when he'd been buried the day before? No one could have heard him under all that dirt. Lorraine was so upset he missed the lunatic invasion." I looked sharply at Tor; he nodded at me from the couch.

"Tell us about the invasion," I said.

"Oh, it was dreadful," she said, shaking her head. "Boats full of big dark men came, and they were so sick they broke all the windows."

"In town yesterday?"

Nana nodded. "Oh yes. We knew they were crazy because they didn't steal a thing."

"Then what happened?" I almost felt bad, pumping her

for information. She was far worse than I'd expected, surely too scatterbrained to safely run a household. I hoped Grandfather wasn't as far gone.

Nana was clasping her hands together and looking up at the ceiling, thinking very hard. "After they invaded us, they ran away," she said finally. "And Gabriel went out in the woods and told them shoo! So you needn't worry, dear. They won't be back."

"Have there been any other visitors lately?" Tor asked. "Besides the invaders?"

Nana brightened. "Oh yes, indeed." Then, without another word, she trotted off to the kitchen.

I went to the couch and sat down by Tor. The springs creaked and the whole thing settled a bit, but it was a comfortable couch all the same. I was more tired than I'd realized.

"Boat loads of invaders," Tor said softly, shaking his head. His face was compassionate.

"How much of what she says can we believe?"

"She's degenerated quite a bit," he said. "I'd heard, but I didn't expect this. It's very sad."

Maybe I was hardhearted, but I was more concerned about finding Farrell Dean than about Nana.

"Yes, it's sad," I said. "But we aren't going to get any reliable information from her, Tor."

"I think your Grandfather's still all right. We'll talk to him."

If we could make him hear us, I thought, as Nana came trotting back into the room, carrying a large wooden box.

"I always keep it in the oven," she said. "It's just exactly the right shape for it. I think it was meant to be kept in the oven, don't you?"

Tor stood up, reaching as if to help her with the box. It looked heavy, and she seemed to be having a hard time holding it. But Nana made no move to hand it to him.

"What's in it?" he asked, letting his hands fall.

"Photographs," she said. "My very own photographs of all the lovely visitors." Awkwardly, with one hand, she opened the lid and tilted the box toward me. It shifted heavily and would have fallen had Tor not caught it.

Nana smiled up at him, then unceremoniously tipped the box completely over, dumping its contents onto my lap.

I picked up one of the fallen objects—it was a piece of stiff paper, about the size of my hand. What were these things? Not sketches. They were done in blacks and grays, and were very detailed—so detailed that they looked exactly like real people. They were amazing.

Slowly I began to look through them, and goosebumps rose on my arms.

"I'll leave you to meet all the visitors," Nana said. "I must go air your rooms. Oh—" her face fell. "This is very awkward, my dears, but as I wasn't expecting visitors today I might have to leave you and run to town for a few supplies, once the tide falls a bit."

She sounded, for the moment, perfectly normal. I needed to answer her, but I couldn't form a coherent thought. The faces in my lap were calling out for all my attention.

"Don't worry, Nana," Tor said. "Fiona and I can go back to town for you. Why don't you make up a list?"

She smiled brightly and trotted off again, leaving me with a lap full of faces.

Smiling faces, pensive faces. Faces that looked wise, faces that looked mischievous, faces that looked sad. Faces that I knew.

I leafed through them, feeling colder and colder as I went, my fingers growing stiff and clumsy. The noises from Nana puttering around the house faded, the room around me faded, until it was only me and the faces in my hands.

Tor had been watching me silently. Now he sat back

down and put an arm around me. I could feel the pressure of his hand on my shoulder, but there was no warmth there. I was made of cold stone, and nothing could warm me.

"You've gone white," Tor said quietly, glancing back to make sure Nana was still out of earshot. "What's wrong?"

The words of explanation wouldn't come. All I could do was name names.

"Carley," I said, touching one of the pictures. "Estelle. Old Louie." I slid them away, revealing more underneath. "Mariella. Robert."

Tor sat up straighter, alarmed, perplexed. "These are people from around here. I know some of them. This one—" he tapped Louie—"is Will Bright. He's on the Council with my father. Has been since way before I was born."

Rapidly, fumbling, I sorted through the pictures in my lap and handed one pile to Tor. "All of these people, I know from Optica," I said. "These others I don't."

He looked at the pictures. "The ones you know are all old people," he said, stating the obvious. "Though some of these—" he gestured at the pile in my lap—"Might be photographs of these same old people when they were younger."

"Where did she get all these? Did she draw them?"

Tor looked blank. "No one drew them," he said after a moment. "They're photographs. You've never seen photographs?"

I shook my head, too numb to care that once again I was the ignorant outsider.

"It's a chemical light process that produces an exact replica of the subject. Nana was very good at it. She always took a snapshot—a photograph—of people who came out here to visit, even just for a meal. And for years she took photos whenever people wanted her to, at weddings or birthdays or whatever. They paid her; it was a job. I'm sure she has other boxes full, as well as this one. Black and white was her favorite, but she did some color too. She only stopped taking pictures recently, in the past couple of years."

I looked down at the pile in my lap. I knew exactly what this must mean, but my brain felt paralyzed, unwilling to spell it out.

The magnitude of what I was seeing made me shiver, and once I started I couldn't seem to stop. It wasn't just me; it wasn't just Rafe. I wanted to hug the pictures to me; I wanted to throw them to the floor. All these faces, these people—there and here, all at once. And these were the people who had raised me, been kind to me, played with me when everyone else was too busy for a lonely little girl. These were the old people, the vulnerable people. These were the people the Watchers in Optica had slated to die.

These were the people I had foolishly hoped Sir Tom would help save—and had he been behind their kidnappings in the first place?

"It's all right," Tor said, tightening his arm around my shoulders. His voice was firm and loud, as if he were trying to call me back from a very long way away. "You're all right," he said again. "Fiona, do you hear me? Red?"

I couldn't answer; my teeth were chattering.

Tor wrapped both arms around me and began to rock me like a child.

Chapter 14

Three hours later I still felt unsettled, but I was on my feet. Tor and I were back in Ionia, shopping for Nana. We had collected fish, fruit, and bakery bread, and next were heading for the candle shop because Nana insisted her table wouldn't be properly set without centerpiece candles.

As we walked I studied faces on the street. I only saw one man who looked exactly like someone in Optica, which made sense given that most of the people I'd recognized were older and therefore less likely to be out and about.

But I did see three or four younger people who bore a strong resemblance to people I knew. They were probably nieces and nephews of my friends back home. Nieces and nephews who didn't even know their aunts and uncles existed, except perhaps as unfortunate babies who'd been stillborn long ago.

We passed a shop selling bicycles, but they didn't look like any I'd seen. They were all shapes and designs. Some were made of wood, others seemed to be made of scrap metal.

"They do a good business," Tor said. "And they'll do even better as more of the trucks fail."

"What do you mean?" I said. "Can't you repair them?"

"Oh, we do. But there comes a point when even our best

mechanics can't keep them running. Sometimes there isn't even much left to try to repair. They rust out."

I remembered something he'd said earlier, about not having an unlimited supply, and a chill ran down my spine.

"Tor," I said, stopping beside a half barrel filled with bright pansies. "Why can't you make more trucks?"

He looked down at me, perplexed. "We don't have the supplies, and we don't know where to get them. That information was lost in the plague. Can you make trucks—or patrol cars, or whatever you call them—in Optica?"

"I don't know," I said. But I did know that we had things in Optica that we didn't produce there—cigarettes, for instance. Things the Guardians and the mysterious "supply drops" apparently had provided for the Watchers and wardens.

Thinking this through slowed my steps, and I had stopped to gaze absentmindedly in a shop window containing baskets full of multi-colored yarn, when Tor suddenly wrapped his arm around my waist and pulled me close, jostling the wicker shopping basket I held.

Irritated, I righted the basket and looked up at him, ready to say something sharp.

He was looking straight down at me, his gray-blue eyes intense. "Is that him?" he said, his voice low. "Be casual. Don't stare."

Carefully I cast one glance past his shoulder, and my heart leapt. Farrell Dean was coming our direction, nodding as he listened to a dark-haired girl who was walking beside him, her arm linked familiarly in his. He looked a little worse for wear—tired and unshaven, with a dark scab on his split lip—but he was alive. He was alive and walking briskly, his head up, as if he felt fine.

"It's him," I said. "But you've never met him—how did you know?"

"He's wearing my shirt," Tor said. "The one you were making for me."

That "you" held a warning.

I glanced at Farrell Dean again. The girl was leaning close, saying something right in his ear. She was, I thought, a year or two older than I was, maybe Farrell Dean's age. Her dark hair was cut short, like a boy's, and though the effect was new to me, I could see that it flattered the lines of her face, her sharp cheekbones. She wore a clingy shirt that emphasized her good figure, and loose black pants. She was very striking, and looked like she knew it.

"Who's that with him?" I said.

"Don't turn around. Watch them in the window."

Tor was really getting into the spy routine, pointing at some yarn in the window as if we were discussing it. Was that even credible, that Fiona would be discussing yarn with Tor? I didn't know, but obediently I pointed to a different basket of colors.

"Who is she?" I said again.

"That's Rain. She's Gabriel's daughter."

In the window we saw them stop in front of the Dream Recorder door. Gabriel came out and Rain spoke to him, gesturing at Farrell Dean as she did so. Gabriel turned toward Farrell Dean and shook his hand.

"See," I told Tor. "Farrell Dean hasn't told Gabriel anything about Optica. They're just now meeting for the first time." So where on earth had Farrell Dean been all this time?

Farrell Dean was talking; in the window we watched as Gabriel crossed his arms over his chest. Even from where I stood, even watching a reflection, I could tell his expression was darkening.

"Uh-oh," Tor said.

Rain, meanwhile, had been looking up and down the street, waving at various passersby. Now she glanced our way and caught sight of me. "Fiona?" she said, then called more loudly. "Fiona Alleyn, is that you?"

We turned, acting surprised, as she came dashing across the street and flung her arms around me, almost knocking me off my feet.

Over her shoulder I saw Gabriel and Farrell Dean following her, crossing the street toward where we stood. I just had time to identify her scent as something citrusy when she let go of me, and then Farrell Dean was right there, not three yards away. I wanted to fling myself at him just like the girl had flung herself at me, but Gabriel was watching, and Tor was giving me an anxious look, and I had to deal with this girl. I had to be Fiona.

With difficulty I tore my gaze from Farrell Dean and faced Gabriel's daughter.

"You look wonderful, Rain," I said, managing what I hoped was a natural-looking smile.

She spun in a circle, holding out her arms. "Indeed I do," she said. "And I'm taller than you now, you itty bitty thing."

She paced around me, examining me. "You look good, though. You hold yourself better than you used to, but that dress could stand to be taken in a bit. You're swimming in it. That pale blue suits you, though. A perfect color."

Now she was back in front of me again, holding both my hands in hers. "I'm so happy to see you, I forgive you for staying away so long."

Suddenly she put her hands to her cheeks and made her eyes go wide, miming dismay. "What am I thinking? I'm so sorry, let me introduce you."

She spun around and, reaching for Farrell Dean's hand, pulled him forward.

"Farrell Dean, this is my cousin Fiona Alleyn, and this is her friend Tor Van Stavern. They live on the other side of the island, so we hardly ever get to see them."

The barest flicker in Farrell Dean's eyes made me wonder whether he'd just registered the cascading family relationship. Rain's cousin. Therefore Gabriel's niece. And therefore *Rafe's* niece.

"Nice to meet you," Tor said, holding out his hand to shake Farrell Dean's.

Farrell Dean returned the greeting, then turned politely to me. I willed my expression to be pleasant but distant.

"I'm glad to meet you," I said. Tor put an arm around my waist and I remembered not to shrug him off.

"And I'm glad to meet you, Fiona," Farrell Dean said, looking straight into my eyes.

Every single cell of my body was focused on him, but no matter how hard I focused, I could see no signal, no recognition. Though I knew him better than anyone else in the world, I couldn't tell whether Farrell Dean knew me or not.

Just then another man walked up, a thin faded man with a mop of graying blond hair and a face lined with dissatisfaction. Gabriel glanced at him.

"Afternoon, Tristan," he said.

The man's eyes were on me and I suddenly realized it was the same man who'd stared at me that morning, the nondescript man with the cold blue eyes.

Tristan … Fiona had mentioned a Tristan. Or maybe it had been one of the brothers. Taking orders from Gabriel Drewblood, that was it. Would Fiona know him?

Just to be safe, I gave him a slight nod.

The man didn't acknowledge my faint greeting. Instead he tilted his head toward Gabriel and spoke as if no one else were present. "She favors Rachel strongly," he said. "Save for that hellish hair."

I didn't know what hellish meant, but his tone said it wasn't a compliment. Tor's arm grew tighter around my waist, but Rain laughed.

"Oh please, Tris," she said. "Time to drop the scorned lover act. It's been thirty years."

"Rain," her father said warningly, and the man named Tristan gave her a cold look before turning toward Tor and me.

"You look like you're in love," he said to Tor, giving an ironic twist to the word.

Tor jerked his head in a noncommittal sort of way.

"Might as well break it off now," Tristan said. "Either she'll take after her mother and abandon you, or she'll take after her father and be a thief."

My face flushed, and beside me Tor stiffened. For a split second Farrell Dean's eyes met mine, and then Rain was in front of me. I wasn't sure whether she intended to block me from Tristan's view, or him from mine, but in any case she stood right in between us.

"Consider Tristan our local color," she said, lifting a strand of my hair and smoothing it down behind my shoulder. "He adds a charming dash of melancholy to every broadcast. Need to bring yourself down a notch? Feeling a bit too cheerful? Just tune in to Tristan and in no time, you'll be feeling low."

I couldn't see the man's face, but he said nothing in response to Rain's nonsense. Gabriel cast one reproving glance at his daughter. He took Tristan by the arm, and the man allowed himself to be led away from us.

I wanted to know what had happened, how that unhappy man knew my mother, but without knowing how much Fiona knew, I couldn't ask.

"Don't mind him," Rain said, her voice low. "He's tiresome, but he did love your mother dearly. However obnoxious he gets, Dad can't forget that fact." She winked at me. "Plus they share an intense dislike of your father. It forms a lovely bond."

Tor made a disapproving sound, and Rain's face changed.

"Stupid me," she said. "I forgot. Do forgive me, Fiona."

I didn't know what she was talking about, but fortunately Tor spoke up. "If Tristan's device had killed Eric Alleyn rather than merely destroying his leg and hampering his livelihood, Fiona would have been orphaned."

Tristan had planted the bomb? Then why did everyone keep saying it was Gabriel? Tristan certainly made better sense. He looked out-and-out mean.

"Even if your father doesn't find crippling a man excessive punishment for a little mechanical tampering, surely he wouldn't punish an innocent child—his own niece—for her father's wrongdoing," Tor was saying. "Surely your father parts ways with Tristan there."

He was laying the groundwork, I saw, hoping Gabriel would go easy on Eric Alleyn for Fiona's sake when the truth about my abduction came out. I still didn't see why Gabriel would be so upset about that, and anyway I didn't suppose that talking to Rain about it would do any good. If she had that sort of influence over her father, surely she'd have used it long ago to help mend the family feud, given how much she seemed to like Fiona.

Now she merely shrugged. "Don't lecture, Tor. I said I was sorry."

The two men had stopped and were conferring in the middle of the street. Tristan's icy stare was fixed on us, and Gabriel had a hand on his shoulder, though whether soothing or restraining, I couldn't tell.

Then Tristan shook off Gabriel's hand and walked away, becoming again a plain, nondescript man. It was strange—when he wasn't staring at you, he seemed like the sort of person you could overlook completely.

A small woman passing by said something to Gabriel. He paused to answer her, looking somehow gallant, and came back to us alone.

"If you'd like to continue our conversation," he said to Farrell Dean, raising his voice to be heard over a sudden burst of noise from down the street, "we can go back to my shop."

Tor stirred uneasily; I knew he wanted to take Farrell Dean aside before he talked with Gabriel, but what could we do? Absolutely nothing.

I gave Farrell Dean a tiny shake of the head—no telling what he'd make of that, if he thought I was Fiona—and then Rain linked her arm in Farrell Dean's and turned with him to cross the street to the shop.

Her father stepped in front of her. "I'm sure you'd like to catch up with Fiona," he said. It wasn't a suggestion.

Rain let go of Farrell Dean and turned back to me, smiling. She opened her mouth to say something. Then she froze, her eyes fixed on something farther down the street.

I thought she was just being dramatic again—so did Tor, because he gave a soft sigh—but all the same we turned to see what had caught her attention, and Gabriel and Farrell Dean turned, too.

Far down the street people were exclaiming and dashing into shops. Doors were slamming. A small child began to cry and his mother scooped him up and ran.

For a moment the milling crowd blocked the source of the disturbance, but as the street emptied, three men came into view. The two on the outside were holding on to the one in the middle. For a second they seemed to be supporting him, then they seemed to be restraining him, and then they were almost carrying him. Though they were still some distance away there was no doubt about who they were: One man with red hair, one with dark, and in between them a dark-skinned man in Optica gray.

I took a step forward. Tor caught me by the arm.

"Here comes trouble," Gabriel said. He glanced at me. "And for once I'm not speaking of your brothers. Looks like they've done what my search parties couldn't."

Then he turned to Farrell Dean.

"Two strangers," he said, and his voice went hard. "Both saying they come from another island. Are you going to tell me this is a coincidence?"

"*Dad*," Rain said. "How *rude*. And you know the lunatic was alone in that leaky little boat of his—half the town saw him arrive."

Gabriel ignored her.

Farrell Dean looked Gabriel straight in the eye. "I don't know how he got here," he said. "We didn't come together. But I do know him. His name is Ezzie. He's a friend. He isn't a lunatic."

Down the street Ezzie flung back his head. He was either laughing hysterically or crying hysterically, I couldn't tell which. Rory's face was pinched and white, and Angus' mouth was open with the effort of hauling Ezzie along.

"Then what's wrong with him?" Gabriel said.

"I don't know," Farrell Dean said. "He was injured a few days ago, in a fight. Helping me escape from the people who were trying to kill me. He's a good man."

Gabriel looked hard at him for a long moment.

"You'll forgive me if I withhold judgment," he said.

A flurry of noise made me turn; behind us, half a dozen men came running. They were carrying guns.

Gabriel's eyes never left Farrell Dean's face. Tor's hand was like a vise on my arm, but I couldn't stand there and let Ezzie get hurt. I opened my mouth to speak, to tell Gabriel that Ezzie had been injured protecting me, Gabriel's own niece, but Farrell Dean spoke first.

"Looks like you're going to let someone else pass judgment for you," he said. "Is that what passes for justice on this island? Men with guns?"

Gabriel gave him a sharp look but turned away, intercepting the armed men a heartbeat before they passed.

"Hold your fire," he said. "Anyone who kills him will answer to me. If necessary, use tranquilizers." Without waiting for a response, he pulled a small device from his pocket and spoke into it.

The men nodded and went on, surrounding Ezzie and my brothers, keeping a good distance back from them, pointing their guns.

Another noise made me turn. Behind us the doors of a tall glass building sprang open and more men ran out; they were wearing white coats and masks and carrying a stretcher.

They hurried past us and, without hesitation, went straight toward Ezzie.

What if he hurt them, infected them? I looked up at Tor and pulled at his hand.

"They'll be careful," he said, his eyes on the scene before us. "He's already announced he was contagious."

Sure enough, when the medical men reached Ezzie they set the stretcher on the ground and then stepped back. I could hear voices, but couldn't make out what was said, and then Rory and Angus pulled Ezzie forward and lowered him, as gently as they could, onto the stretcher. He seemed, now, completely limp.

Once they had him down they straightened his limbs, and then the medical men wrapped restraints around his chest and knees, tying him to the stretcher.

They spoke with Rory and Angus a little longer, and then the whole strange procession—men with guns, men carrying Ezzie on the stretcher, and my brothers—moved together past us, down the street, and into the tall glass building.

"Where are Rory and Angus going?" I said to no one in particular. I wanted to talk to them, wanted to find out what had happened.

"The doctors will need to check them over," Tor said.

"And security will want to know where they found the stranger," Gabriel said. "They might be awhile, Fiona. But I'll stay and keep an eye on things."

Tor looked decidedly unhappy.

Gabriel spoke into his small device again, then turned to Farrell Dean.

"As I said, I'm reserving judgment," he said. "But in the meantime, I'll do what I can to keep each of you in one piece."

He nodded at the street where, one by one, people were beginning to emerge from shops and houses. Some carried objects clearly meant as weapons—long clubs, knives, and a few even held guns. Then, as I watched, there in the distance two men on horses appeared. The Dream Recorder's thugs? I couldn't tell, but the horses were the same dark brown.

"This is not a good day to be a stranger," Gabriel said.

As he spoke, a man with cropped hair appeared at his side. He wore a holster under his arm and a belt with a knife in a sheath. His gun was in his hand.

"This is Earl," Gabriel said. "He's going to escort you to my house and offer you my hospitality—food, clothes, a bath, a bed, whatever you need. But he's not going to let you out of his sight, for your protection and for ours. Is that clear?"

Farrell Dean nodded. "Perfectly."

"I look forward to our conversation," Gabriel said, and then he turned and started toward the glass building. The sign over the door, I now saw, said "Hospital." In the rows of windows above, dozens of figures in loose white gowns peered out. Some supported others; a few were leaning on canes or crutches. As I watched, blue-garbed people appeared and seemed to be urging the patients away, no doubt back to their beds and chairs.

A dozen yards away from us Gabriel half turned.

"Rain," he said over his shoulder, still walking. "Go home. Take care of your mother."

Chapter 15

It was a mile from town to the grandparents' house, and another half mile up a long gravel road to the Drewblood's house. No wonder the basket was getting heavy on my arm.

I extricated my other arm from Rain—she seemed to always be touching someone, and at the moment I was the only person in range—and shifted the basket to a more comfortable position, glancing over my shoulder as I did so.

Farrell Dean and Tor were twenty yards or so behind us. They were talking, but both of them looked reserved. The security man, Earl, was bringing up the rear, another ten yards behind them. I wondered whether he could hear what they said.

"Where did you meet him?" I asked.

"He's gorgeous, isn't he?" Rain said. "That strong, sure, salt-of-the-earth type is so appealing."

I wanted to tell her he wasn't a "type," he was Farrell Dean. Fortunately she was still talking and I got a grip on myself before she stopped.

"Maybe we can persuade him to settle down here," she said. "We need some fresh blood on this side of the island, don't you think? Most of the boys are such sissies. No spunk whatsoever. People say they're really better than they seem, except around me, because they're afraid of Dad. But what good does that do me, I ask you? It's not like I can stop being Dad's daughter. And it's no fun at all—who's going to ask me to go dancing when they're afraid of getting crossways with Dad? Only stupid boys, or ones with a death wish. It's a no-win situation, Fee."

Her boy trouble didn't interest me at all.

"Did he say why he's here?" I asked. "What did he tell Gabriel?"

"Oh, something about his homeland being in trouble."

"Another island, he said?" I gestured toward the inlet, toward the sea, though we couldn't see it from here. The trees were too tall.

Rain turned to me, her eyes sparkling. "That's right. Fabulous, isn't it? I always said there was bound to be life on other islands. Why should we think we were the only ones? And I was right."

"What sort of trouble is it?" I asked.

"Oh, oppression and what not." Rain waved her hand. "I wasn't really listening. I was busy noticing *you*, my lovely long lost cousin. Good thing you have that stunning red hair—I might not have known you otherwise, it's been so long since I've seen you. You weren't going to go away again without coming to see me, were you?"

I was only half listening. I couldn't pull my mind away from Farrell Dean, from the things we needed to talk about, the decisions we needed to make.

He seemed all right—he looked a little tired, but not unwell. But where had he been? Had he spent two nights alone in the woods, walked forty or fifty miles? That was not at all what the doctor had advised. Had he had eaten? Had he met with any trouble?

I shot another glance over my shoulder, trying to be sur-reptitious.

Rain laughed. "Look but don't touch," she said. "I saw

him first. And besides, you've got Tor. But then, you've always had good old dependable Tor. Don't you intend to ever have a little fun?"

I flushed. Rain cast a sideways glance my way, then bumped me with her hip. "Don't look so serious, Fee. Tor's great. I mean, he's even an artist and all that. I'm probably jealous or something. Dad always says he should tape my mouth shut."

"And Carol?"

She shot me a glance. "Mom doesn't mind what I say. She still lives in her own little world, if that's what you're asking." She tipped a hand to her mouth, miming drinking. "Dad pours it all out, Mom buys more. Whatever."

"What does she do all day? Does she work?" I shouldn't have asked that—Fiona would already know—but Rain didn't seem to notice.

"Nope," she said. "Not a day in her life. Why should she? Dad has plenty for us all to live on."

She leaned in close. "That's why I'm extra glad to see you—I'd be glad anyway, naturally, but I'm extra glad today. Mom won't know how to react when Earl shows up with Farrell Dean. Should she treat him like a guest? A prisoner? A charity case? An invader? An exotic alien life form? Mom likes her social situations clearly defined, and this one most certainly is not."

"And exactly how do I help matters?" I said.

Rain waved her arms expansively. "You distract her, of course," she said. "You're a minor social problem, and that's exactly what she needs to take her mind off the major one. Should she ask after your father and brothers? If you say they're well, should she say she's glad, or would that be hypocritical? She won't know. So she'll dither around you, and we'll whisk Farrell Dean through without throwing her into complete meltdown."

Just then Tor caught up to us, taking my hand as he came alongside me. Was he going to do this the entire time? Between him and Rain I hardly had an arm to call my own. I glared at him—it was safe to do, since he was on one side of me and Rain on the other—but he merely smiled sweetly at me and kept hold of my hand.

"Did you leave the new boy all alone?" Rain said, and dropped back to wait for Farrell Dean.

"Is he okay?" I hissed.

"Shh," Tor said. "He's fine."

"Does his back hurt? Are his ribs okay? Where has he been—"

"*Fiona*," Tor said, "he's fine. I told him I knew your family, and suggested that if he wants to stay in Gabriel's good graces, it would be wise for him not to mention having a previous acquaintance with *any* of you. He said he'd gathered as much."

"What else did you tell him?"

"To stay clear of the two men on horseback."

"And what else?"

"That's all. That's enough."

"I want to talk to him," I said, looking back. Rain was beside Farrell Dean now, laughing up at him but keeping, I noticed, a good three yards between them—Earl's orders. In fact, Earl was closer now, almost right behind Farrell Dean, his attention completely focused, his gun held loosely but at the ready, down by his side. He looked like the sort of person who lived for this sort of thing, like one of our more enthusiastic wardens. He probably was hoping Farrell Dean would make a move just so he could jump him.

Farrell Dean's eyes met mine just as Tor pulled me frontwards again.

"We have to be careful," he said. "Security is watching and that girl is like a sieve—can't keep a secret to save her life. She'd probably let it slip on purpose, come to that, just to watch the fireworks."

I didn't care about Rain's character. "But I really need to talk to him," I said.

"But you really can't. It's very simple, Fiona. He's fine. We'll get through this evening as carefully as we can, and then go home in the morning."

"Already?"

Tor looked straight ahead. "Rory and Angus have been intercepted and warned, Farrell Dean has been located and warned, and a random lunatic has been rescued and hospitalized. Mission accomplished."

"Your mission, maybe, but not mine. I want to talk to Farrell Dean about Rafe. I need to tell him about the photographs. I need—I need to talk to him."

"No," Tor said.

I yanked my hand out of his and stamped my foot. "You can't tell me what to do!"

Rain's laugh rang out. "You tell him, Fiona. Now, before it's too late."

She and Farrell Dean caught up to us.

"Don't encourage her," Tor said, throwing an exasperated look at Rain. "Unless you want to be the one to catch her next time she faints, that is. I was merely telling her she'd better rest awhile, once we get to your parents' house, but she wants to try out the coracles."

"Oooh, did you faint?" Rain said. "How dramatic of you."

I was a little disconcerted by how well Tor could lie.

"I was hungry, that's all," I said. "I'm fine now. But Tor won't let me forget it."

I felt Farrell Dean's eyes on my face, but I kept mine averted. If I looked at him, he'd probably send me a look that said he'd stolen food for me every day for years, and what was I doing fainting from hunger now that we were in this land of plenty?

And if he didn't send me that look—if he thought I was Fiona—I'd probably burst into tears.

This masquerade was way more complicated than I'd expected.

Chapter 16

While Aunt Carol fluttered around me, behaving exactly as Rain had predicted, Earl took Farrell Dean and vanished into the depths of the house. Was Earl taking Farrell Dean to the place where he'd be confined? I wished I knew the layout of the building.

Maybe I could get some information out of Rain later. At the moment she was sending her mother for tea and cake, or trying to. Carol kept taking a few fluttering steps in my direction, exclaiming under her breath, then backing away. Whenever she got within a few feet of me I caught the vinegary scent of wine. My Aunt Carol was very pretty, in a leftover sort of way, and very drunk.

Rain was flushed with embarrassment, which surprised me after the blithe way she'd talked about her mother. Tor was doing his best to appear oblivious, standing in front of a bookcase, apparently deeply fascinated by what he saw there, but Rain's discomfort seemed more directed at me. At least, I was the one she kept shooting quick glances at. When I caught her eye I gave her a sympathetic just-between-us-girls smile, and her expression eased a little.

"Come show me what you baked this morning, Mom," she said again, steering her mother toward the door—not the same door Farrell Dean had taken. "And let's get out the special stoneware, those plates Gilda Morrow glazed. Fiona hasn't seen those."

This time Carol allowed herself to be led away.

Tor turned away from his bookcase. "They have a housekeeper and a cook," he said. "But Carol might fare better if she actually had something she was respons—" he broke off. "What are you doing?"

I was sliding the heavy curtains back from one of the windows. "Checking the windows," I said.

"Why? Are you afraid Farrell Dean won't be safe here? The security men aren't going to let anyone past the fence."

I didn't answer. I already knew I could climb that fence, but it wouldn't do me any good if all the windows in the house were locked.

It also wouldn't do me any good if they had dogs, but there was no point in worrying about that just yet.

There. Now one window was unlocked. They might check it before bedtime, but at least I had a chance of getting in there.

Putting the curtains back as I'd found them, I hurried to the hallway where Farrell Dean had vanished.

"Have you been in this house before?" I asked Tor, who was looking at me as if I were crazy.

He shook his head.

For a second I paused, listening. Somewhere in the distance dishes clattered. Surely Rain would stay with her mother, help her.

Cautiously I took a few steps down the dark hallway. It was laid with a thick rug that muffled my steps—that was good. On the other hand, the rug also muffled other people's steps, which is why, a moment later, I came face to face with Earl.

I let out a little shriek. "You startled me!" I said, putting one hand over my heart.

Earl crossed his arms over his chest and said nothing.

"Rain's helping Aunt Carol," I said, then lowered my voice to a whisper. "And I need to ... " I gave an embarrassed little shrug.

Earl's expression registered nothing, but he dropped his guard dog stance and stepped aside.

Okay. That was good.

I took a few more steps and looked back. He was still standing there, watching me.

"It's this way, isn't it?" I asked, pointing vaguely.

He nodded. Did the man even have a voice?

I turned around and kept walking. On the right I passed a room that contained only a couch and a large black object with a matching bench, then a room full of books. On the left was a bedroom, then a bathroom. Without looking back at Earl I hurried inside and locked the door behind me. So far, so good.

There was a window. I unlocked it.

Another door led to the bedroom I'd passed, or so I assumed. I left it shut but checked, very quietly, that it too was unlocked.

There had been more doors beyond this room, and two had light showing beneath the closed doors; that must be where Farrell Dean was, in one of those rooms. I stood still and listened, staring at myself in the big mirror. Water was running—it seemed to be just on the other side of this wall. Another bathroom, then, right beside this one. Maybe Farrell Dean was cleaning up.

The thought made me feel grubby.

I'd splashed my face with cold water that morning at the Grateful Fields—had it only been this morning that I'd woken in the woods with my brothers and Ezzie?—but I'd walked a long way since then.

Quietly I slipped open a drawer. I didn't think Rain

would mind, but I felt self-conscious with Earl lurking just outside. I found a brush and combed my hair, then washed my face and hands. After a moment I even slipped my dress down and washed under my arms. No need to give Rain any cause to remark on stinky country cousins.

In the room beside me, the water stopped.

Someone knocked and I jumped, but it wasn't my door. "Clean clothes on the bed," someone said. So Earl really could talk.

"Thanks," Farrell Dean called back.

Having accomplished all I could at the moment, I came out of the bathroom, nodded at Earl—he was standing guard outside Farrell Dean's door—and headed back to the room with the couches.

Tor was sitting on one of them, reading a book. "I wouldn't mess with Earl, if I were you," he said without looking up.

Ignoring him, I went straight to the foot of the staircase. The better I knew the lay of the land, the safer I'd be when I broke in.

I had taken several steps up the stairs when Rain and her mother returned. Rain was carrying a tray.

"Oh, that looks delicious," I said, starting back down.

"Fiona, my dear," Carol said, leaning forward and air-kissing me. "How nice to see you. Welcome."

"Thank you, Aunt Carol," I said, avoiding Rain's eyes. It was exactly as if Carol had just seen me for the first time, as if all that fluttering and muttering had never taken place. Surely she couldn't have sobered up that quickly?

"Do you like the staircase?" Rain said, setting the tray down on one of the low tables and coming up the stairs to meet me.

"I love it," I said, running a hand along the banister. "Our house is only one story."

"We were in a one-story for a long time," Rain said. "Remember? And when Dad decided to build this house, I *begged* for a staircase." She laughed. "He used to say I'd be happy with a staircase leading to nowhere."

"May I go up it?"

"Of course," Rain said, reaching for my hand and leading me up the curving stairs. "I'll show you my room. It has a balcony. Back in a minute, Mom," she called, and I caught a glimpse of Tor's face—resignation quickly masked with politeness—as Carol turned toward him.

Upstairs a wide open area looked over half of the room below. I could see the front door from here, but not where Tor sat on the couch and—this could be important—not the window I'd unlocked.

Rain pointed to a door on the far side of the area. "Mom's and Dad's room," she said. "Here's mine."

Rain's room was enormous, and striking in the same way Rain herself was, with simple lines and starkly contrasting colors. The wood floors were stained a rich dark brown and were partly covered by a thick pale blue rug, so pale it was almost white. Her bed, too, was covered in that same pale blue, and matching gauzy curtains billowed around open windows.

She cast me a sideways glance. "Now you see why I love your dress," she said. "I covet it. That's my favorite color."

Without a word I pulled it over my head.

"You can have it," I said, handing it to her. "Only you'll have to give me something else to put on. My change of clothes is at Nana's."

Rain looked astonished, then delighted.

"You'll want to wash it before you wear it," I said. "I wore it all the way here."

Silently I apologized to my sister for giving away her clothes; but, then, it was her father I was trying to protect. If it weren't for him we could just level with Gabriel and be done with it.

Rain was examining the embroidered borders. "It's beautiful," she said, looking up at me. "You have the best eye of anyone on the island, Fiona. You really do." Draping the dress over one shoulder, she went to one of two mirrored doors and opened it, revealing a long row packed tight with dresses, pants, and shirts.

"I know exactly what I'll give you in return," she said.

She hummed happily while she dug through her closet, and I realized I was smiling. It was fun to be able to give someone a gift. I had never had that in my power before.

Rain found what she was looking for. Kicking some shoes out of the way, she shut the closet door and turned toward me, holding out a handful of midnight blue fabric. When I shook it out I saw it was a long shirt. Like everything else of Rain's it had simple lines, but it was very soft and when I pulled it over my head it fell to my thighs and clung in all the right places. I actually looked like I had a figure.

"It's too small for me now," Rain said, looking me over critically. "But I've kept it because I loved it more than anything else I've ever had. Now I know I was saving it to give to you." She met my eyes and smiled. "It looks as if it were made for you."

A wave of guilt washed over me, but I talked myself through it. I wasn't manipulating Rain just to manipulate her; I was trying to keep peace in the family. And I was looking for an ally in case things went badly for Farrell Dean. Those were noble causes, both of them, and anyway all I was doing was being nice.

Rain slid a drawer from under her bed. "You can't wear it with those brown stockings," she said. "Here. Try these." It was a pair of loose black pants, similar to the ones she wore. They were a little big in the waist, but the shirt hid the gap.

"Perfect," Rain announced, pulling my shirt up and tightening the pants' waist with a pin. "We'll be the most gorgeous girls on the whole island."

"We'll be the hope of all the men and the despair of all the women," I said, straightening my clothes.

"Tor will lock you up for fear you'll be stolen away," Rain said.

"I'd like to see him try," I said darkly, and Rain started to laugh.

"You're an odd pair," she said, crossing to a glass door. "You suited fine when we were younger, but now I can't quite make you fit together. To each his own, I guess."

She swung the door outward. "Come see my balcony," she said.

We stepped outside onto a platform six feet long and four feet deep. It had a waist-high iron railing and looked out across treetops, to the shining inlet. Beside us another balcony jutted out from Gabriel's room.

Rain was watching me expectantly.

"How lovely," I said, gesturing at the inlet. And it was lovely—but the view didn't interest me as much as the iron ladder extending from Rain's balcony to the ground. It looked like the sort of thing that could prove useful.

"What's this?" I asked.

"Fire escape." She shrugged. "Dad has enemies, you know. So there's the fence, and the security men, and the house made of stone instead of wood, and the fire escape in case all that fails and someone manages to set the place alight."

"What about surveillance cameras?" I said. "Or dogs?

Rain gave me a look I couldn't read.

"We have a dog," she said. "Dad doesn't like cameras."

"Oh," I said, trying to sound casual. "Well, we'd better go back down, hadn't we? Aunt Carol will be waiting."

Rain stayed where she was for a long moment, studying me, and my heart began to race. Had I tipped her off?

Then she smiled. "You're right," she said. "Let's go."

Downstairs, Tor was sitting on one couch looking peeved, and Farrell Dean was sitting on another looking courteously blank. Aunt Carol was standing by a window, gazing out as if no one were in the room with her. Every now and then, absently, she tried to poke a stray strand of fading blonde hair back into her disorderly bun.

Earl was standing near the front door, looking much more alert than Carol. He was obviously keeping a clear line of sight to Farrell Dean.

"There you are," Tor said, getting up and coming toward me. "Finally. What were you doing up there? Playing dress up?"

Rain looked at him in disbelief. "Artists are supposed to be gallant," she said.

Tor rolled his eyes. "I never claimed to be an artist," he said. "Just a hardworking craftsman."

"But *look* at her," Rain said. "Even a craftsman has eyes in his head."

An indefinable expression crossed Tor's face. He held up his hands in surrender.

"I'm sorry," he said. "You're quite right."

He bent in an elaborate mock bow. "My dear, you look absolutely beautiful," he said, then straightened up and looked me in the eye. "But we do need to leave now. Your Nana will be wanting her supper supplies. And her supper guests."

"I'll see you in the morning," Rain said, hugging me hard. "Thank you again for the beautiful dress. And you really do look gorgeous." She gave Tor a reproving look. He returned it and reached for my hand, clasping it too hard, as if he thought I might try to pull away.

I smiled at him with exaggerated sweetness, and turned toward my aunt. "Goodbye, Aunt Carol."

Carol looked away from the window just long enough to wave at us. Farrell Dean had gotten to his feet but remained across the room. He no longer wore Tor's clothes, and I was so irritated with Tor that I was childishly glad. Instead Farrell Dean was wearing black pants and a crisp white shirt with the sleeves rolled up. I had to say they suited him very well.

But of course I couldn't say that.

"Have a good evening," he said, looking somewhere between Tor and me. His expression still polite but blank, just as if he were in a room of complete strangers who weren't behaving very well.

He thought I was Fiona. He really did.

And all I could do was go away and leave him alone in Gabriel Drewblood's house.

Chapter 17

Supper was awkward, between Nana's baffling conversation and my irritation with Tor. He watched me out of the corner of his eye, a longsuffering look on his face, until I asked whether I could see pictures of my mother. That delighted Nana and kept the conversation on safe topics—because however addled Nana was, Grandfather, it turned out, was perfectly sharp. Hard of hearing, yes; but sharp.

My mother had been a sweet-looking girl, with long dark hair that often hid her face from her mother's camera. Her parents had stacks of photographs of her, but only until she was about my age. And she did, in fact, look a lot like Rory and Fiona and me, only quieter, somehow. Shy.

Gabriel always came about to her shoulder, and he looked alternately mischievous and sulky.

"He caught up with her soon enough," Grandfather said. "But for years he thought he'd always be smaller than his sister. He was younger, and anyhow boys get their growth later, you know."

I fingered through the pile of photos. One showed Rachel standing on the river bridge beside a fair-haired boy. He was smiling, but it was a tight cynical smile. He looked like he had a chip on his shoulder, as if he didn't think the world ever gave him his rightful due.

I held it up to Grandfather.

"Tristan," he said. "Tristan Oldfamily." I could tell the name didn't taste good in his mouth. He twisted a button on his sweater, and then he took the picture of Tristan and turned it over, face down, as if he didn't like to see it.

The faded man with the cold eyes. But he had loved my mother—that's what Rain had said.

"We don't talk about that man," Nana said, getting up to clear the table.

Shortly afterwards she went to bed. Then Tor and I sat on the creaky sagging couch visiting with Grandfather. At least, I was visiting; Tor kept yawning widely and, I thought, pointedly—but I had no intention of going to bed. I had too many questions, and Grandfather seemed to like answering them. He had a storyteller's manner, one that wouldn't be rushed, one that wanted you to hear the flavor and not just the words.

"I didn't want to upset Nana," I said at one point. "But I don't know much anything about Tristan Oldfamily, except that he's a friend of Uncle Gabriel's."

Tor roused himself long enough to give me a warning look, and I widened my eyes at him. I was allowed to say Gabriel's name.

"I suppose you have a right to know your family history," Grandfather said slowly. His old eyes were sad. "Your mother would have told you herself, if she'd lived. She would have wanted you to learn from her mistakes."

"I'm sure she would," I agreed, and Tor slumped back on the couch, apparently considering ancient history a safe enough topic.

"Tristan was a neighbor," Grandfather said. "Back when we lived in town. His folks lived down the street from us, and their boy was just a bit older than our girl. And when those two got to be young people, Tristan took a fancy to Rachel."

He paused, collecting his thoughts. "Now, you have to understand that Tristan is clever with gadgets. Mechanics, electronics, all sorts of contraptions. He came up with a way to record sounds and send them out through the air, on the radio—quite clever.

"But Rachel was smart, too, in different ways than he was. And that got to bothering him, once they were courting. And his being bothered—well, that bothered Rachel. She'd never been a talkative girl, your mother, but she got to where she wouldn't say a word for fear of showing up young Tristan. Showing him up in his own mind, that is. Nobody else ever thought that her being bright made him dim."

He looked at me to see if I understood, and I nodded that I did.

"Well, the quieter your mother got the more worried your grandmother and I became. Finally, after discussing it between ourselves, we spoke to Rachel about it. And that's an awkward thing, coming between your child and someone she loves. We knew any interference on our part could make matters worse—it could harden her resolve to have him, and separate her further from us. Young people are funny that way. But we had to try. We felt we were losing her anyway. And we were afraid for her."

Grandfather was gazing out at his shabby comfortable living room, but I could tell he wasn't seeing it. He was seeing his daughter.

"Rachel heard us out, not saying a word, and then we all sat there staring at each other, each of us thinking our own thoughts. And after a time Rachel nodded like she'd made up her mind. 'I won't marry him,' she said. 'I love him, but I can see that you're right. There are parts of me he doesn't love.'"

Grandfather paused and picked up a pipe from a little table. He took his time emptying it, and refilling it, and tamping it down, and lighting it. His pipe tobacco didn't smell quite like the cigarettes in Optica; it smelled damper and fruitier, somehow. I liked it.

Beside me, Tor's head had fallen back against the couch; his eyes were shut. Grandfather looked at him and lowered his voice.

"So she ran away," he said, giving a gentle wave of his pipe. "Everyone said she ran away from *home,* but your grandmother and I knew it wasn't us she was running from. She was running from him."

"She went away without telling you where she was going?"

He nodded. "She left without a word to anybody. We were that worried. But she did send a message as soon as she could. Sent it by way of the milk truck. She had gone to the other side of the island, you see, which in those days was just farms, not even enough people to make a proper town. And she'd found a job working as a milkmaid."

"For Eric Alleyn," I said.

Tor's head came down on my shoulder and he began to snore softly. I elbowed him—more or less gently—and he sat back up, blinking.

"She didn't work for Eric so much as for his father," Grandfather said. "He was around in those days."

"Because they didn't move away until later." I was trying to sound like I knew at least bits of family history. Tor had said Eric Alleyn's parents had been living off in some remote place when Fiona and I were born.

Grandfather looked a little apologetic. "Well, yes. That was before they moved. But what I actually meant was that Eric's father was around at that particular time. He had a sort of tendency to come and go. Not without warning, mind you, but not always conveniently, either. And then there was the swimming ..."

He broke off. "Your Papa never talks about his father?"

"Not to me," I said truthfully.

Grandfather nodded. "Eric has had a hard life," he said. "I suppose living through it has been hard enough, without talking about it too."

"But you'll tell me?"

Grandfather chewed thoughtfully on his pipe stem. "Yes, I'll tell you," he said. "Children should know their families, is what I think. So. Your other grandfather, Eric's father. He was quite strong, quite fit. About my age, but restless in a way I never was. He walked a lot, off on his own. And sometimes he'd light out swimming until he was nothing but a tiny speck in the distance, and sometimes not even that.

"It was worrisome to his family, the way he'd go off. But I don't believe he could help himself. He was something of a troubled soul. Good with wounded things, though. People, animals. And in any event Eric Alleyn turned out well, thanks in part to his own stubbornness. And to his mother."

He smiled and began talking more quickly, as if glad to change the subject.

"Ah, that Rosie," he said. "Now she was a force to be reckoned with. I'd heard tell of her, and I knew Rachel was in good hands, staying at the Alleyn farm with Rosie Alleyn. And Eric was a good lad. He wasn't much older than Rachel herself. Seventeen to her sixteen. And before a year had passed they'd married."

For the first time I felt a little real warmth toward my father. No matter what Tristan said, Eric Alleyn hadn't "stolen" my mother. He'd been her refuge.

I glanced over at Tor. Sure enough, he was asleep again, his head tilted back at a painful angle, his large nose pointed straight up in the air. I tried to gauge just how quietly I could speak—it had to be loud enough that Grandfather could hear me, but quiet enough that Tor wouldn't hear the dreaded name and wake up.

"Why are Tristan and Gabriel such friends?" I said. "It seems odd, given what happened."

Tor gave a single snore but didn't wake.

"Well, they had something in common," Grandfather said. "They were both angry."

"But it seems like Gabriel would be mad at Tristan," I said. "For driving his sister away."

Grandfather sighed. "Gabriel was never an easy child. He took things to heart. Your grandmother thought he felt his dead brother's absence, or maybe that was just an excuse to be moodier than the rest of us. But Rachel always could soothe him, even when your Nana and I couldn't. Gabriel loved her, you see; he loved her very much. And then she left him."

"So he blamed her instead of Tristan."

Grandfather nodded. "And then, of course, when she got married and began having babies of her own, that made matters worse. Gabriel was jealous. Jealous, or just plain lonesome for his sister. And Tristan was right there being angry at Rachel too, but pretending to himself he was angry at Eric Alleyn. They were both wronged, you see, Gabriel and Tristan. At least in their own eyes."

It made a sad sort of sense.

Grandfather ran a gnarled hand over his messy, half-shaven chin, and looked past me at Tor. Then he leaned closer to me and said, his voice low, "Perhaps Rachel didn't handle the situation in the best possible way. Perhaps she should have explained to Tristan's face why she wouldn't have him, or at least have written him a letter. But she was afraid."

"Afraid he'd hurt her?"

"Afraid he'd make her stay. Rachel was a mild girl, and she knew it. She knew she wasn't strong-willed enough to tough it out here. Tristan would have bullied her into staying with him until it was too late ever to escape."

He patted my knee and again peered around me at Tor. I got the point.

I couldn't exactly profess my undying love for Tor, so I settled for a reassuring smile. "I can be stubborn," I said. "Nobody is going to bully me into making a bad decision."

"Good girl," Grandfather said.

A patter of raindrops hit the windows. Beside me Tor stirred, opened his eyes, then shut them again, his torso sliding away from me, toward the arm of the couch. Out of affection for Fiona I picked up a small cushion and wedged it under his head.

"And then Rachel died," Grandfather said, and his whole face seemed to sag with sadness. "Matter of fact, Tristan was the one who brought us news of her death, glad to tell us the end result of our meddling, glad to point the finger at Eric one more time. By that time Gabriel had been avoiding Rachel for years, giving her the cold shoulder whenever she came to see us. And then she was gone."

Gabriel must have felt terrible; his sister had died while he'd been acting like an idiot. No wonder he'd rather blame everything on my father.

And, I supposed, my death had been wrapped up in Gabriel's loss of Rachel. My loss had been one more he could lay at Eric Alleyn's feet. No wonder the two men didn't get along.

A soft tapping at the door made Tor sit up and rub his eyes. Grandfather got to his feet and peered cautiously out the window.

"It's the boys," he said, unbarring the door.

Rory and Angus came in, being as quiet as the two of them knew how, and still they seemed to crowd the small house. I scanned their faces anxiously—was Ezzie all right? Were they? I couldn't think how to ask in front of Grandfather, not without giving something away.

Grandfather solved my problem. "Nana's asleep, and now that you're safely in, I'll head on to bed too," he told the boys. "Fiona told us what happened, you finding the lunatic and all. You're all right? The doctors gave you a clean bill of health?"

Rory nodded. "We're fine. Go on to bed—we'll see you in the morning."

Grandfather padded off without another word, pausing only to pat me on the head as he went.

"I'm going, too," Tor said, yawning again. "The three of us are in the room upstairs," he said to my brothers. "Fiona's been put in the small downstairs bedroom. Goodnight."

Since it was just my brothers, he didn't bother to say a special goodnight to me, and I was glad. I'd about had all of the Tor-and-Fiona act I could take for one day.

Chapter 18

"How's Ezzie?"

I asked the question as soon as the others had gone, and Angus collapsed on the couch, grimacing at me.

"Can't you even feed us first, you heartless woman?"

"Come to the kitchen," I said.

With a groan Angus heaved himself up again, and with an exaggerated stagger made his way to a kitchen chair. Rory followed less dramatically and helped me set out plates and food—bread and butter, fish, green beans, and baked potatoes.

Knowing Nana would want it, I even set a match to her beloved centerpiece, a ring of twelve short candles sitting on a round mirror.

The boys ate as if they were starving, and I waited as patiently as I could, watching their faces in the flickering candlelight. Finally Rory wiped his mouth on his napkin.

"We didn't want to bring him to town, but we didn't know what else to do," he said. "You saw how he was scratching himself? He tried to stop but it got worse and worse. So then we tied his hands, but he started gnawing on his lip."

"Just about bit it through," Angus said, and I grimaced. "Just saying," he said.

"So we untied his hands," Rory said, "and he stopped

193

biting and went back to scratching. Meanwhile he was getting less and less coherent, and telling us really scary things about your island, about wild men and time of the ashes and city meetings and so forth."

"He wasn't ever mean, though," Angus said, his mouth full. "Or violent. Just confused."

"So we brought him in," Rory finished. "We didn't want to wait until it was too late."

"You did the best thing," I said. "Thank you. What did the doctors at the hospital say?"

Rory and Angus looked at each other.

"They sedated him and started an i.v. drip to get him rehydrated," Rory said. "And in the meantime they ran tests on some blood samples. Serology tests."

"What's an i.v. drip?" I said. "What's—oh, never mind. Go on."

They looked at each other again.

"It's a little hard to explain," Rory said apologetically. "It's … he's …"

"Just tell me," I said.

"He has some mutation or variant of canid sylvatic cystic hydatid disease," Rory said, speaking carefully, as if he'd memorized the words. "They think."

That meant absolutely nothing to me, mutated or otherwise, but it sounded awful.

"It's a wild animal disease," Angus offered, waving his butter knife. "Wolves get it, or wild dogs, foxes, things like that."

"Canids," Rory said. "Anything in the dog family. Sylvatic—wild animals, not domestic ones."

"And they pass it on to deer or other herbivores," Angus went on. "It makes a sort of cycle, wolf to deer to wolf and so forth. But humans aren't supposed to get it, not anymore. The doctors haven't ever seen a single case of it. They only know about it from some really old books. It was supposed to have died out a long time ago. Humans became inhospitable hosts to that particular parasite, or something."

I was going to scream if they didn't get to the point. "But what *is* it?" I demanded. "What does it do? Will Ezzie be okay?"

Rory took pity on me. "This parasite, this worm thing, gets into the host," he said. "And it starts making cysts. If the cysts get big and burst, they kill the host. Anaphylactic shock. But sometimes they calcify instead."

The host. Ezzie.

"Can they help him?" I said.

"Absolutely," Angus said, but Rory looked worried.

"They're going to try," he said. "They did some imaging scans and found a big cyst growing in his brain, which is why he's acting peculiar. They've started him on some heavy duty chemo drugs and tomorrow they're going to try to remove the cyst—hopefully without bursting the thing or damaging the brain around it."

"They're going to operate on Ezzie's *brain*?" That would have been unthinkable in Optica. In Optica they operated for appendicitis, and to sterilize people after the breeding years. Every other treatment, so far as I knew, involved leaving the body nicely shut.

"They're good at that," Angus said. "Neurological research, Dream Clinics, all that mind and brain stuff. They're better at brains, on this side of the island, than at setting broken arms. Way better."

I looked at Rory. He nodded, looking as apologetic as if he'd caused all this himself. "They're good," he said. "And if they don't operate, it's only going to get worse, his dementia. And the bigger the cyst gets, the more likely it'll rupture."

Angus started to speak but had to stop to swallow. "That's why he was itching," he said. "The doctors said he probably had a couple of little cysts that ruptured. In small amounts the cyst gunk doesn't kill you, just makes you itch like crazy."

He took a drink of water and swallowed wrong, spewing it all over the floor as he coughed. Rory sighed and grabbed a towel.

"And how can they be sure you're okay?" I asked, watching Angus wipe his streaming eyes. I had a sudden anxious image of Shawna, sitting up all night drawing pus out of Ezzie's wounds. She had worn gloves, hadn't she?

"Apparently this thing spreads pretty much instantaneously, once you've got it," Rory said. "They tested our blood when we got there, and we were clear. Then they tested us again a little while ago, and we were still clear."

He shifted in his chair. "And the thing is, the doctors said it was passed through fecal matter."

"I'm *eating*," Angus protested, holding out a piece of buttered bread as evidence.

Rory and I ignored him. "So it isn't passed through blood or spit or air," I said, thinking about Ezzie's injury. He had been clawed, and no doubt the wild man hadn't washed his hands any time in recent memory.

"So maybe Ezzie isn't all that contagious," Rory said. "In fact, for all we know, he might not be contagious at all— maybe only those wild men can pass it on." He glanced at Angus. "We didn't know how much to tell the doctors," he said. "But we did tell them he'd had a direct run-in with an unidentified wild animal."

"We had to tell them that much," Angus said. "Because before they figured out it was this fecal matter thing, some of the doctors were arguing that Ezzie should be put down, and his body burned—quarantine the parasite, you see? They were trying to persuade Gabriel it was the only safe thing to do. So we had to let them know that maybe it was harder to catch than they thought. They were thinking it could be passed from person to person, right? And that might not be true."

I was speechless. The doctors had wanted to kill Ezzie?

"And that guy you said doctored Ezzie?" Angus went on. "He must have done something right. Managed to at least slow the cyst growth, or something. Because according to that old book, the cysts grow so fast that most people die within 48 hours."

Hmmm. I wondered—if Ezzie had stayed with Sir Tom, would the old man's medicine have cured this? Or had Ezzie saved his own life by running away to die?

Angus wiped his plate with another piece of bread. Rory began washing up the dishes.

I stood. "I guess I'll go to bed," I said, giving each of them a hug. "Thank you for taking care of Ezzie."

And I did go to bed, lying there fully clothed, until the creaking stairs told me Rory and Angus were safely tucked away for the night.

Chapter 19

The security man wasn't utterly predictable, but predictable enough to suit me. He sometimes went all the way around the wrought-iron fence but mostly stayed by the gate, in the shadows, where he was hard to spot. The fence had lights fixed at regular intervals, pointed not at the house but at the lightly wooded grounds just outside the fence. Child's play, after what I was accustomed to in Optica.

Except for the dog.

I crept through the trees and around to the side of the house, out of sight of the security man at the gate—and out of sight of Gabriel's bedroom windows. Moving slowly, keeping low to the ground, I eased toward the fence, stopping just beyond the exposing light.

I'd brought some leftover fish with me, and now I tossed a bit of it toward the yard area. The first piece hit the fence and bounced back, but the second one made it in. The dog didn't bark when it found the fish, but it did look in the general direction of the security man—out of sight around the corner of the house—as if it knew it wasn't supposed to be eating unexpected treats. It had longish hair, pale and wavy, and in general looked less intense than Angus's dog Rex.

After it had eaten the bit on the ground, I tossed another bit in, keeping my distance. Then I came a little closer, into the exposing light, and tossed in another piece. Now it saw me—the source of the tidbits—but it didn't bark. Instead it cast another guilty look toward the front of the house.

I wanted to talk to the dog, like I talked to the stray cats in Optica, but I was afraid the security man would hear me. So I settled for creeping closer and closer, feeding it bit by bit. Finally, when I was right up by the fence and it began to act curious about its mysterious benefactor, I let it smell me—with its muzzle poking through the fence and my hand more or less safely outside it.

It snuffled wetly at my hand, then rubbed its face on my sleeve—in fact, my sleeve seemed to interest it more than my skin did. I let it take its time, smelling all up and down my arm. Finally it sniffed my hand again, whining softly in some sort of protest, and then it shoved its head against my hand. It wanted to be petted.

I smiled. I was already reaping a reward for giving Rain my dress. The dog knew I wasn't her—it kept peering up at my face, snuffling at my hand, then whining at the sleeve—but apparently I smelled enough like Rain that it didn't feel inclined to take my hand off.

Just to be safe, I left the fence twice, coming back at different places. Every time the dog found me, and every time it wanted to be petted, even when I ran out of fish.

Only then did I risk scaling the fence.

The dog wasn't sure what to make of that, and crouched down on the ground, making that same confused whining noise, but louder.

"Shhhhh," I told it, climbing down and offering it my sleeve again. I hoped it hadn't been cleverly luring me inside, planning to bite me once it could get a good clear shot.

It didn't. Once I was on the ground it seemed pleased that I was inside the fence with it, and ran happily along beside me as I moved into the shadows of the house.

I was heading for the back of the house—I had decided to try the bathroom window first—when the dog suddenly sprinted off, warning me that the security man was making his rounds.

There was nothing to hide behind—no bushes, no trash cans—but except for the glare of the guard lights by the fence, the night was pitch black, no moon, no stars. Rain's shirt was dark blue, and I had my trusty black cap to hide my hair. So I crouched down against the wall of the house, against a flat decorative pillar that broke the smooth expanse at least a little bit, and hid my face in my arms. I'd thought about darkening it with mud before I came, but then there would be no talking myself out of trouble if I got caught.

The security man was moving closer. I could hear the sound of his steps crunching on the dry winter grass.

"There you are, you lazy brute," he said. In the silence of the night his voice seemed loud, though in truth he was speaking very quietly. "No, I do not want to play. We'll play in the daylight, when I'm less likely to break an ankle tripping over you."

The dog whined, then gave a high-pitched yip. He wanted to show off his new friend.

For a long moment there was silence. I held my breath, imagining the security man scanning the area, looking for anything that didn't belong, any flicker of movement.

Finally he spoke. "You need a friend, is what you need," he said. "A doggy friend." Then he moved away. The dog ran back and snuffled at me, then ran to the security man, then back to me. But he didn't yip again, and the security man didn't come back.

Still I stayed put, counting to three hundred before cautiously lifting my head from my arms. The dog promptly licked my face.

As best as I could tell in the darkness, the security man

really was gone. Slowly I slid around the corner of the house, beneath Rain's balcony. Her light was on and I could hear voices. Every now and then a shadow moved across the square of light.

For a moment I hesitated. Then curiosity got the better of me. Carefully, slowly, I began to climb the fire escape ladder.

Beneath me the dog made a confused noise. "Shhhh," I whispered. "It's okay." He stood there for a moment, looking up at me, and then ran off, probably to try to interest the security guard in this strange happening.

I sped up, climbing as quickly as I could without jarring the metal rungs and making them ring. At the top of the ladder I stayed low, squirming on my stomach until I was lying against the house, just beside the big glass doors. They were shut, but the window was still open, and through it I could hear Rain's voice.

"… can wait until morning," she said. "He's exhausted. He went to bed ages ago."

"I'd hoped to get home before everyone was asleep," a man's voice said. Gabriel. "But as I said, one thing led to another."

"It sounds like quite a day," Rain said. "Especially with the Alleyns involved."

"Rory was actually a help," Gabriel said. "Not Angus, though. Do you think that boy is quite right?"

"Hard to tell," Rain said.

There was a pause, then Gabriel spoke again. "All right, Rain. If I'm to let the young man downstairs have his beauty sleep, you can at least tell me what you know about him. Where did you find him?"

"Apparently he'd been wandering around town asking for you," Rain said. "Delia Overland pointed him in my direction, and I said I'd take him to find you."

"Did he say anything else? Then, or tonight? He did eat supper with you and your mother, didn't he?"

Rain sighed. "He ate with us, but he didn't talk, not about anything that matters. I tried, I truly did. I asked him all kinds of questions, and I was harmless and nonthreatening and harebrained, and he still gave me nothing but politely evasive non-answers every time. Or else he talked at length about utterly useless things, like what sort of apples Mom likes best for pies. She wasn't much help herding him into any corners, I'll tell you that."

A cold feeling formed in the pit of my stomach. Rain was sounding perfectly sensible. She wasn't rattling on about clothes or giggling and acting boy crazy. I tried to think back—if she'd been acting a part that afternoon, was it just because of Farrell Dean, or was it for my sake, too?

"If he's in cahoots with those Alleyn boys, things could become awkward between you and Fiona," Gabriel said.

That made it sound like he, at least, thought Rain was up front with Fiona. And she'd been less flighty, hadn't she, when we were alone in her room?

Gabriel was still talking. "The Alleyn boys knew more than they were telling," he said. "They acted as if everything they knew, he'd told them in the ten minutes it took to get him from the woods into town. I'm not buying it. Not in the state he was in. They were with him longer, or else they knew him beforehand."

Rain was silent for a moment. "We saw him come ashore," she said finally.

"Yes, but he could have set off from the southern beach," Gabriel said. "It would be just like Eric Alleyn, to ship a sick man up here to run wild and make mischief."

"So you don't think he's really from another island?"

"I've no way to tell," Gabriel said. "Not without talking to that boy downstairs."

I froze. Gabriel's voice was suddenly very close to the window; he might even be looking out.

"And you know as well as I do," he went on, "that suddenly discovering life on another island isn't very likely. It's much more likely that Eric Alleyn is up to his usual tricks."

"I can see that Eric Alleyn might well have sent the dark man to make mischief," Rain said. "But what would be the point of sending Farrell Dean?"

Above me Gabriel's voice was grim. "I can think of reasons," he said. "He says he wants me to help him. Help his people. Well, if Eric Alleyn—through this boy—can get me to set off in a boat, out to sea, into the unknown … Rain, you know we aren't sailors. In the whole history of this island, no one who set out in a boat has ever come back again. And then Eric Alleyn could finally rest easy."

"But why would Farrell Dean be willing to go along with him?" Rain said. "Why would he conspire to kill you—a man who has never wronged him, a man he doesn't even know?"

"That's exactly what I'd like to find out," Gabriel said. "And, speaking of people who'd enjoy my funeral, I'd also like to know why Fiona didn't mention that her brothers were around. She sat there in my shop and said not one single word about them."

Rain laughed. "You know exactly why she didn't. If she and Tor were hoping for a peaceful visit with Nana and Grandfather, the last thing they'd do is mention the boys to you."

"You think I'm too hard on them," Gabriel said.

"A little bit. They're irritating, especially Angus, but they aren't like Mick and Rufus. They still think it's some sort of game."

"Well, I'd take any one of them over Sean," Gabriel said. "That boy doesn't care about right and wrong. He only cares about peace, as if peace can exist in a vacuum."

There was a movement above me, and when Gabriel spoke, his voice was quieter. He must have turned around to face his daughter. "I'll let you get to sleep now," he said. "And I suppose your boy's not going anywhere."

"Door's locked, Earl's in the other guest room, and Morris and Woof are outside," Rain said. "He'll be there when you want him."

They told each other goodnight. Footsteps sounded, and then a door opened and shut. I started to move away from the window, back to the fire escape ladder, but Rain spoke again.

"He's not my boy," she said quietly, and her voice was troubled. "Not the way he looks at Fiona."

Chapter 20

Her words echoed in my head as I carefully descended the ladder. The implication was painfully clear: Rain had an answer to the question of why Farrell Dean might go along with Eric Alleyn's plots against Gabriel. If Farrell Dean were hoping to cut out Tor and win Fiona, he well might be trying to win an ally in her father.

But Rain hadn't mentioned this to Gabriel. I wondered why not.

I hoped it meant she felt some sympathy for me—or Fiona, rather. Some loyalty that kept her from exposing me to her father.

Halfway down the fire escape I felt a jolt in the rungs, as if someone else had stepped on the ladder. I froze, my heart leaping into my throat.

This would be a terrible time to get caught. Could I say I was just now climbing up, going to surprise Rain? It depended on how long the security man had been watching me. And sneaking around at night would be entirely out of character for Fiona, but what else could I say?

I was afraid to look down—I almost felt as if as long as I didn't look, he wouldn't be there, coming up after me. But of course that was nonsense.

So, my heart in my throat, I looked down; and then I

almost laughed with relief. It was the dog, his paws planted on the bottom rung, gazing up at me happily.

"You scared me," I told him softly when I'd climbed the rest of the way down and was scratching him behind the ears. He panted still more enthusiastically and tried to lick my face.

Now for the bathroom window. Would it still be unlocked, or would someone have checked it?

Gently I tugged. It was stiff and hard to move, but it opened silently. Good. I had to be extremely quiet—this bathroom was connected to a bedroom, and Earl was sleeping there. Or lurking, more likely. That seemed more his style than sleep.

I waited outside the open window for a long time, listening. The last thing I needed was to climb in and surprise Earl taking a midnight trip to the bathroom.

All was silent. He could come in at any moment, of course, so now the sooner I got through the window and out of his way, the better.

The sill was a little high off the ground for me, but I was motivated. I held to it tightly and walked myself up the wall, my fingers cramping painfully before I managed to get one leg up and through the window. Very slowly, very carefully, I eased inside and lowered myself to the bathroom floor.

Peering through the darkness, I saw that I had extra reason to be quiet: The connecting door to Earl's bedroom was open.

Softly I slipped across the room toward the hallway door. My image in the mirror crept along beside me, a dark shadow. Rain's words came back to me—how exactly did Farrell Dean look at "Fiona"? As if he were trying to figure out if she was me? Or in the way Rain meant?

The hallway door was closed. Gently I turned the knob and eased the door open, and then, holding my breath, I moved very slowly out into the hallway—slowly, because Rain could have been wrong; Earl could be sitting outside Farrell Dean's door, or pacing the hall. But he wasn't. The hall was empty and silent.

Farrell Dean's door was locked, but luck was with me and the key was in the keyhole. Carefully I turned it, and the lock opened with a soft click.

I didn't know what to do with the key. I thought I should probably leave it in the keyhole, so that if Earl checked, everything would look the way he'd left it. But I didn't like the idea that someone could come along and turn the key and lock me in. There were windows, though. Farrell Dean couldn't escape out them without alarming Woof the dog, but I could. So I left the key in the lock and slipped into the room, closing the door quietly behind me.

It was very dark, but I could hear Farrell Dean's even breathing, and a memory hit me, sending sudden tears stinging in my eyes. Not quite a week ago I'd broken into another locked room, looking for Farrell Dean. I'd found him bloody and beaten, chained to a wall, and while I was with him, assuring him we'd get him out somehow, Meritt was intercepting the wardens, protecting us, putting himself in danger.

How could that have been only last week? So much had happened since then, so much had changed.

Standing there in the dark, my hand still on the door, I struggled to focus. This was not the time to cope with everything that had happened. This was the time to speak with Farrell Dean, the time to be grateful he was alive and, though a prisoner, not in any immediate danger.

Neither was I, come to that. The last time I'd broken in to see Farrell Dean, if the wardens had caught me I'd have been executed, possibly on the spot. Now I'd have an angry uncle to contend with—and Tor's fury as well—but nothing deadly like guns and bullets.

I'd known the difference all along, of course. That was why I'd actually been enjoying myself. That was probably why the dog let me alone; I not only smelled like Rain, I also didn't smell afraid. But now everything had come crashing in on me, and I was standing there in the dark trying not to bawl. This was ridiculous. I couldn't get all emotional and mess things up now.

Taking a deep breath I stepped carefully into the pitch-black room. If I ran into anything I'd have to do it quietly.

Six steps into the room I bumped into something. Cautiously I reached out to feel it—sure enough, it was the bed. When I felt a little further, I found Farrell Dean's foot under the covers. I climbed over the footboard and onto the bed, and crawled up beside Farrell Dean.

He didn't even move. As Rain had said, he was completely exhausted.

I was, too. I don't know how long I sat there in the dark, propped up against the headboard, listening to Farrell Dean breathe, letting him sleep. I knew I'd have to wake him up eventually. We had to talk before Gabriel interrogated him the next day. But he'd been through so much, and now he was finally sleeping in a real bed, probably his first one in days and days.

At one point I put a hand on his shoulder, intending to nudge him awake, but instead I let it rest there, unmoving. The warmth of his skin, the rhythm of his breathing, drew away my worries, my tension. He was all right. He was safe, hadn't been attacked out in those woods, hadn't fallen ill out there alone, hadn't left me on this island all alone.

We'd figure out a way to convince Gabriel to trust him. We'd get help for our friends back home. It would all be okay.

There in the warm darkness I had almost started to drift off—knowing I couldn't, just toying with the lovely idea of curling up and letting sleep take me, instead of having to elude the dog and the security man, climb the fence, make my way back to the grandparents' house in the dark chilly night—when a hand reached up and grabbed my wrist.

I jumped about three feet straight up, but I didn't make a sound.

One hand still holding my wrist, Farrell Dean sat up and felt my face, my head. He pulled off my cap and ran a hand down my hair, and then pulled me into his arms.

"You okay, Red?" he said, his breath tickling in my ear. He was warm and smelled good, like sleep and safety, and a great wave of something I didn't understand washed over me.

Hastily I pulled away from him.

"Red's fine," I said, giving it Fiona's lilt. "It was too dangerous for her to come, but I promised to check on you."

Farrell Dean laughed under his breath.

"Nice try," he said. "But I know you."

Something in his voice made me flush, and I was glad the darkness hid my face.

"Where have you been?" I said in my own voice, feeling a little out of breath. "I was so worried."

"Yeah, I'm really sorry about that," Farrell Dean said. "It was Gabriel—well, you've seen him. I saw him in Doria and tried to catch him, but he took off all of a sudden, and then I was afraid that if I lost him I'd never find him again. So I hitched a ride this way."

"You didn't walk through the woods?"

"No, I—"

"I wish I'd known that," I said. "I was so worried. There are men out there looking for you. Riders on horseback."

"Tor told me."

"So if you got a ride, what took you so long? I beat you here, and I left later than you did, and I walked. Where have you been?"

In the dark I felt his silent laugh. "I'll tell you, if you'll let me get a word in edgewise," he said. "I got mixed up with this man who gave me a ride in his wagon. This woodcutter. He's —look, Red, let's come back to that later." He was speaking very softly, scarcely audible even as close as I was. "Tell me about Ezzie—what's he doing here? Do you know?"

"He didn't want to expose anyone in Optica to whatever he has," I said, and described the scene Ezzie had recounted—the fight on the cliff top, Ezzie's frightening rage, the wardens. And then, there in the darkness, I told him about what Meritt had done to help.

"So Meritt's working with Angel," Farrell Dean said thoughtfully. "And they took down the wardens and let our guys go."

I didn't reply.

"That's a good sign, Red," Farrell Dean said. "Meritt had a plan."

Suddenly I was struck by how utterly decent Farrell Dean was. As Cline had so forcefully pointed out, as far as Farrell Dean was concerned, Meritt might be a friend, but he was also a rival. And yet here he was, sounding nothing but pleased that perhaps Meritt would be vindicated in my eyes.

It was a relief, too, to know that I didn't have to argue with him about it, didn't have to hash the whole thing out. We both knew that Ezzie's account didn't prove anything, and we both knew that Meritt would at least be tempted to use me as a pawn if the situation demanded it. That was just Meritt.

The only question was whether I was okay with that, whether I was willing to play the game to win, whatever it took, even if it meant not only dying—I could do that—but letting someone else, someone I loved and who probably loved me, hand me over to die.

Neither of us had to say any of those things. They were

understood. And that got to me—the relief of having some-one who understood things without being told because he *knew* me, knew my past and my present, knew me well enough to tell me apart from my sister.

And it was late at night, and I was very tired, and too much had happened in the past few days. And Rain was right. Farrell Dean was good looking and strong and sure, and I had felt so lost and lonely while we were apart in this strange place, and it was dark and I was so tired I almost felt that I was dreaming.

And so I leaned forward, put my hand on his cheek, and kissed him.

He pulled me to him and then he was kissing me back. His mouth was warm and soft and I could feel the ridge where Angus had split his lip.

Then he broke away. He didn't say a word, just turned his head. Then he shifted so that a good two feet separated us.

My cheeks began to burn. I was glad he couldn't see my face, but I wished I could see his. In the darkness I could only tell that he was sitting with his elbows on his knees, his head in his hands.

"I'm sorry," I said at last. "I shouldn't have …"

He raised his head and cleared his throat. "I'm glad you did," he said. "But if you do it again I might start to think you mean it." He said it matter-of-factly, not being cruel, just tell-ing me the truth.

Cline's angry face swam before my eyes—he was right, I was horrible, Farrell Dean deserved far better than this—and then I was crying, hot tears streaming down my cheeks. "I meant *something*," I said in a strained whisper, trying not to sob. "But I don't know what."

For a long moment he hesitated. Then he took me back into his arms and held me, comforting me for not knowing whether I loved him or his rival best.

It was not my best moment.

After a long time he shifted away from me again and spoke, changing the subject.

"So this thing with Ezzie," he said. "What else do you know about it?"

If he was trying to lower the temperature in the room, he couldn't have picked a better topic. I took a deep breath and told him about the parasite and the cysts and the surgery.

"Rory and Angus think he caught it from the wild man," I said. "But what if he caught something else from the wild man, something that makes him capable of getting ..." I couldn't make myself finish.

Farrell Dean saw where I was going. " ... capable of getting diseases only wild animals get. And then maybe he picked up this parasite later."

"That would mean he's going wild," I whispered, shivering.

"But maybe he isn't. We need to talk to Sir Tom, try to get a clearer picture of this illness."

"There's something else we need to ask Sir Tom, though he probably won't tell us the truth about it." I told Farrell Dean about the box of photographs, the uncanny ghost images of people identical to people we knew back home, and about the suspicious plague that created amnesia, so similar to Optica's collective amnesia.

"All those identical twins," Farrell Dean said. "Not just you and Rafe. Do you see what this means?

"This island is connected to the experiment," I said. The thought had struck me immediately, and I had pushed it away.

"Someone divided twins into two groups and watched them both," Farrell Dean said, his tone matching my own mingled sense of indignation and astonishment.

"But watched us both do what?"

"I don't know. It could be anything. Drug testing, nutrition, genetics, eugenics …"

In the darkness I felt him shift. "One set of twins might be the control group," he said, and he was being tactful. If there was a control group, the ones allowed to more or less go on with an ordinary life, we both knew it wasn't the people of Optica.

It was odd—I had been in Optica for years and years, and here for only hours. But this world was the one that felt ordinary to me—it hadn't at first, but now that I was getting used to it, I could tell that this way of doing things was natural and Optica's was contrived.

What had been done to us, to Rafe and Louie and me and all the other twins? What changes had they made to us, so they could compare us to our normal siblings?

"Don't tell anyone," I said, feeling faintly sick to my stomach. "Not yet. I … you're so lucky, Farrell Dean. You know your mother. You know you aren't a twin. Who knows what they did to me?"

"It'll be all right, Red," he said. "You'll be all right."

"But please don't talk about it—"

"I won't. Not until you're ready. But at some point they're going to wonder. They're going to want to know why half of all their twins were taken."

"Only Tor knows about that," I said. "He was with me when I saw the pictures. But he doesn't care—he's mostly concerned about keeping me quiet." I explained why Tor was so determined I should keep my resurrection a secret.

"I really can't believe Gabriel would kill Eric Alleyn in cold blood," I said. "But he is pretty intense, and he seems sure that Eric Alleyn would like to kill him. He basically thinks you're Eric Alleyn's weapon, sent to lure him away so he'll get lost at sea."

"So we hold off on telling him about you," Farrell Dean said, beginning to put the last pieces of the family puzzle together. "He doesn't need another reason to be angry at Eric Alleyn just now."

Farrell Dean reached for my hand. "I guess I'd better go ahead and tell you," he said. "That man I met, the one who let me ride with him—you remember the midwife? Rowena Marchrest?"

I nodded. How could I forget about the woman who handed me over to Sir Tom, who told my family I'd died and was buried beneath the willows?

"The man I met in the woods was her son." Farrell Dean's voice took on a tone I knew all too well, the tone that said he wanted to protect me from something painful. But he'd promised not to keep secrets from me, and he didn't keep one now. I wondered if I would regret bullying him into making that promise.

"Bear in mind that he might have been passing on a rumor," Farrell Dean said. "Or a flat-out lie. Maybe even a malicious one."

"Go on," I said. "Tell me what he said."

Farrell Dean laced his fingers through mine. "He said the man who took you off the island didn't steal you. He bought you."

It took a moment for the words to penetrate. I'd been *sold*?

While my mother lay dying, I'd been taken out of Rory's arms and *sold*. Like a piece of merchandise. To populate an experiment.

"There's more." Farrell Dean's voice was uneven. "According to Evan Marchrest, the midwife wasn't the one who sold you."

He couldn't mean what it sounded like he meant.

I turned it all around in my mind, searching for another

option, but there wasn't one. No one had been there with the children but my dying mother, the midwife, and my father. My father, whom I'd only just begun to like, who had been my mother's refuge, her choice over bitter, twisted Tristan. I felt as if the wind had been knocked out of me.

"Evan Marchrest said his mother was afraid of Eric Alleyn," Farrell Dean said. "So she went along with his story about you dying. And then, when Gabriel wanted your body—which no one could have predicted—then Eric Alleyn blamed her. He said the midwife was the one who had buried you, not him. That was his excuse for not being able to tell Gabriel where to find you."

It couldn't be true, I told myself. The midwife was lying.

But even as I was telling myself this, my mind was going back to that peculiar tension in the Alleyn house when Rufus came in and saw me, his remarks about keeping me safe, the cryptic argument between him and Mick. I remembered the look on Eric Alleyn's face when he first saw me, a look of shock, of dread.

Farrell Dean was still talking, his voice low, his breath warm against my cheek. "When Eric Alleyn kept blaming the midwife, when he really did seem to be losing his mind, she ran away. She came to this side of the island and has been living here ever since, counting on Gabriel to protect her if your father ever comes after her. That's her story, anyway."

Two girls. Identical. One expendable.

"How much did I fetch?"

"That's what doesn't make sense," Farrell Dean said. "I wouldn't have pegged Eric Alleyn as the mercenary sort."

I didn't answer; I was thinking about my sister, piecing things together. This information explained a lot. Fiona hadn't known the truth about what had happened to me. That's why she'd let Rory and Angus start out for Ionia—she didn't think her uncle would haul off and kill Eric Alleyn at

215

the bare mention of my return.

But then Tor had shown up, and chances were he knew that Eric Alleyn had sold me—because he was the Council Chief's son. He knew all sorts of things.

And he must have told Fiona. That was why she'd suddenly decided he had to go after her brothers and keep them from talking. But she couldn't bring herself to tell me the truth, and Tor couldn't, either. He'd been talking around it all day, trying to make me believe Gabriel might kill my father, but not wanting to tell me exactly why. Their history was a keg of gunpowder and I was a match, that was what he'd said.

Farrell Dean broke into my thoughts. "Remember this is just a rumor."

I shook my head. "It's true. Tor knows it is. He's the Council Chief's son, and he knows what happened back then. He doesn't like Eric Alleyn—he said it would solve a lot of problems if Fiona gave him too much medicine—he said—" Another thought distracted me. "Did my father know what they were going to do to me? Did he know he was selling me to be a lab rat?"

"Stop it," Farrell Dean said, taking me by both shoulders. "Listen to me: we don't know if this is true. It all comes down to the midwife's word against your father's, and she wouldn't even talk to me. I got the whole thing secondhand, from her son. I tried and tried to get her to talk to me, but she wouldn't even let me in the house. I kept hanging around, helping her son with the wood, trying to get in her good graces so she'd let me in the door. But she never would. Don't you think that sounds suspicious?"

"I think it sounds like she's afraid of my father."

Another thought hit me: Rufus wasn't afraid of my father, but he was angry with him. And now, as I thought it over, I realized that Rufus hadn't asked who had taken me, and neither had Mick. That should have been the first thing they wanted to know, but they didn't ask because they didn't need to. They already knew who had sent me away.

"It fits the facts," I said, and my voice came out cracked.

"The best lies always do. So bracket it off for now. I wouldn't even have told you until I'd gotten more information, but I bet Gabriel knows the story and believes it. That's got to be why he hates your father so much."

Gabriel hated Eric Alleyn not because my father's backward ways delayed the medical care that might have saved my mother and me, and not because he failed to protect me from a kidnapper. Because he sold me. He sold Gabriel's niece. Rachel's baby.

And if Gabriel suddenly found proof that the midwife's tale was true—if, for instance, his dead niece turned out to be alive, having escaped from the experiment into which she'd been sold—then Tor's wild predictions wouldn't be farfetched at all. Eric Alleyn would be a dead man. If Gabriel didn't kill him, Rufus very well might. And what would happen to the family then?

Did I care?

That's what I was wondering when the key turned in the lock.

Chapter 21

The unlocked door was what saved us. The intruder thought he was unlocking the door, but instead he locked it, and that bought me a precious few seconds—not enough to get out a window, but enough to get into the bathroom and behind the door.

In the bedroom the door opened and a light flicked on.

My cap! I'd left my cap on Farrell Dean's bed.

Cautiously I peered through the crack in the door. Farrell Dean was half sitting, one hand shading his eyes from the light, the other under the covers. I saw no sign of my cap.

Standing at the foot of the bed was Gabriel Drewblood.

"Sorry to wake you," he said, not sounding sorry at all. "But I want answers, and I want them now."

Behind him, out of my line of sight, the door shut. Who else was there? Earl?

I'd heard about this sort of interrogation technique; it happened sometimes in Optica. Wardens surprised someone during the night, disorienting him, causing him to speak in a panic after being jerked out of sleep.

"How do you know Eric Alleyn?" Gabriel said.

"I've met him," Farrell Dean said. He swung his legs out of bed and reached for his shirt, draped over a nearby chair. "I've had one meal with him. That's all."

As he turned I saw his back clearly for the first time, and I pressed a hand to my mouth in dismay. Long dark scabs slashed the full length of his back, crossing each other here and there. In places the scabs had come off, leaving puckered and angry red streaks.

Gabriel was looking at the wounds, too, but they didn't affect his demeanor. "How well do you know Eric Alleyn's daughter?" he said.

"Not as well as I'd like," Farrell Dean said, pulling on the white shirt. "But my understanding is that she's spoken for. More or less."

I deserved that.

But even as I felt heat rise in my face I knew Farrell Dean wasn't aiming to wound me. He was focused on the man in front of him, the man we hoped would help us. He was thinking about Fiona and Tor, not about me.

Farrell Dean stood up and began pulling his pants on over his pajama bottoms. Gabriel stepped forward and reached for something on the bed.

"How do you explain this?" His thumb and forefinger were pinched together. I couldn't see what he was holding— from where I was, there seemed to be nothing but air.

Farrell Dean leaned forward as if to get a better look. "A red hair?" He shrugged. "Did your maid forget to change the sheets after your niece's last visit?"

Gabriel's face darkened and I stifled a groan. Farrell Dean really did not need to antagonize this man. But then, what could he say about that tell-tale red hair? Sorry, Gabriel—your niece broke into your house and was curled up on my bed until thirty seconds ago, and now she's hiding in the bathroom?

"Don't play games with me." Gabriel's voice was low and dangerous and he moved toward Farrell Dean, crowding him.

Farrell Dean didn't step back.

He returned Gabriel's gaze calmly for three or four seconds, then pulled the chair sideways, sat down, and began putting on his boots.

"Your sick friend showed up with two of the Alleyn boys, none of whom I'd trust further than I could throw him," Gabriel said.

"I don't trust the Alleyns either," Farrell Dean said, glancing up at Gabriel. "But you've only got my word for that." He finished tying his boot laces and stood up.

"You're not leaving this house until you've answered my questions," Gabriel said.

"Fine. Ask away."

"I'll give you another stripe on your back for each lie."

I winced, but Farrell Dean merely looked impatient. "I don't have time to waste on lies," he said, "and I expect you don't either."

Gabriel stared at him for a long moment. The two of them were face to face, both grim, both tense. They looked incongruous in the comfortable room with its mellow golden-yellow walls, with its plush white comforter and array of soft pillows. Optica would have made a more suitable background. Would the civilized room keep Gabriel from carrying out his threats? I doubted it.

Gabriel crossed his arms over his chest. "First question. Where did you come from?" he said.

Farrell Dean answered without hesitation. "As I told you this morning, I came from another island, from a small city called Optica. It's walled in and controlled by a group of tyrants and their thugs. They're killing off my friends. That's why I came to this island—to get help."

"How did you get from there to here?"

"In a boat. I assume it's still on the beach on the south side of the island, if you care to send someone to look for it.

It isn't fancy, but I'm pretty sure it's made of a wood you don't have here on your island."

"And after you landed?"

"I walked up a path from the beach and came to the Alleyns' house. That's when I met Eric Alleyn. Angus gave me this." Farrell Dean pointed to the half-healed split on his lower lip. "Then he was sorry and showed me the way into Doria, to the doctor's clinic. Later I saw you eating dinner in a building with a big front window, and a man was standing beside the table talking to you. I started to go in to speak to you, but you went out a side door and got in your truck and drove away before I could catch you. I think now that maybe that man told you about Ezzie, but then I didn't know Ezzie was here. After you left I started asking around, trying to learn where I could find you. When I did, I followed you."

"On foot?"

"At first," Farrell Dean said. "I followed the footpath until it came out on the bigger road, and then a man named Evan Marchrest came by and let me ride in his wagon."

At the name, Gabriel shifted slightly.

"When I got to Ionia this morning, I started looking for you again," Farrell Dean said. "Someone pointed me to Rain, and the rest you know."

"And why did you go to all this trouble to track me down?" Gabriel said. "Why me?"

Farrell Dean paused, just for a fraction of a second. "Because I recognized you," he said. "You look exactly like your brother."

It was so quiet I was afraid they could hear me breathing. Gabriel didn't move a muscle. I almost thought he hadn't heard Farrell Dean's words.

When he spoke, and I had to strain my ears to hear.

"I should give you another flogging for that," he said. "I should beat you until you can't stay on your feet."

Farrell Dean's gaze was level. "Only if you beat people for telling the truth," he said. Gabriel started to retort but Farrell Dean raised his voice and kept talking.

"Your brother's name was Rafe," he said. "Short for Raphael. He was my instructor in school. He wrote books and drew maps and he lived with a woman named Lonna. I think they had two children, but in Optica babies are separated from their parents at birth, so it's hard to know for certain who they are, or even if they survived infancy."

Rafe had children—I'd known that—but only now did I realize that meant I probably had cousins in Optica—if, as Farrell Dean said, they'd survived infancy. Did Rafe even know? Surely he did. Surely he at least had a guess.

"Rafe hated that he couldn't raise his own children," Farrell Dean was saying. "He hated the walls around our city, hated being constantly watched, constantly controlled, constantly manipulated, and he taught the children in his classes to hate those things, too. He taught us to want freedom. He taught us to want justice. He was a good man."

Gabriel stared at him silently for a long time. I couldn't read his face, but I was sure there was no easing of tension in it.

"I'll give you credit for cleverness," he said at last, and his voice was strained. "You've been talking with Tor Van Stavern. Or Fiona."

Farrell Dean shook his head. "I knew your brother," he said. "They never did."

"*My brother is dead!*"

I clapped my hands over my ears at Gabriel's shout, but Farrell Dean didn't flinch.

"Yes," he said. "He's dead. He died ten days ago, at a few minutes past eight o'clock in the evening. The entire city saw him die." Farrell Dean's voice was even. Only the tenseness of his jaw told me how hard this was for him.

"He was shot as a thief," he said. "Ostensibly. But really he was shot for leading a covert rebellion against the Watchers. I was helping him. I wanted to save his life—I'd have died to save him. He was Optica's best hope—the rest of us were just his extra eyes and hands and feet.

"But I couldn't save him, no one could save him, and then there were other executions. They went on and on and on. We couldn't stop them. And there will be more, unless you help us. That's why I'm here—to ask Rafe's brother for help."

Gabriel had shifted and I couldn't see his face any more, but I could see his hands. He was clenching and unclenching his fists, and though I was still afraid for Farrell Dean I felt so sorry for Gabriel—all in the same moment he'd learned his brother had lived, and had died. Surely he wouldn't shoot the messenger—surely he'd trust Farrell Dean, and help us.

Though he didn't know there was an "us." He didn't know I was me. If he knew, without doubt he'd help. After all, his vengeance, his anger—they were because my father hadn't protected my mother and me. He loved me, Gabriel did, even if he didn't know me. He had dreamt of a redheaded Lost Child. And he was Rafe's brother—Rafe, who had been a better father to me than my real one ever was.

I should tell him. I should step out from my hiding place and tell him who I really was. Even if I had to explain that we were experiments, Rafe and I. Even if Eric Alleyn got hurt because the truth came out.

But before I could move, the bedroom door opened. Farrell Dean looked that direction and gave a slight nod. Who had come in? Earl? But I thought he'd been inside the room the whole time. Had Gabriel's yelling woken Rain?

Then she came into my line of sight. It wasn't Rain—it was Carol.

She was wearing a long plain nightgown and her fading

blonde hair was loose around her shoulders. She went straight up to her husband and stepped in between him and Farrell Dean.

"Gabriel," she said softly. "Come to bed."

And like a mother with a very small child, she took him by the hand and led him away.

"I'll be just outside," Earl said. "I suggest you stay put. He's not finished with you."

As soon as the door closed Farrell Dean was with me. "Go," he said. "Go now while they're distracted."

"We should tell him. We should tell Gabriel who I am."

Farrell Dean shook his head. "Not yet," he said. "Once we tell him, there's no going back. He'll go after your father and chances are one or the other will die, whether the midwife's story is true or not."

He twisted my hair and crammed it under my cap, then unlocked the window and shoved it open. For a long moment we listened—there was no sign of the security man, but I heard Woof panting and moving about down below.

"Be careful," Farrell Dean said, lacing his fingers together. I stepped in his cupped hands and, as he boosted me up, swung one leg out the window.

"You too." Then I was out, and the window was closing behind me, and Woof was ecstatically licking my hands.

My instinct was to run for the fence and get out of there as fast as I could, but I forced myself to take the same care leaving that I'd used coming in.

Finally I was outside the fence—Woof moaning piteously behind me—and moving stealthily through the wooded area toward the path that led to Nana and Grandfather's.

It was very dark, that night—there was no moon, and the clouds hid the stars—and so I had to go slowly, feeling my way step by step. I wasn't willing to take the exposed path because it was in full view of the security man's position, but

I stayed as close to it as possible. I didn't want to get lost in the woods.

It shouldn't have been difficult to get back to my grandparents' house, even staying off the path. It hadn't been bad earlier, when I'd gone up the hill to Gabriel's.

But I'd been happy then, knowing I was going to see Farrell Dean, playing spy games without any real danger involved. Now I was miserable. My father—my own flesh and blood—had sold me. The news distracted me, narrowed my vision, and even the trees and underbrush seemed to resent my intrusion. They sprang up out of nowhere, grabbing at my cap or thrusting low branches out to trip me.

I knew it was only half a mile to Nana and Grandfather's house, but in the dark, groping practically blind, it felt like ten. I was so very tired, and the farther I got from Farrell Dean, the more tired and disheartened I felt.

Something snagged my pants and I stopped to free it from the briery vine. It took forever—about a million tiny thorns had to be gently disentangled, one by one. I had a depressing vision of myself still there, at daybreak, trying to explain to a scolding Tor why I had sneaked out on him.

Finally Nana and Grandfather's house came into sight, its bulk darker than the other darkness. I walked faster now, almost jogging, across the level mowed yard. As I rounded the corner, heading for my bedroom window, I was thinking about Farrell Dean. What would Gabriel say to him come morning? Would he look for the boat to verify our story?

That was smart of Farrell Dean, I thought, to mention the wood the boat was made of. Was it true? Did that sort of tree not grow here, or had Farrell Dean made that up on the spot?

Thinking these thoughts, so very close to safety and sleep, I forgot to be careful.

That's when he grabbed me.

Chapter 22

I woke feeling nauseated and when I sat up, the room spun and a splitting pain shot through my head.

Clenching my eyes shut I waited for the dizziness to pass, for the nausea to subside. Gradually it did, and then, cautiously, I opened my eyes.

I was on a dingy brown couch in a room that looked uncared for. A jumble of wires and metal pieces lay on an old scarred table alongside a black metal box with knobs and dials on its side. Dust balls drifted across a mud-tracked floor, and light filtered through a dirty window with half-open curtains.

Where was I? What time was it?

Very carefully I got to my feet, afraid I'd pass out again and hurt myself falling. But though my head still hurt, the dizziness seemed to be gone, and I was able to make my way to the window and look out on a muddy path and a wall of dark trees. The sky was cloudy and gray, but clearly morning was well along. How had I gotten here?

I turned away from the window, looking for a way out, but just as I spotted the door, it opened. It was the nondescript man from Ionia—the man who'd loved my mother. Tristan.

"Ah. Princess Fiona is finally awake," he said, eyeing me

coldly. "I was beginning to think you'd sleep all day."

"Why am I here?" My throat hurt when I spoke.

He was carrying a bottle of something dark.

"First things first," he said, shaking the bottle. "Come into the kitchen."

I backed away from him.

Tristan raised his eyebrows. "You're here because I caught you," he said. "And you deserved to be caught. You were acting like your mother, sneaking around, leaving poor gullible Tor to bear the consequences of your desertion."

My head hurt so much I wasn't even afraid of him.

"I didn't desert anybody," I said. "I couldn't sleep and I went for a walk."

"That's right," he said, coming toward me. "You took a little walk and went to visit your secret lover."

"I went to visit my cousin Rain."

He gave me a look filled with contempt. "I'm not a fool. Now come on. We have work to do."

He took hold of my arm and I tried to muster the energy to run, to fight, whatever I had to do, but I was so unbelievably tired. I tried to make myself a dead weight, but he gave an impatient yank and I half-fell against him, and then, as I regained my balance, a loud crackling noise filled the room.

Tristan turned toward the table. It was the black box—one of its knobs had lit up and was shining green in the dimness of the room.

I vaguely remembered hearing this same sound earlier, through a welter of baffling dreams.

And had I heard Gabriel's voice? I thought perhaps I had. He had said something about not drinking breakfast. Had he been here?

Surely he hadn't followed me from his house—I'd been careful leaving, I knew I had been. I'd been careful until I thought I was safely back at Nana and Grandfather's. And wherever I was now, it certainly wasn't Gabriel's neat, clean house, or his shop in town. Was this Tristan's house?

The box began to produce human voices, and for the first time I saw Tristan look pleased—or at least smug. Dropping my arm he went to the box and turned a dial, and suddenly Farrell Dean's voice was in the room.

"What do you mean, she's missing?" he said. "Since when?"

Someone else said something I couldn't make out. Tristan set down his bottle and fiddled with the dial again.

"But it's past noon," Farrell Dean said. "Nobody's seen her at all today?"

"It looks like she slept in her bed," Rory said. "But nobody's seen her since Angus and I got back from the hospital last night. When we realized she was missing Tor went into town to look for her—it was still early, and high tide, so he took a coracle—but nobody he spoke to has seen her since yesterday either. Angus and I have been all around the inlet and through the woods, but we can't find any sign of her, not anywhere."

Gabriel said, "How well can she swim?"

"Not at all," Farrell Dean said, just as Tor said, "Like a fish."

Then Farrell Dean said, "Not if she hit her head," just as Tor said, "Assuming she's not injured."

There was a brief pause. Then Gabriel said, "Earl, call out the men. Have a couple of them drag the inlet. Leave one man at the hospital and divide the rest between the south woods and Ionia. She could be in a shop, in a house, anywhere. Make no assumptions. Knock on every door. I'll take the truck to Doria in case she caught a ride home. It seems unlikely, but it's a logical place to check."

"No," Tor said, his voice rising. "Don't go there—not yet. Eric Alleyn—he—it'll—his daughter—he isn't well. Let's keep looking around here. Fiona wouldn't have gone home without me. There's no need to upset him."

"Eric Alleyn's nerves are not my concern," Gabriel said, and then his voice changed. "And just where do you think you're going?"

"To the midwife's." It was Farrell Dean. "To find Fiona." The quotations marks around the name were so loud they were practically visible, but apparently Gabriel didn't notice or didn't know what to make of it.

"Why would she go see the midwife?" he said.

"Because I told her about meeting the midwife's son, and she was curious."

There was a blank silence. As far as the others knew, Farrell Dean and I had never been alone together to have any such conversation.

Tor didn't know what was going on, but he tried to cover Farrell Dean's mistake anyway. "That's right, you did," he said. "At least you told me, and I told her, and ... But I don't think she'd go there. That's ancient history."

"Not anymore." Farrell Dean's voice was more muted; he must have been moving toward the door.

"Wait!" Tor said.

"He could be right," Rain said. "She has always been fascinated by Rowena Marchrest. The last time she was here she wanted to go meet her, but nobody else thought it was a good idea."

"We thought it was morbid." That was Angus. "Because it was."

"I should have taken her myself," Rain said, and Tor began to object, but Farrell Dean spoke over him.

"So she might have thought someone would stop her, or maybe she didn't think, maybe she just woke up early and took it into her head to go, and so she went." The hope in Farrell Dean's voice made my heart ache. He desperately wanted to believe I'd walked off of my own free will, in pursuit of the truth about my birth.

"But the midwife's place isn't very far away," Rory said. "If Fiona went there, she should have been back ages ago."

"It won't hurt to check," Gabriel said. "Let's go."

"But someone should stay here in case she comes back." This was Tor, sounding panicked. "Farrell Dean, you stay. And Angus and Rory. I'll go with Gabriel."

"No," Farrell Dean said, over Angus's angry mutter. "I'm going."

"No, you're not."

"Yes, I am. You can't stop me."

Tor said something else to Farrell Dean but Gabriel spoke, too, and he was louder. "Fiona is our concern, not yours." His voice was carefully even, too even. "You're out of line."

"Good thing I am," Farrell Dean said. "Given that the rest of you just want to stand around and argue."

Several voices rose in protest, interrupting and obscuring each other. Angus, sounding aggrieved, said, "I've been looking all morning and I haven't even stopped to eat!"

Rain said, "There's too much testosterone in this room."

And Farrell Dean said, "Red could be hurt, she could be lost, and all you care about is F—."

There was a scuffling sound and many voices rose clamorously, cutting across each other. Something fell hard and there was a crash and the sound of glass breaking.

"Tor?" Angus's voice was incredulous.

Were they actually fighting, Tor and Farrell Dean?

Across the room from me, Tristan laughed. "Like panicked ants," he said.

"Enough!" That was Gabriel.

In the wake of his roar came a brief window of silence. Then Farrell Dean spoke.

"I'm going to the midwife's," he said.

"Then I'm going too." That was Tor.

"They'll be at each other's throats the whole way," Rain said. "I'd better go with them."

"No!" That was Tor. "We won't be at each other's throats. We—I—"

"You both have a thing for Fiona," Rain said. "I get it. But the important thing right now is to find her. Then she can sort the two of you out."

"I don't have a thing for Fiona," Farrell Dean said—snarled, really—and Tor said, "Oh yes, you do!"

"Maybe Angus and I should go to the midwife's." That was Rory.

"I don't want to see that old witch," Angus said. "She gives me the willies. Let's go back to the hospital instead and see if Fee's gone to check on Ezzie."

"Why on earth would Fiona check on Ezzie?" That was Gabriel.

"Because she's tenderhearted." Tor was still frantically trying to put out fires the others were busily setting. "You know Fiona, always looking out for other people—I mean, just look at how she's taken care of Eric Alleyn all these years, and when my father was sick and Mother was away Fiona was the one who kept our house going, and when Judith Erskine had her accident and all her children were frightened it was Fiona who arranged for regular meals to be brought in to them and came herself to read to the children every day and she didn't even live in town—"

He broke off, and a slight pause followed his outburst.

"It's true!" Tor said. "Fiona always takes care of other people!"

"Nobody's saying anything against Fiona." Gabriel sounded like he was reining in his temper with great effort. "I know you're upset, Tor, but try to focus."

"Wait!" Rain called out. "I'll go with you."

Farrell Dean, sounding further away, said something that I couldn't catch. Gabriel muttered something nearby.

Rain said, "Of course I will. Maybe it'll finally come in handy. And Tor is going too, safety in numbers and all that. So don't worry. I'll see you later."

"Rory and Angus, you two check the hospital," Gabriel said. "I can't see why she'd visit Ezzie, but if she's been injured someone might have taken her there. The men and I will split up and cover other territory. If anyone finds Fiona, bring her straight back here. If we don't find her by nightfall, I'm going to Eric Alleyn's whether Tor likes it or not."

Tristan was watching me with cruel amusement. I was gripping the edge of the table so hard my fingers hurt. From the black box came the sound of more movement. Voices rose and fell in the background, blurred and distant. Doors opened and closed.

Then there was a long silence. Everyone had gone—they were all out looking for me, and even I didn't know where I was.

Tristan reached to turn the dial, but then, out of the silence, a single voice spoke.

"That poor child," a woman said. Carol, I thought. It must be Carol.

"That poor, poor child," she said again. "Please protect her. Bring her safely home."

If someone answered her, I couldn't hear the words.

Tristan adjusted the dials again, clicking one off, then another on.

"That was Gabriel's living room," he said. "I have bugs all over." He was absolutely cheerful.

"Bugs?"

"Listening devices."

"Like where?" I said, trying to sound conversational,

hoping he didn't have one in the guest room where Farrell Dean and I had talked.

"Too many to list," Tristan said, waving a hand. "Listen." He spun the dial once, then again and again. I caught snatches of conversations in voices I didn't know.

"Two for the price of one," someone said.
"But I only need one," another voice answered.

"Rainy season. It makes them multiply."
"Awful things breed in the damp."

"This isn't a good time. He'll be back any moment."
"It's never a good time. How will we get it finished before his birthday?"

"… stay here, but you go look. I know you want to."

I caught my breath. The sound was obscured by heavy static, but I recognized Nana's voice.

"This one is always bad," Tristan said. "Leave it to your grandparents to make trouble." He adjusted the dial, and then Grandfather's voice came through, not as clear as if he were in the room with us, but clear enough.

"Yes, lovey, it's true I'd like to go," he said. "But I can't. What if you have one of your foggy spells?"

"I'll try very hard not to."

The anxiety in her wavery old voice brought tears to my eyes.

"It's all right, lovey," Grandfather said. "We'll be the lookouts. If Fiona turns up here, you can feed her milk and cookies and I'll go tell Gabriel. It'll take both of us, you see? One to tend to Fiona, and one to call off the search."

Tristan turned down the volume. "You see?" he said,

smirking. "Everything I need to know, right at my fingertips. I even have one at the Marchrest house. A leftover, in fact, from a little problem a long time ago. Never thought it would come in handy today."

"But none on the other side of the island?" I was thinking about Eric Alleyn's home.

Tristan stared at me with his vivid blue eyes. "Across the *island*? Don't you know anything at all about surveillance?"

I thought of the banks of computer screens in Optica's watchtower, the cameras, wired and wireless, the telescopes and patrol cars and wardens. But I didn't say a word.

"I thought not," Tristan said, smirking at me again. Why had my mother ever loved this obnoxious man?

He hadn't answered my question. That meant he didn't have devices on the other side of the island, or else he'd have bragged about them. His technology must not be good enough for that distance. In fact, his system seemed primitive, compared to Optica's. No visuals, only staticky sound, and he could only monitor one location at a time.

"Now," Tristan said, bringing me back to the current crisis. "Into the kitchen."

I didn't want to do anything he said, but my head was so fuzzy I didn't think I could manage an escape just yet. Plus my limbs felt heavy, slow, like they belonged to somebody else. What had this man done to me?

The best I could do was make a virtue of necessity. Maybe if I acted cooperative now, he'd underestimate me later. And at least it seemed he was working alone—surely I could get away from just one man. None of Gabriel's other men seemed to be around.

"Gabriel's not going to be happy about this," I said.

Tristan smiled. "Gabriel doesn't own me," he said. "I let him think he does, but he never has."

The kitchen was as grimy as the other room. Did Tristan

live here, in this squalor? It wasn't a bad house—the walls were square to each other, and someone had obviously spent considerable time framing the windows with scrolled trim work—but the place was filthy and depressingly neglected. Worse, from my perspective, it seemed to be completely isolated. The kitchen window, like the other one, showed nothing but trees all around.

Tristan pushed me down in a chair and draped me in a sheet. Then he snapped open a box of white petroleum jelly and began rubbing it around my forehead and all over my ears, humming softly to himself all the while.

I didn't like his hands on my face, but I made myself sit still. What on earth was he doing? At least it didn't involve guns or knives.

"Now lean over the sink so I can get your hair wet," he said, grabbing my wrist and pulling me to my feet.

That sounded like a fairly vulnerable position, even with no weapons in view.

"This won't hurt, Fiona," Tristan said. He looked straight into my eyes and didn't blink, as if that would convince me of his truthfulness.

"Why do you want my hair wet?" I said.

"Because it's the first step," he said, picking up a piece of paper from the counter. "See?" He waved the paper as if I could read it from across the room. "Wet hair thoroughly."

"And what's the second step?"

He smiled. "Apply dye."

I backed away from him.

"No thanks," I said. "If I'd been given a choice I might not have picked red, but I'm used to it now." Not only that, but it was my *name*, for pete's sake.

Tristan shook his head. "This isn't open for debate," he said. "The doors are locked. I'm stronger than you. And if I have to, I'll get out the chloroform again. We can do this the

235

easy way, or we can do this the hard way, but we're going to do it."

Chloroform. *Again.*

That explained why I couldn't remember how I got here. I vaguely remembered reaching for the window at my grand-parents' house, and I remembered instinctively elbowing backwards when someone's arm went around my neck.

After that there was only darkness until I'd woken, nau-seated and in pain, on the couch. He'd drugged me.

"It's only hair, Fiona," he said, as if I were an idiot. "I ought to cut it, since it's a bit longer than hers, but I won't even do that. I only intend to color it."

For a moment I didn't understand. Did he know about me? Was my hair longer than Fiona's—or, since he kept call-ing me Fiona, was hers longer than mine? I was confusing myself.

Then it hit me.

"My mother?" I said. "You're dying my hair to look like my mother's?"

Tristan nodded. His eyes were too bright, too vivid. They scared me.

"It's the right time," he said. "You're sixteen. You're the same age Rachel was when she left me for that redhead fool."

The right time for what?

Was he making me into an imitation Rachel, a proxy? And then what would he do to me? My skin crawled and panic rose in my chest. I had to get away. But how could I, with these heavy limbs? My own body was trapping me, mak-ing me stay.

Fighting to stay calm I caught hold of a passing thought: My mother had been young, as young as me, when she crossed the island on her own to escape from this man. She had done it. If she could get away from him, so could I.

I could do it. I'd have to bide my time, that was all. I'd

have to be cooperative until the effects of the chloroform wore off, which would be soon, I hoped, very soon.

I took a deep breath. "All right," I said, and walked over to the sink. It wasn't very clean, but it was big enough that I didn't think I'd have to touch my face to it.

Let him dye my hair. That would take time, and meanwhile my body would be coming back to life, my arms and legs waking up, my headache dimming. Time was good. Time was on my side.

I didn't like bending over, leaving my neck and back completely exposed. But all Tristan did was pour cold water over my head until my hair was drenched.

After that he gave me a towel to protect my face, and then I smelled chemicals as he poured the dye into my hair and worked it in. The feel of his fingers on my scalp made my skin crawl.

"Now I wait ten minutes," he said. "Can you breathe down there? I'd let you raise up, but if that dye runs down your neck it'll stain your clothes."

"I'm okay," I said. I didn't make the mistake of thinking he was concerned about me. He just didn't want his project marred.

It wasn't comfortable, down in the sink. All the blood was rushing to my head. But at least down here I didn't have to face Tristan. Down here I could focus, I could think.

People were looking for me. Someone would find me. But how? Had he left any trace, any clue to where I'd gone?

Behind me Tristan moved around, speaking to me now and then, but mostly humming to himself.

Where was my cap? I'd had it on when he grabbed me, but I didn't have it now. Had it fallen somewhere on the way? Maybe someone would find it.

Farrell Dean was on the wrong track about the Marchrests' house. But he was right that if I'd left on my own, that's exactly where I would have gone. I wanted to know why my father had sold me.

Tears welled in my eyes and I blinked them away. My mother had somehow gotten involved with one bad man after another.

I couldn't think about this now.

I had to think of a way to get free from Tristan. Whatever he was planning, he obviously was up to no good. Maybe he would hurt me, maybe he wouldn't, but something bad would happen, to me or someone else. Tristan, for all his creepy cheerful humming, was out for blood.

I wished Farrell Dean wasn't wasting time going to the midwife's house. I wished he were coming straight here, wherever here was.

"Where exactly are we?" I asked from my cave of a sink.

Tristan stopped humming. After a long pause, he said, "What do you mean?"

Uh-oh. We were someplace Fiona should recognize.

"My head really hurts, Tristan," I said. "Everything looks familiar, but then it looks unfamiliar, too. Like I'm remembering a dream. I think you gave me too much chloroform."

He didn't answer. Was he suspicious? But how could he be—I looked like Fiona, exactly like Fiona, and I really did have a headache and he'd drugged me with chloroform. Fiona really could be confused, just like I was.

His silence was scaring me.

"Tristan? Can I get up now?"

"Not yet. I have to rinse your hair."

Again he poured cold water, and rubbed at my scalp, and poured more cold water, and still more, until I was shivering. Finally he wrapped a towel around my head and let me stand up.

"Rub it as dry as you can," he said, and watched while I

did it. Then he handed me a comb.

"You don't look good," he said, leaving the room. "I'll turn up the heat."

I scanned the room for a means of escape. The window was sealed all around, with no way to open it. Could I find something to break it?

But then Tristan was back. He crossed his arms over his chest and examined me critically.

"You're green," he said. "How am I supposed to make you look like Rachel when you're green?"

"I'm queasy. The fumes from the dye must be getting to me," I said. That, or being chloroformed, but I thought I'd better not mention the chloroform again. Tristan was looking pretty testy.

I knew it would make him suspicious, but I had to try. "Maybe some fresh air would help," I said, trying to sound casual.

He pursed his lips and didn't answer, but after a moment he took my arm and pulled me through the room with the black box, through a sort of entryway room that was crammed with fishing poles and nets, and then outside, onto a deck that went all the way around the back of the house, extending out over a rapidly flowing river.

"We'll stay back here," he said. "And if anyone comes down the path, you'd better be quiet." He pulled something out of his back pocket and showed it to me. A knife.

I nodded, hardly listening, I was so relieved to recognize where I was.

"We're at Grandfather's fishing cabin," I said, and then was struck by a frightening thought. This was where Angus, Rory, and Ezzie had been. How long had they stayed? Several hours? "Do you have a bug here?" I asked.

Tristan shook his head. "What would I hear? No one ever comes here anymore. No one but me, and obviously I don't need to listen to myself."

Hope was rising in me. Someone else *had* been here, and maybe—just maybe—either Rory or Angus would think about that odd collection of wires, that black box. Surely they'd noticed it.

"No wonder it felt unfamiliar," I said. "I haven't been here for years."

Tristan shrugged. "And it's seen better days," he said.

I didn't think he was setting a trap for me, but just to be sure I didn't respond. For all I knew, this place had always been a dump.

The river rushed by beneath us, fast and brown. It was a barrier, limiting the direction I could run—but if I could get away, we were only three-quarters of a mile or so from Ionia. And we were right on the path to Doria. Eventually someone would come this way, heading to the other side of the island to look for me. When they did, how could I get their attention?

Tristan was eyeing my hair.

"It's darker than hers," he said, frowning.

"Will it look lighter when it's dry?"

"It better," he said, and it sounded like a threat.

"My own hair looks darker when it's wet than when it's dry," I said, and Tristan shrugged and took my arm.

"You don't look as sallow now," he said. "We'll go back inside. You can eat while we listen to the next installment."

Did he think he was being funny? I couldn't tell.

My legs seemed to behave marginally better, but I was still headachy and unnaturally tired. Casting one longing look up the path to town, I obediently climbed the stairs and went inside.

Chapter 23

Tristan brought out some cheese and bread, and though my stomach still felt odd I made myself eat. I'd need the strength.

I was sitting on the couch, working at combing my coal-black hair, when the box crackled to life again. This time a different bulb turned green. Tristan leaned over and fiddled with dials for a moment, and then a male voice said, "—same as yesterday."

"You invited him to come back?" That was a woman's voice, high and quavery. She sounded ancient.

"I didn't invite him, but he *is* back, looking for a friend who's gone missing. Fiona Alleyn, as a matter of fact. I told him we haven't seen her in years, but I don't think he's going away until he hears it from you as well."

"It's a strange group. This young man, and Tor Van Stavern, and Rain Drewblood. Do you suppose Tor has thrown over the Alleyn girl for a Drewblood?"

"I've no idea, Mother."

"And why is this other boy leading the search? Doesn't the Chief's boy have any natural leadership ability?"

The man said nothing.

"It's obvious what has happened. Fiona Alleyn got her feelings hurt and ran away because the Chief's son was canoodling with Rain Drewblood. That would be a wise move for Tor, politically speaking."

The man didn't respond, but Tristan did.

"It would be poetic justice," he said, his eyes fixed on the black box. "Let her see what it feels like." It was as if he had forgotten I was there.

"Eric Alleyn is a political liability, nowadays," the old woman continued querulously. "He once was a force to be reckoned with, but those days are long past. And it serves him right. I don't like living on this side of the island. I liked the other side much better, and I could have stayed there if not for him."

"Yes, Mother. Can you please deal with your visitors now? I have work to do."

After a loud creak and some rustling noises, we heard other voices. At first they were indistinct, distant. I started to think the entire conversation was going to take place at the front door, too far from Tristan's bug for us to hear. Then Farrell Dean said, "…while we're here. It'll only take a moment."

"No," the old woman said. "I don't like speaking of that."

"I'm not asking," Farrell Dean said.

The old woman grumbled a bit, but finally said, "Very well, then. But I must sit back down. I am old, as you might have noticed. It isn't polite to keep old people on their feet too long."

Tor said, "We'll wait outside."

Rain said something I couldn't catch, some sort of angry protest that grew muted.

The rustling moved closer. The loud creak sounded. What was that? Her chair?

Then Farrell Dean spoke. "Your son told me about what happened the night Rachel Alleyn died."

"Everybody knows about that," she said dismissively. "People like to discuss other people's hardships. I can't think why you've never heard the tale before."

"I have. But your son didn't tell the story the way other people tell it. He said the other baby didn't die. The twin."

"Dorians don't discuss that," the old woman said. "You're going to get cross-ways with Eric Alleyn, if you go around talking about that."

"I'm not from Doria," Farrell Dean said. "And I don't care about getting cross-ways with Eric Alleyn. I just want to know the truth."

The midwife was silent for a moment. "Locrians aren't usually so well-spoken," she said finally. "Or so nosy."

Farrell Dean ignored the comment. "Your son said you didn't know about– he called it the *transaction*—until after it was over."

"That is correct. Naturally I would have stopped it, otherwise."

"And yet Rory Alleyn says you took that baby out of his arms and told him she was dead. That sounds as if you were part of whatever happened that night. You took a living baby out of his arms, and carried her outside, and she never came back again."

There was a long silence.

"Rory Alleyn was all of five years old," the old woman said. "He was practically a baby himself. What can he re-member, after all this time?"

Farrell Dean said nothing.

"His father planted that evil seed in his little head," the old woman said. "Eric Alleyn taught that child what to 're-member.' The truth was something very different."

"This is no use to me," Tristan said, standing up and reaching for the knob.

"No, please—" I leapt to my feet as well and hurried to

243

the table. "Please let me hear—"

"It was all Eric Alleyn's doing," the old woman said, and Tristan's hand stopped. "He was distraught. Rachel was feverish, suffering a post-partum hemorrhage presumably due to retained placental tissue. Her condition didn't respond to the usual treatment, not to manual uterine massage, nor to oxytocin. I am not and have never been a surgeon, young man. There was nothing I could do. And mothers sometimes die. It happens, even in the best of circumstances. But Eric Alleyn apparently believed his wife should be miraculously exempt from all risk. He simply couldn't accept that there were complications. Eventually I was forced to bar him from the sick room. I told him he must go outside and calm himself, for his wife's sake. He did, but not until he'd managed to disturb the infants. One of them would not be quieted."

"Which one?"

"The one who stayed. The firstborn. She screamed and screamed, and Rachel grew distraught and that's not what was needed. So I left her and took the screaming babe outside to calm her, intending to send Eric back to his wife. But he was out at the gate speaking with a man. I couldn't see who it was, not with the darkness and shadows. Then Eric called out to me, telling me to take the screaming mite inside and bring him the quiet one. So that is what I did."

Was that the deciding factor? Fiona screamed, and stayed. I was quiet, and was taken.

"And then?"

"He came to meet me at the door. He took the child, and sent me back inside. He was her father. He wanted to show his babies to someone, to a friend, a relative, and no one wants to show off a screaming baby. That was what I thought."

Tristan's cold blue eyes met mine. I don't know what he was thinking—I wasn't even sure he really saw me.

"The man who took the baby away," Farrell Dean was saying, and once again Tristan reached for the knob, and this time I shoved his hand away and pushed in between him and the table. "What did he give in exchange for her?"

"Medicine. The stranger said he had something new, something that would work. Something that would save Rachel. And the price was a baby. That is what Eric said, when he came back into the house with it, and without the child."

Tristan took me by the shoulders, forcibly moved me aside. "I don't have time for this," he said. He clicked off the knob and the voices ceased. "You don't need to hear this," he said, pointing a finger at me. "It has nothing to do with you."

Nothing to do with me? My father had sold me. He had sold me for a chance to save my mother. And how could I blame him for that? He only had one wife, but he had an extra baby.

Tears stung my eyes and I turned away so this horrid man wouldn't see.

"You should have listened to me," Tristan said behind me. "I told you. Now you're upset, and I don't have time for that. I have work to do."

I ignored him and wiped my eyes on my sleeve.

My father had tried to save my mother's life, and he'd failed. No wonder he was tormented and bitter. No wonder he didn't seem to know how to look at me, what to say to me. He'd gambled me and he'd lost. He'd lost my mother, and he'd lost me too.

And if it had succeeded? If the medicine had saved Rachel's life, would it have been worth the price? Would *Rachel* have thought it worth the price?

It was like a nightmare that wouldn't stop. I was a pawn. In every world I found, I was a pawn—and an unsuccessful one, at that. My mother had died. Optica was dying. Eric Alleyn had gambled and lost. Meritt—

245

"Your hair is dry enough," Tristan said. "It's time to go."

Chapter 24

He dressed me in a cream-colored dress with woven lace edges. He did it himself without saying a word, stripping Rain's shirt off me and dropping it on the floor, then pulling the other over my head, smoothing it down, looking me over with his cold blue eyes.

I didn't want the dress to be my mother's, but I thought it must have been hers. I was sick at heart, stricken, and felt somehow as if wearing her clothes, her hair, I might become her, might crumble to dust as she was dust.

"Take off your pants," Tristan said.

I backed away from him, shaking my head.

"Take them off," he said impatiently. "She never wears pants. The dress is long enough without them."

With fumbling fingers I did as he said, trying to hurry, afraid if I didn't he'd pull them off me himself.

When I stood in front of him, barefoot, barelegged, he scanned me up and down and gave one nod. Of approval, I supposed.

Then he took out a package of cosmetics and began working on my face. "Her color is higher than yours," he said. "She always has roses in her cheeks."

He'd started talking about her in present tense.

I braced myself not to recoil from the touch of his

fingers. He was tapping one foot on the floor, twitching, tense. I didn't want to set him off.

"Time to go," he said finally, setting aside the pencil with which he'd blackened my eyebrows. "But first, look at what I've done."

I didn't want to look. But he took me by the shoulders and walked me to an oval mirror on a stand. A strange woman looked back at me—a dark-haired woman whose face was shaped like mine, whose eyes were the color of mine, whose dark brows and eyelashes stood out against her pale skin. Her cheeks were pink and her lips were red, far redder than anyone's naturally were. She looked unreal, like a painted doll.

She would be horrified by this charade. I could almost feel her, my mother, standing behind me, looking over my shoulder in disbelief at what he had made me be.

"No!" Tristan said, pinching me hard on the arm. "Don't cry! You'll ruin the makeup."

When he took me outside and led me up the path, away from Ionia, I walked slowly, dragging my feet. We were out in the open, on a public path, a place people traveled. Surely someone would come along.

"Hurry up," Tristan said.

"I can't. That drug you gave me makes my legs so heavy."

He snorted but stopped hauling away at my arm. He still kept a grip on it, though, and a tight enough one that I didn't dare try to pull away.

"We might be missing something on your box," I said.

"Doesn't matter. I've heard all I need to know."

"Like what?"

Tristan smirked but said nothing. After a little while we passed the turn-off to the footpath and the bridge. I'd never been past the bridge, not on this road. The path was broader here, and still empty. Why weren't any people out? Weren't

Gabriel's men supposed to be looking for me? I'd even settle for the men on horseback who were hunting Farrell Dean.

"Where are we going?" I said.

"My truck."

"Is it at your house?"

He gave me a scathing look. "Do you think I'd take you to my house? What if Gabriel came to ask me to help search for you?"

"Do you think he'd do that?" It seemed like a good idea to keep him talking—or maybe it was just that I was scared and couldn't stop talking myself.

"Of course he would. We're as close as brothers." His tone was sarcastic.

"I thought you really were," I said. "Rain said you were."

He snorted. "Not anymore. He lost the fire."

I wasn't sure what he meant, but I could guess. "He doesn't hate Eric Alleyn like you do?"

"Oh, he hates him. But no one hates him like I do." Tristan glanced at me. "I was referring to your mother."

"Gabriel never hated my mother."

"Yes, he did. He hated her for leaving him. But he couldn't hang on to it."

There wasn't any point in prolonging this discussion. I'd only make him angrier. Already he was stalking along, gripping my arm so hard it hurt. I thought I'd better change the subject. "If we're not going to your house, then where's your truck?"

"There's a pull-off up ahead," he said. "I hid it there."

Not that I cared where his truck was; I wasn't about to get in it with him. He could be taking me anywhere, and once we were in the truck there would be no escape. Trucks went too fast—I couldn't jump out. I couldn't leave any sign of my passing, any clue for Farrell Dean to follow. Trucks, I wholeheartedly agreed with Eric Alleyn, were a bad idea.

The sky above was dark with heavy clouds. What time was it? My head felt better, but everything that had happened today felt distorted. It had been after noon when Farrell Dean learned I was missing. Now it must surely be getting on toward evening—and tonight Gabriel would start out for Eric Alleyn's and would come down this road.

But by then it would be too late. We'd be gone from this place in seconds.

There was Tristan's truck, a dark gray one.

When we drew close to it I forced myself to relax. "I've always liked trucks," I said. "You know my father won't keep one, but they seem very handy. Do you like yours?"

Tristan shot me a cold glance. "Don't ask stupid questions," he said. "You know quite well I do."

"I was just making conversation," I said. "It's called being nice."

"Well, don't bother," he said. "No one else does."

"Maybe they just got tired of trying."

Tristan didn't reply. He was pulling open the truck door with one hand, and still holding my arm with the other.

"Get in," he said, shoving me toward the truck and pushing down on the top of my head.

I went down faster than he expected, all the way to the ground, scrambling away from him as he grabbed at me.

He caught the hem of my dress but I yanked away—I'd have left the whole thing in his hand if I'd had to—and started running, as fast as I could, back up the path toward Ionia.

But my legs were still too heavy, too unwieldy. I'd only made it twenty or thirty yards before Tristan caught me by my hair, jerking me backwards and off my feet.

"Get up, you little tramp," he said, hauling me up by my hair. Then he grabbed me by my shoulders and shook me so hard my teeth rattled.

"Do that again and I'll kill you," he said. His breath was

hot in my face. "You are not your mother. Don't ever forget that. *You* are expendable."

Then he dragged me back to the truck, not even slowing when I stumbled and almost fell.

"And *don't cry*," he said, shoving me inside and slamming the door.

Then he was in the seat beside me and the truck was moving, speeding down the lane away from Ionia.

I had never been in a car or truck before. The windows sealed off the normal outdoor sounds, birds, insects, wind. The seats were smooth and a panel of controls was laid out in front of Tristan. I paid close attention to what he did; I wasn't counting on having to drive this thing to get away from him, but I had to be prepared.

The road sped toward us, faster and faster. I thought about what Tor had said—deer in the road, pedestrians. Surely Tristan was going far too fast to stop for anything in his path. We were hurtling, flying along. The trees flashed past my window so quickly I began to feel queasy, or maybe it was the aftereffect of the chloroform.

That gave me an idea.

"I'm going to be sick," I said.

Tristan ignored me.

"Really," I said, pressing a hand to my mouth. "I am."

When I made a gagging sound, he pulled over to the side of the road and reached across me to open my door. He kept a grip on my hair and my dress as I leaned out.

"Don't get it on the dress," he said. "Keep it clean."

He yanked at my hair as he said this, and I nodded that I understood. Then I made the fake gagging noise again and leaned further from him. But his grip was relentless; I leaned against it as hard as I dared, but before I could try to yank away, he said, "That's enough drama," and pulled me back in.

We were moving again instantly.

251

At least now I knew how to open the door from the inside.

We rode in silence for a long time. I kept hoping he would come to his senses—this was a stupid thing to do, abducting Eric Alleyn's daughter—but every time I glanced at Tristan's profile he looked the same, bitter and determined.

"Do you have any water?" I asked.

"No."

"Then please, can we stop for a drink? Is there a well anywhere near?"

"No, we cannot. We have a schedule to keep."

"Why? Where are we going?"

"That's for me to know and you to find out," he said, glancing at me with a frown. "You've smeared your makeup," he said. "Your mother never looked like that. She was always clean, always elegant."

"Even when she was being drugged and abducted?"

He backhanded me before the words were all the way out.

"See what you've done?" he said. "Now you'll have a bruise. I'll have to try to hide it with more makeup."

I bit back a sarcastic response and pressed the back of my hand to my cheekbone. Turning my face away from him I looked out the window, watching the dark lines of trees scrolling past. Where *were* we going? Was this the road Tor and I had briefly been on, the one that joined the footpath for a little ways? I couldn't tell. It was just a road, with trees lining both sides.

I watched for other trucks, but saw none. We passed one man on a horse, but his back was to us until we sped past him. Then mile after mile ticked past empty, with no one to see me, no one to help—mile after mile, while I watched anxiously for someone, anyone at all.

Then we reached a turning I recognized. This was the

same road I'd been on before—we were skirting Doria, edging onto a smaller road, a much smaller one.

It was the road to Eric Alleyn's. Tor and I had walked this way. He had been helping me change my voice, my accent. I knew where I was, exactly where I was.

At a wide place Tristan pulled over. He smeared more makeup on my face, wrinkling his nose as if he could scarcely bear to touch me, which was fine with me. I sat still while he worked on my face, pretending I was somewhere else—in the boat with Farrell Dean, away from this horrid island—and wondering, from my safe position in that boat, what exactly Tristan was planning to do with me.

If we were going to Eric Alleyn's, was that a good thing or a bad thing?

I didn't know. The role of dead woman seemed like a dangerous one to play, especially when that woman was in the middle of an old feud. Then again, at least it looked like Tristan wasn't taking me off someplace where we'd be alone. I'd been afraid he was planning to make me his very own secret Rachel bride.

It was definitely better to go to Eric Alleyn's and get killed.

Then we were back on the road. It grew bumpy—this road was meant for people and horses, not trucks—but Tristan didn't even slow down.

At the Van Stavern house, Tor's little sister swung on the gate, her eyes wide as she watched us go jolting past. A man came out the door and stood on the porch—Tor's father? Maybe he'd guess that trouble was brewing, and come down to Eric Alleyn's.

There was the bend in the road.

And there was the collection of buildings belonging to the Alleyns, the two barns, the henhouse, the house.

The long slow twilight had set in, softening angles,

graying out colors. When we pulled to a stop the deep shadows of the trees obscured but didn't hide the truck.

Tristan opened the door and got out, yanking me out too. He pulled me around to the back of the truck, where he opened a big metal box and took out a knife. He slid it under his belt, then reached into the box and took out a long gun.

Rex came barreling out of the barn and toward us, barking as he ran. When he got within ten feet of us he stopped. He looked at me, then at Tristan. Then he growled and dropped to a crouch, the hair on the back of his neck rising. *Jump*, I urged him silently. *Kill him.*

As if he'd heard me, Rex sprang.

Tristan lifted the gun and shot him dead.

I screamed. Rex's body fell to the ground with a thud that I heard but didn't see, because Tristan had let go of me and I leapt away from him and ran, but there wasn't any time, Tristan already was right behind me. He grabbed me again, yanked me back against him, dragging me down the road, around poor torn bloody Rex, toward the house with its windows shining cheerfully in the evening gloom.

They must have heard the gunshot, but everything still looked so peaceful. A thin stream of smoke rose from the chimney, and I could smell something baking. From the barn beyond the house I heard a cow lowing, a horse's whinny.

As we reached the little gate a shadow flitted across one window and disappeared, and suddenly I remembered Fiona. I'd been so fixated on Tristan's hatred for Eric Alleyn, so determined to be Fiona myself, I'd forgotten that Tristan knew nothing about me.

Please don't let her get hurt, I said to the invisible stars above me. Please let someone else be here. Let Rufus or Mick be here, anyone who can help us.

Please.

Chapter 25

Tristan gripped my arm hard and pulled me up against him. "This gun will be pointed directly at your back," he said in my ear. "If you say a single word, if you make any move, you die. Got that?"

I nodded. He shoved me in front of him prodding me in the back with the end of the long gun. About twenty feet from the house, still outside the little fence, we stopped.

"Eric Alleyn!" Tristan called. "Come out. Alone and unarmed."

A curtain twitched; I couldn't see who was behind it.

"Hurry up!" Tristan called, then muttered, "I don't have all night."

What else did he have on his to-do list? Kidnap a girl, taunt Eric Alleyn, buy groceries?

He poked me with the gun again, as if I could speed up Eric Alleyn. My heart was pounding painfully in my ears and I felt like I couldn't draw a full breath. I kept seeing the dog jerk and fall, the spray of blood, and then instead of Rex I was imagining me on the ground, Rachel's creamy dress dark with blood, her black hair spread out around my dead face. That's how Farrell Dean would find me, dead like Rafe, like all the others.

Tristan jabbed me with the gun again. Would he go

ahead and shoot me if Eric Alleyn took too long? I hoped he'd remember that the man had a bad leg, that he couldn't get to the door quickly.

The front door opened, spilling a rectangle of light into the gray dusk.

"Greetings, cripple," Tristan said.

Eric Alleyn stood there leaning on his cane. He was wearing brown pants and a battered leather jacket, and when his eyes fell on me he gave a choking sort of cry and took one uneven step forward, his free hand rising as if to reach out for me—for Rachel—and then falling back to his side.

"Pretty, isn't she?" Tristan said. "It's been a long time since I've seen her. I'd almost forgotten how beautiful she was." His voice was deliberately, mockingly conversational.

Eric Alleyn said nothing. His eyes were fixed on mine, but he looked stunned.

"It's been a long time since I lost her," Tristan went on. "A long time since you stole her from me. All these years I could have had her, could have seen her every day—every morning as I awoke, every night as I went to sleep, and all the hours in between. Almost two hundred and sixty three thousand hours. I counted them up. *Two hundred sixty three thousand*. Imagine that—but you can't, can you? It's unimaginable, what you owe me. Thirty years with Rachel."

Eric Alleyn seemed to recover from the initial shock. His eyes cleared, and the hand on the cane was steady.

Surely he'd realized what he was seeing. Surely he knew it was only me, out here in the dying light, masquerading as his dead wife. And surely, though he'd sold me, he'd help me now.

If he wouldn't, or if he couldn't, then I was lost. I couldn't think of a way out of this—forbidden to speak, forbidden to move, and with the gun prodding at my back every few seconds while Tristan worked himself up to murder.

"You owe me!" he said loudly, and I flinched. "You stole her, and then you killed her."

His voice grew quiet but very hard and cold, as if he were packing his fury down into the smallest space imaginable. "You forced her to have child, after child, after child. It was a ticking time bomb. We all knew it. Sooner or later she'd be too weak, too old, too worn out to survive it but still you went on, putting my Rachel at risk."

Eric Alleyn's head tilted as if he were giving careful consideration to Tristan's words, but in the deepening twilight I couldn't see the expression on his face. He was silhouetted against the lit doorway. He made a perfect target.

The gun jabbed me hard between the shoulder blades and I staggered forward a pace. I could hear Tristan breathing behind me, angry and hard.

"You took my Rachel and you used her up and killed her," he said. "You killed her as surely as if you put a gun to her head and pulled the trigger."

Slowly, Eric Alleyn nodded.

"I've told myself the same thing many times," he said, and for once his voice was quiet. "A man's wife dies in childbirth, he has to blame himself. But Rachel—" he smiled, my father actually smiled—"Rachel knew her own mind. And she wanted those babies, Tristan. She wanted every last one. And so did I."

My cheeks were wet with tears. He wasn't talking to Tristan. He was looking straight at me, and I knew he was talking to me.

Tristan practically spat with fury. He started to speak, but Eric Alleyn made one small gesture with his free hand and suddenly Fiona was standing beside him, framed with him in the lit doorway, her bright hair glowing and shifting around her shoulders like a living thing.

Then everything happened very fast.

Tristan cried out, one sharp fearful angry cry. I flung myself sideways, away from him, away from the gun. He swung it to his shoulder and put his eye to the sights—not at me, he wasn't aiming at me, he was aiming at my sister.

"Demon! You came back!" he said, and I leapt toward him, grabbing the gun barrel and shoving it hard as he fired once, twice, three times, and Fiona and Eric Alleyn vanished—fell, leapt—dead, alive, injured, I didn't know—into the house.

Tristan dropped the gun and grabbed me by the hair. As he yanked me around I caught a glimpse through the open doorway of bright blood, unmistakable on the pale wood floor. He'd hit Fiona, or he'd hit my father, someone was bleeding, and then Tristan was half-dragging, half carrying me back the way we'd come. My hands ached from the hot gun barrel but I fought him, biting and scratching.

"Not her," he said, struggling to pin my arms. "She's not the one. She's with him so it's you—you're the demon. Why did you come back?"

I was too busy fighting him to make any sense of his words, and then we reached the truck and he was shoving me inside, pushing himself in after me, crushing me, climbing over me to the driver's side.

Then he was starting the truck and we were moving fast, speeding in the direction the truck had been facing—past Eric Alleyn's house, past the barn, jolting up the rough path past the cows' meadow, past the willow trees where I'd been buried, through the woods and down the path that Farrell Dean and I had travelled when we'd first arrived, the narrow leaf-strewn path down to the sea.

There was nothing out here, no one to help me. Better to fall from a moving truck. I jerked open the door and Tristan grabbed me, pulled me back, and I threw myself into his pull and we fell backwards hard and he cracked his head against the driver's side window.

He shoved me off him and hit the accelerator but I grabbed the wheel and twisted it so he lost control and the left side of the truck ran up the side of the narrow path, dug into the side of the hill where the ground was soft, and we came to a jerking stop.

"Demon!" he said again, and he shoved me out the open door, falling with me onto the ground, then he was up and dragging me up, pulling me down the path, out to the open beach.

A strange blaring noise split the air but I saw nothing and we'd reached the soft sand, and he lost his footing and fell, hard, on top of me. His breath was on my face, his hands bruising my arms, and he struggled upright and hauled me up, too, pushing forward—why was he pushing me, there was nothing out here, nothing but the sea—

"I watched you go," he panted, splashing into the water. He dragged me out until I was waist deep in the icy waves, then turned me to face him and shook me, hard.

"You were the price, and I paid you. I watched you go!" Tears were streaming down his face and everything was moving, I was shaken about by him, by the wind, the waves. "A life for a life," he said. "That's all it took. He could do that, he had power, he was some sort of sorcerer, beautiful and powerful and strong, and he could save Rachel and all it took was you. A trade. A life for a life. It was that easy. We struck hands, and he promised, and I watched you go."

Tristan shook me again and my feet slipped in the cold wet sand but he held me up, hurting me, his face inches from my own.

"But you came back," he said, his icy blue eyes bright with fury. "You came back, and Rachel died. *I want her back.*"

Then he gripped me under the arms, lifting me up and

into the air, water streaming off my clothes, and I knew this was the end. He would shove me down and fall on top of me, holding me under the blue green waves until my breath ran out and my lungs burst and I died, drowned, dead in the sea.

It only took four seconds, maybe five, but time slowed down and I saw everything, things past and present, and things long past that I could never have seen. I saw the chestnut horse hurtling down the crooked path, impossibly far away, and then I went crashing down into the cold water and the world was only the rushing of the waves in my ears, and I saw Farrell Dean in Optica gray pulling the boat ashore with me at his side.

Then Tristan yanked me back up and shook me, and I saw Eric Alleyn leaning forward, urging the chestnut horse on, its hooves throwing sprays of sand. Then the water was over my face and I was trying to hold my breath but Tristan was shaking me, shaking the air out of me, and I saw the boat setting out to sea and Angel in it, a baby in his arms, the lantern in the stern bobbing with the waves. Blood pounded in my head and my lungs screamed and then there was another light, a smaller light, making its way back up the crooked path as Angel's light grew distant on the sea.

Then Tristan pulled me up again, screaming in my face, and I saw the horse's wide nostrils and the long knife glinting in Eric Alleyn's hand, and then the horse was upon us and Eric Alleyn shouted a command that I couldn't hear but understood and I kicked out with all my might, twisting away from Tristan as the horse plunged and the knife flashed and Tristan fell and I rolled away with the water all around me, in my eyes, my ears, my mouth.

Then I was choking and gasping and scrambling to my feet and there was blood in the water, oily vivid blood on the gray blue waves.

And my father reached down and I reached up, and I

was on the horse and in his arms.

Chapter 26

Keeping one arm tight around me, my father guided the horse away from the sand and the sea, away from Tristan's body drifting in the red-soiled waves, toward the path home.

"Fiona?" I gasped, shivering so hard my teeth chattered.

"She's all right," my father said, tightening his arm around me, pulling me back closer against his chest. "Some broken glass cut her, but she's all right. We'll go to her now."

"Hurry," I said, and he nodded and spurred the horse with his heels.

I was cold, so cold, but the horse's back was warm and so was my father, and I shut my eyes and breathed the clean brisk air, the smell of pine trees, the scent of my father's leather coat. I could feel his good leg against mine, and the hard metal of his artificial leg nudging against my other foot. He could ride. I hadn't known he could still ride.

"You're safe," he murmured in my ear. "It's all right. It's all over. You're safe." I felt the rumble of his voice in his chest, his throat, and I leaned back against him and let exhaustion take me, let him hold me up, limp and shaking, wet and cold, dressed as a dead woman, but alive.

We cantered up the leafy path, skirting Tristan's wrecked truck, and had made it to the top of the hill by the willows when figures came running up the path toward us. I couldn't see who they were but down below I could see other trucks, two of them, and shadows moving back and forth across the open doorway.

Then the men were closer—Gabriel and Farrell Dean.

"What do you think you're doing?" Gabriel shouted, planting himself in our path. He had a handgun in one hand and was pointing it at us before he registered what he was seeing. Then his hand fell and his eyes went wide. "Rachel?"

"Don't be a fool," Papa said, sounding like his old self. "And get out of the way. She's half frozen and in shock."

"Red?" Farrell Dean shoved past Gabriel and took hold of my foot. "Red, is that you?"

Mutely I nodded.

Gabriel looked baffled. He glanced back toward the house, then at me.

"You called Fiona that," he said. "You called her Red. And Tor hit you."

"It wasn't Fiona," Farrell Dean said. "It was Red. We were looking for Red."

Gabriel shook his head. "I don't understand. Who is this?"

"Valentina," Papa said, nudging the horse with his heel. "This is Valentina, my lost child. Now get out of the way or I'll run you over."

Gabriel moved and Farrell Dean reached up and I gave him one hand, and with the other I kept hold of my father's arm, and in this way we made a slow and awkward processional back home, my father strong and warm behind me, Farrell Dean holding my hand so hard it hurt, and Gabriel keeping pace beside us, gun hanging loose by his side, all of us utterly silent all the while.

At the house my father said, "Take her," and slid me down into Farrell Dean's waiting arms.

Rory and Angus came to help their father off the horse and Farrell Dean pulled me against him and hugged me so hard I gasped and he loosened his hold just enough to let me breathe.

"What did he do to you?" he said against my ear, fingering my black hair, pulling back to study my face. With his thumbs he traced the lines of my darkened eyebrows, and then he ran his fingertips gently across my swollen cheekbone.

I met his puzzled angry eyes and felt—I don't know why—a wave of shame, of horror and humiliation. I couldn't speak. I wanted to sink into the warm earth and not come back until I was myself again, not Rachel, not Fiona, not even Valentina, but just plain Red. I wanted to disappear.

Instead, Farrell Dean pulled me back into his arms. He held me while people moved around us, exclaiming, asking questions, giving orders and directions; held me while Fiona called out a series of rapid instructions, while Rain and Tor got into a violent argument and had to be separated by Gabriel; held me while a voice I didn't know—Tor's father? Earl?—said something curt, and my father answered with a short bark of laughter.

Then someone threw a blanket around us both and, hidden in its safe dark folds, my face against Farrell Dean's chest, I cried and cried as if my heart were breaking.

Chapter 27

"It was Ezzie," Angus said, leaning over me.

"Get out of the way." Fiona elbowed him and kept scrubbing.

I was lying on the kitchen counter, my head over the sink, a rolled up towel supporting my neck. Fiona, wearing her rubber dishwashing gloves, was working something that smelled like lemons into my hair, something she'd insisted Angus go straight into town to fetch.

"You're ruining my prospects," he told us when he got back. "How am I ever going to find a wife now that half the town has seen me banging on a beauty parlor door, begging the owner to open up for a hair tonic emergency? And she asked me questions—permanent, semi-permanent, demi-permanent, temporary? I'd no idea. Black, that was all I could tell her. It's really … black."

Now he kept leaning over me, checking to see if his tonic was working, telling me snippets of what had been happening during the long day while I was drugged and isolated. Fiona kept scrubbing, a determined look on her face, while behind her Rain busily gave orders to Tor and Rory—the three of them were trying to fix supper without getting in Fiona's way.

Over by the fire Tor's father was listing all the things he

expected of my father, now that he knew Eric Alleyn still could ride. Gabriel sat with them, but he wasn't really listening to them. I had seen the play of expressions across his face, so like Rafe's, and I knew there would be questions, hard ones, and soon. Right now he was biding his time, sorting out what he knew and did not know about Optica, and his brother, and my reasons for coming to Aislin.

Farrell Dean was standing beside Fiona, leaning across me, shielding me with his body from as many prying eyes as possible. But people kept coming up on Fiona's other side, looking at me, checking on me, and every now and then someone I couldn't see straightened the blanket around my legs or patted my feet.

"It was Ezzie who did what?" I asked Angus.

"He found you. He asked us whether Grandfather's surveillance equipment might be useful in tracking you down."

Angus laughed, his freckled face upside down to me. "We thought he was still delusional. I mean, there he was, just out of surgery and with his head all bandaged, talking about bugs and radio waves and listening devices. We hadn't given that mess at the fishing cabin a thought, Rory and I. We'd been too busy trying to keep Ezzie from clawing his cysts out by hand."

I shuddered.

"Go away, Angus," Fiona said. "You're upsetting her."

"No I'm not. Ezzie kept on at us until he got us to listen, which took some doing because we were thinking you had fallen down a ravine or drowned in the inlet or been mauled by a bear—we sure never imagined that Tristan was playing some sick game with you, dressing you up like a—"

"Angus, go away," Fiona said again, and swatted at him with a wet gloved hand.

"She wants to hear this!" He appealed to me. "You want to know how we found you, right?"

I nodded, sending a trickle of water running toward my eyes. Fiona sighed, snatched up a towel, and blotted my forehead, shoving Angus out of the way as she did so. "Be still," she told me sternly.

"We didn't know for certain that Tristan had taken you," Angus said, looming into view again. "But it was his radio spy gear at the cabin, and he's the one who has always been fixated on this family, and Earl couldn't find him to help search for you, so it seemed like a good possibility. In fact by then it seemed like the only possibility, because we'd searched everywhere else. That's pretty much what today was, the search-for-Valentina day.

"So when Ezzie told us about the spy gear we went straight to the cabin, but you were already gone, and then we fanned out looking for Tristan, and Tor found someone who had seen his truck parked on the path to Doria, near the cabin. Then we knew for sure it was him, and we came here."

By the time he finished he'd managed to squeeze Fiona almost entirely away from the sink.

"How am I ever going to get this out of her hair if you keep getting in the way?" she said, elbowing him hard. "*Go away.*"

"I like my other sister better," Angus said. "She's nicer."

"She won't be once she knows you as well as I do."

Angus sulked for a split second, then kissed Fiona's cheek, patted my forehead, and wandered off.

I looked at Farrell Dean. "So you went to the cabin."

He nodded, his face grim.

"I kept hoping that you would," I said. "The whole time I was there, listening to you talk about where I might be, no one ever said a word about the cabin. But I still kept hoping you'd come."

"I was too late. You were gone." Farrell Dean's hazel eyes darkened. "All that was left was your blue dress."

I saw in his face how terrible that moment had been. He'd had no idea what it meant, the discarded dress in the fishing cabin. For all he knew, I was already dead.

"And then you came here," I said, wanting to move him away from that moment.

"Yeah. But we didn't know if you'd be here. It was only a guess. And we didn't get here soon enough."

I touched his arm. "It's okay. I'm all right."

"We handled it," Fiona said. "Red rescued me, I rescued Papa, and Papa rescued Red." When I'd grabbed Tristan's gun to keep him from shooting Fiona, she had grabbed Papa and pulled him inside on top of her, not trusting his artificial leg to get him out of the way in time. "We all saved each other."

"Everyone but my poor dog," Angus said from somewhere. "Nobody saved poor Rex."

"Angus, go away!" Fiona said, as I tried to block the image of Rex's bleeding body from my mind.

"But before I rescued you, you rescued me," I told Fiona. "When you stepped out you startled him and threw him off balance."

"That was Papa's idea. It was all we could come up with on the spur of the moment. And anyway you rescued Papa every bit as much as I did. Look at him—" she glanced over her shoulder, seeming uncharacteristically at a loss for words.

Farrell Dean shifted and beyond him I could see our father sitting by the fire, gesturing with his cane and talking in a downright animated manner as Tor's father listened intently. Eric Alleyn's eyes were bright and his shoulders straight.

"Couldn't get a clear shot," I caught over the other conversations in the room. "Had to use the knife."

Then Farrell Dean leaned back over me, rightly guessing that I didn't want to relive my near-drowning just yet.

"How's it coming?" Rain said, leaning in from Fiona's

other side.

Fiona cocked her head and eyed my hair narrowly. "It's a little lighter now, don't you think?"

"Must be," Rain said. "Look at how much black is running down the drain." She looked at me fondly. "I knew there was something funny about you," she said, and vanished from sight.

Fiona reached for the bottle and squirted more lemon-scented liquid on my hair.

"She probably did know," she said. "I was more worried about Rain catching on than anybody else." Then—because she was wearing wet rubber gloves—she lifted one shoulder and rubbed it against the bandage on her cheek. "This thing itches."

"Be careful, or you'll knock it off," I said.

One of Tristan's shots had shattered a window and she'd been cut on her cheek, and on her ear—which had bled profusely—and on her wrist, but none of the cuts went very deep. The one on her cheek scared me, though. It had come so close to her eye.

Fiona's eyes met mine. "If it scars, we won't be able to trade places anymore."

"She wasn't very good at it anyway," Tor said, appearing beside her. "No offense," he said to me.

Farrell Dean stiffened and straightened up. He gave Tor a hard look and then, without really relaxing, went back to gazing at me. I didn't think he'd taken his eyes off me for three seconds at a time since the moment he saw me in my father's arms on the chestnut horse.

"I think she played the part wonderfully," Fiona said. "And frankly, it doesn't sound like you were much help, sleeping while she was outside pacing around, trying to figure out what to do next."

I hadn't just been pacing around outside, but I didn't

correct her. That could be Farrell Dean's and my secret.

"If she could have counted on you," Fiona went on, "Tristan would never have caught her alone."

She was being too hard on Tor, given that he'd set out at her command, without any forewarning, to protect her father from whatever havoc a rogue sister might wreak.

But Tor had a black eye that I was pretty sure Farrell Dean had given him, and I certainly wanted to stay in Fiona's good graces, given her current determination to get my hair back to normal. So I didn't come to Tor's defense other than to look at him sympathetically—at least, I tried to. Like everyone but Fiona and Farrell Dean, Tor was upside down.

His face was expressionless. He stared at me for a long moment, then nodded once.

"You're right," he said. "Valentina, I'm sorry."

"Red," Fiona and Farrell Dean said together.

Tor sighed. "I'll talk to you when you're in a better mood," he said to Fiona.

Then, to me, he said, "I only meant I like you better as yourselves than as each other. And I'm glad you're all right, Valen—Red. I'm very glad." Then, with a wary glance at Farrell Dean, he left.

Fiona gave me a small smile. "Go get the kettle," she told Farrell Dean. "I need to mix more solvent."

As soon as he was gone, my sister leaned in close. "Do you like him?" she asked.

"Tor? I guess so. For you, anyway—not for me."

She smiled, then glanced over her shoulder at Farrell Dean. "You really scared him," she said.

"I know."

"Has he broken the enchantment?"

Meritt's face flashed before me, his dark unruly hair and quick grin.

I shut my eyes. "I don't know, Fee," I said. "I can't think

about that now."

Then Farrell Dean was back, resuming his protective position, twining his fingers in with mine.

Two hours later Tristan's body was lying in the barn. Tor's father would have him collected by Doria's Death Family—they took care of burials when the person had no family or friends able to do it. Tristan's friends, it seemed, weren't helpfully inclined after what he'd done to me today. At least Gabriel wasn't, and everyone else would follow his lead.

Tor's father had gone home and Earl had taken one of the trucks back to Ionia to let Nana, Grandfather, and Carol know they'd found "Fiona."

Everyone else was still at Eric Alleyn's, nine of us. The boys had pulled the table back and brought in extra chairs to group around the fire. The gas wall-sconces were turned low, and the flickering firelight made everyone look warm and sleepy and content.

I'd been dosed with hot tea, bathed, dried, dressed in clean clothes, and fed. I was stiff and dozens of bruises had begun to bloom all over my body, including a fairly impressive one on my cheekbone, but I was safe and my hair was back to its normal flaming red, more or less. It was still a little damp, so I was sitting right beside the fire, in between Farrell Dean and my father. Both of them were sitting a bit close—our knees kept bumping—but I didn't mind at all.

Fiona came over and handed me something. "I should have shown you earlier," she said, with a sideways glance at our father. "But I was jealous."

It was the one photograph of Rachel and all her children. She was propped up on a pile of pillows in bed, five laughing little boys grouped around her, a baby in the crook of each arm. A young, happy Eric Alleyn leaned over the bed on her right, smiling down at his family.

It was strange, finally seeing her. I'd seen childhood pictures at Nana's, but this was the first photograph I'd seen of Rachel as an adult, a mother. My mother.

Her face was fuller than before, and her hair wasn't black, as Tristan had made mine, but a rich dark brown. In the picture she looked a lot like Fiona and me, and we didn't look like ourselves. We were just little blanket-wrapped bundles with red hair on top.

"That's you, in her left arm," Fiona said, pointing. "You're the one she's looking at. We can tell because I have a ribbon around my ankle—that's what the midwife did to tell us apart." Her voice dropped. "I used to look at this picture and feel so left out," she said. "Because Mama was looking at you and you were looking at her, as if the two of you were already in your own world. As if you were already planning to go away and leave me."

Eric Alleyn made a disapproving noise and I stood up and hugged my sister.

"We'd never have left you on purpose," I said, and she nodded, her eyes wet. Then, without another word, she went and sat down by Tor and leaned her head against his shoulder. He put an arm around her and gazed owlishly at me over his beaky nose, and I couldn't quite stifle a smile.

Gabriel was leaning forward with his elbows on his knees, studying first Fiona, then me, then Fiona again. He'd been doing it all evening, moving between the two of us, examining us as if he'd be tested on the subject of his twin nieces.

"It's an amazing likeness," he said, and looked at Farrell Dean. "And my brother and I were as much alike?"

Farrell Dean nodded.

"He had a little more silver in his hair," I said. "That's the only difference I can see."

"How did he end up on your island? Did the same man

who took you steal him as well?"

Farrell Dean answered before I could. "We don't know," he said, and I knew he was trying to avoid the experiment issue, to spare me having to make that revelation to my family, at least for tonight. "We have a lot of questions and not many answers."

"At least they were together," my father said. "I find some comfort in that. Rachel's brother was with my daughter."

Gabriel didn't look impressed. "They didn't know they were related," he said.

"Rafe looked out for me all the same," I said. "I used to pretend we were related, and once he said he wished I were his daughter."

I wanted to talk about Rafe, wanted to somehow convey how wonderful he'd been, how necessary to me, but I didn't know how to begin. How to explain that after he'd been stern, when I'd gotten in trouble, his eyes would twinkle and I'd know I'd been forgiven. And that he might be mistaken for someone easygoing, even careless, but beneath it all there was a deep stillness, a watchfulness. He was always paying more attention than you thought.

And so many other things— he'd been assigned to Lonna but then had loved her and stayed with her; he'd been respected by everyone; he'd done his best to protect his fellow conspirators, dying alone rather than giving Meritt away for a chance at clemency.

I looked at Gabriel, at his hungry eyes, and I knew that someday I'd tell him all this and more, everything I could remember. But here, now, with so many listening, I felt shy. I didn't know where to begin.

"He called her his lost child," Farrell Dean said quietly, and I shot a surprised look at him.

"Not to everyone," he said. "Only to Meritt and me. He

knew he wouldn't be able to see her much, once she left school. So he told us to take care of his lost child, to always watch out for her."

Tears welled in my eyes, and suddenly I wondered—had Rafe known? Had he caught some glimpse of the truth through Gabriel's eyes?

Maybe that was what he was trying to say when he died. Maybe it hadn't been about the map at all, but about me— about us—about all the lost children of Optica.

I wondered if I'd ever know exactly how much Rafe had known.

Gabriel had covered his face with one hand. When he looked up again his eyes were very dark. "I called you the same thing," he said. "The lost child. I called you that for years."

"Until I told him to stop it," Rain said. "It was so darned dramatic. And anyway we didn't really know you were lost. You could just as well have been dead."

"Dead Child," Angus said. "Now that has a ring to it."

Tor shut his eyes, looking pained, but everyone else ig-nored my youngest brother.

"Was Rafe dreaming my dreams?" Gabriel said. "Or was I dreaming his? Or was it coincidental, that our circumstanc-es made us both worry over a little lost redheaded girl?"

My father shifted uneasily beside me. I couldn't see his expression; he was looking down at the floor.

"About that," I said. "About the abduction. The first one, I mean, when I died."

The expressions on the faces around the circle told me my childhood abduction was the last thing anyone wanted to talk about.

I didn't want to talk about it, either, but I had to. No one else knew what Tristan had said to me, out there in the cold sea, and they deserved to know. But where to begin?

"The midwife told Farrell Dean that I wasn't kidnapped," I said, lighting at random on a starting point. "She said I was sold. I guess you all know that."

But clearly, not all of them did. Rain and Tor nodded, and Fiona looked sick; Gabriel's expression was unreadable; but Angus and Rory looked startled.

"You were *sold*?" Angus said. "That's *sick*. What sort of person sells babies?"

"According to rumor, a person like me," said Eric Alleyn, ever blunt.

"You?" Angus said. "Why would you sell Valentina?"

"For medicine, so the story goes. For your mother."

"And people believed this?" Rory said. He looked at Tor. "You knew this story?"

Tor nodded. Beside him Fiona shifted uneasily.

Rory looked back and forth between the two of them.

"And he told you," Rory said to Fiona. "He inflicted this rumor on you."

She made a helpless gesture. "He only told me yesterday morning," she said. "He felt he had to, once he heard Red was back again."

Rory—the calmest of my brothers, I had thought—looked downright dangerous. "So you believe it," he said, eyeing Tor with disdain. "You actually believe that Papa sold Valentina."

Tor's sleepy blue eyes were resigned. "I've never known what to think," he said.

Angus reached over and removed Tor's arm from around Fiona's shoulders.

"Don't be too hard on him," Eric Alleyn said. "It's a lie, but a clever one. Rufus more than half believes it." He looked at Gabriel, sitting silent and expressionless across the circle from us. "And Rufus isn't the only one. I've always been thankful that no one felt the need to repeat that miserable tale to the younger children."

"I didn't believe it," Fiona said, glancing at Tor.

Eric Alleyn started to say something more but then stopped, looking at me, his brows coming together. I reached over and put my hand on his knee.

"I know it isn't true," I said, and my father covered my hand with his own.

Gabriel was watching us, his face hard, his eyes cynical. Obviously he thought I'd been deceived, that my father's recent rescue of me had clouded my reason.

Eric Alleyn saw his expression. He sighed and, dropping my hand, leaned forward, elbows on his knees.

"I've said this before, Drewblood, but for the sake of my children I'll say it once more. I loved your sister; I loved her more than life itself. But I also loved each child she bore. I would never have sold our daughter, not for any reason, and Rachel would never have wanted me to. Not even to save her life. That's the simple truth." He sat up straight. "But I can't prove it. I've never been able to prove it, and heaven knows I've tried."

"You dug," Fiona said softly, and Papa nodded.

"I dug. And I didn't know what I wanted to find. My dead child? How could I want to find my daughter dead, when there was a chance she was alive? I didn't care what people thought of me—my reputation weighed less than nothing against my hope that she might live.

"But if she was alive, who had her? What terrible things might be happening to her? I almost went out of my mind thinking about it. I *did* go out of my mind, for a time, until the other children brought me back. Until I realized I was abandoning them, leaving them for the darkness of my own thoughts, just as my own father left me for the darkness in his."

I swallowed hard, shaking away the image of my desperate father out in the field, under the willows, and a cold anger rose up in me. Tristan had paid; but Angel should pay as well. Angel who, with his own beautiful little boy back in Optica, had been running here and there stealing other men's children, destroying families, sowing discord and despair—because I wasn't the only one he'd kidnapped. He was too young to have stolen Rafe, but there had been others. I might have been the last, but I wasn't the first.

I knew it had been him. Tristan's description—beautiful, powerful, strong—could only fit Angel. And besides, Angel had stood on the beach outside Sir Tom's cave and said that I was his, that he'd bought me. He wasn't talking about giving poor Jensen something for bringing me to him, that night in the wilderland; he was talking about buying me when I was a baby.

Distracted by my own thoughts, I'd been silent longer than I'd intended. In the flickering firelight, Gabriel was staring at Eric Alleyn with cold, flat eyes, and my father was glowering back at him. Everyone else was avoiding eye contact. They didn't have an explanation for what had happened, other than the one the midwife had given. I had to tell them the truth.

"It was Tristan," I said. My throat was so tight I could barely speak. "He took me."

Every face turned toward me. Most of them looked blank, but a couple—Rory, Fiona—looked alarmed.

"We know it was Tristan," Rory said gently. "We saw him."

"But he's dead now," Fiona began. "He can't hurt you—"

Farrell Dean interrupted her. "Tristan," he said. "He—what, you mean he took you before? He took you *twice*? He's the one who sold you when you were a baby?"

I nodded.

"But he wasn't here that night," Rory said. "No one was here but Papa and the midwife. That was the problem—there was no one who could go for the doctor. Angus and I were too little to be of any help."

I shook my head. "Tristan was here," I said. "Grandfather said so. He told me that Tristan was the one who brought the news that Mother had died."

"That's so," Gabriel said, and shut his eyes as if in pain. "He did. I never thought to wonder how he knew."

"Tristan told me himself," I said, turning to my father. "Out there in the water, before you came. He said that Angel—" beside me, Farrell Dean moved sharply "—the man who took me, a man from our island—told him Rachel's life could be bought, could be saved. A life for a life. So in exchange for Rachel's life, Tristan sold me. I was expendable, he said. He handed me over and, just to be sure, watched me be taken away across the sea. He thought it was some sort of magic, I suppose. A magical bargain."

Other than the ticking of the clock, the silence was complete. The circle of faces stared at me, every one of them blank, startled.

"And then tonight, when he saw there were two of us—" I started shaking, and Farrell Dean put an arm around my shoulders. "He knew then that I had come back, and he was confused, I guess time was running together in his mind, and he thought that because I'd come back, the bargain had been broken. He thought that was why Rachel died."

I was trying to speak clearly but I wasn't sure if I was making sense, and I could hardly breathe.

I got out one more sentence. "I think he imagined that if he drowned me, if he sent me back to the sea, if he kept his side of the bargain, then Rachel would be alive again."

Gabriel got to his feet so quickly that his chair fell over with a bang. "If he weren't already dead I'd kill him," he said, and his voice was quiet and cold and I looked at his face and I believed him.

Unexpectedly he took two quick steps toward Eric Alleyn but Rory and Angus leapt to their feet and so did Farrell Dean, all of them moving between the two older men.

"Get out of my way," Gabriel said. "I'm not intending to hurt the man."

They hesitated, didn't move.

"You heard him," Eric Alleyn said, bracing his cane on the floor and getting to his feet. "Get out of the way."

Farrell Dean looked at me. I nodded and he backed away, and after a moment's pause so did Rory and Angus.

Gabriel came and stood directly in front of Eric Alleyn. "I was wrong," he said. "Wrong about Tristan and wrong about you."

Eric Alleyn studied him for a long moment. "You were deceived," he said finally. "Like most everyone else."

"Yes, I was, but from the day you married her, I—she—it was—" Gabriel broke off. It was the only time I ever saw my uncle at a loss for words.

My father nodded. "You were jealous," he said. "Rachel always said you'd grow out of it. Can't say I thought it would take thirty years."

Gabriel gave a short laugh, but his eyes were full of pain. He dropped to his knees at Eric Alleyn's feet.

"Forgive me," he said formally, bowing his head.

"I will. I do. Now get up before I get a crick in my neck looking at you." Eric Alleyn extended his hand to his brother-in-law and pulled him to his feet.

But Gabriel wasn't finished. "There should be recompense," he said. "Whatever you ask of me, Eric. I'll resign from the Council. I'll—

Eric Alleyn waved an impatient hand. "Stop your babbling," he said. "I'll tell you exactly what I want from you,

Drewblood. I want you to get that blasted truck of Tristan's off my path."

"Of course," Gabriel said. "But—"

Eric Alleyn cut him off. "I'm a stubborn cuss," he said. "I didn't make it easy for you to see me differently. I'm sorry for that. Rachel would have expected better of me."

Fiona was weeping quietly. Rain was flushed and looked half angry, half embarrassed.

Angus broke the silence. "Can we desecrate the body?" he said.

Rory cuffed him, and then everyone was talking at once.

"Obviously Rowena Marchrest was involved," Farrell Dean said to Rory. "Someone had to hand Red off to Tristan, and it must have been Rowena. Because you really do re-member, don't you? You remember her taking Red away. No one planted that idea. You remember what actually oc-curred."

Rory nodded his head, his eyes on me. "It's a real memory," he said. "Being told your baby sister died in your arms makes quite an impression on a five-year-old."

"And to think that man was listening to people all the time," Rain said. "No wonder he always had gossipy tidbits for his radio show. What a creep."

"Red lived with that in Optica," Fiona said, wiping her wet cheeks on her sleeve. "They watch people there all the time. Someone is always watching, even in the shower."

"Well, that's not the way we do things here," Rain said, sounding very much like her father. "If we'd known we'd have put a stop to it."

"So the two lights Old Silas saw—one was Tristan, mak-ing sure his bargain stayed sealed?" That was Tor.

"Little lights for souls," Angus intoned. "What a crock. Drunk old Silas saw kidnappers, and had to go dressing them up in fancy poetry."

"But I liked the lights for souls," I said, and Farrell Dean turned and smiled at me.

"I should have spoken to you later on," Gabriel said to Eric Alleyn. "I knew you were out of your mind with grief. I should have come back and discussed it later, once you were rational."

"But what else could I have said? How do you fight a rumor? Especially if you do have a missing baby, and unexplained medicine in the house."

That brought everything to a halt. We all turned, staring at my father.

"There really was medicine?" Rain said. "What was it?"

Papa shrugged. "I'll get it," he said, and stumped away, leaning on his cane, into his bedroom.

The rest of us waited silently in the fire-lit room. What did this mean, that there really was medicine?

The Guardians had some impressive skills—I supposed it was possible that Angel had given Tristan something that actually might have helped my mother.

I glanced at Farrell Dean; he met my eyes and shrugged.

In a moment Eric Alleyn came back out of his bedroom.

"The midwife said it was a new formulation, experimental, to use only as a last resort. It never crossed my mind to wonder where it had come from—I thought she had it with her all along, I suppose, and by then I was willing to try anything, experimental or not. But Rachel died before we could finish the dose."

He stopped in front of us, leaning on his cane.

"Maybe it would have helped, if we'd had it earlier, if we'd gotten it all down her. I don't know. In any case, here it is. This is what Tristan got in exchange for my daughter. We've never seen the like of it."

He opened his hand.

In it lay the remains of a silver-wrapped square of something dark.

Farrell Dean picked it up and sniffed it.

"Chocolate?" I said.

Farrell Dean nodded. His face in the firelight was grim, inexorable, and I knew my expression was the same.

Oh, yes, I thought.

Angel would pay.

THE END, Book Two

The Red Series

Acknowledgements

All four books in *The Red Series* were family endeavors:

My husband—a professional writer and editor, and former creative writing professor—provided invaluable editorial feedback, copy editing, and proofreading.

My mother—also an English professor—served as another proofreader. Any remaining errors are my fault, because I just kept fiddling around ...

My sister—yet another English professor—gave me a much-needed boost of enthusiasm at exactly the right moment, as did my sister-in-law Laura.

My father gave me a collection of Yeats poems for my nineteenth birthday, thus permanently fixing "The Stolen Child" in my psyche.

And my three (then-teenage) children not only talked me into writing these books to begin with, but also offered constant encouragement and insightful feedback every step of the way.

I am grateful to all of them for their help.